Golden North

Dangerous Times, Book Two

by

Ilona Fridl

Golden North: Dangerous Times, Book Two

COPYRIGHT © 2010 by Ilona Fridl

Cover Art by *Rae Monet*

The Wild Rose Press
PO Box 706
Adams Basin, NY 14410-0706
Visit us at www.thewildrosepress.com

Publishing History
First Vintage Rose Edition, 2010
Print ISBN 1-60154-801-X

Published in the United States of America

You'll also want to read
SILVER SCREEN HEROES,
Dangerous Times, Book One

What happens when a motion picture studio in 1920 is taken over by a crime family? Addy and Zeke, a stunt double and a director's assistant, work with the police to bring the gangsters to justice. But Addy's cousin has married into the crime family. When Addy is given a key to bring down the family and the studio, will she use it?

"Silver Screen Heroes has it all. Suspense, romance, mystery, history. I enjoyed that Addy was part Mexican and that the writer chose to highlight the strained relations between Mexicans and whites during that era. The insight into mob life was also interesting. Both Addy and Zeke were likable and believable and I found myself drawn into the story on several levels."
~Vee, Night Owl Romance Reviews (rated 4.75 out of 5 hearts)

"Wow! What a story. It starts off with a bang, or should I say fire, that kept my attention and made me want to read more. Poor Addy and what she goes through.... Zeke, who also works at Majestic, is attracted to Addy, but they have different backgrounds, a different ethnic heritage.... Once I sat down and started reading, I couldn't stop. I got involved with the characters, related with the situations, and felt I was a part of the story. Romance will never die no matter how much water some people toss on to douse the flames. Read *SILVER SCREEN HEROES* and join the magic of an era long past and feel the miracle of true love. Excellent read!"
~Marianne Gibson, Between the Lines

Muriel's heart went out to Josh.

He had put his head in his hands and leaned his elbows on the desk as Muriel told him what happened at Millie's, and now he looked the picture of despair. He slowly raised his head. "Well, that's it, isn't it? Muriel, I'm sorry you had to come into this. You seem to have traded one problem for another."

Muriel caressed his shoulders. "I'm sure Sarah and Amos can find out what really happened. When they do, the townspeople will come around."

"We may not be here by that time." He straightened and threw his hands up. "I really wanted to prove to myself that my father was wrong, that I could make something of my life. Well—" One hand slammed down on the ledger.

Muriel's chest tightened. He could be right about having to leave. She didn't want to think it, but her eyes swam with tears. How could he blame himself, though? He had worked so hard.

Josh looked at her through the mist in his own eyes. He stood and took her in a gentle embrace, then pulled back quickly. "I'm—I didn't mean to—"

Muriel put her fingers on his lips. "Don't apologize." She drew him toward her again, and they gazed at each other for a moment before she put her hand on the back of his neck and kissed him.

Dedication

To my family and friends, of course.
And in memory of my grandma, Grace,
who believed I could do anything.

Chapter 1

May 1921

Josh Shafer peered into the heavy mist. *I know they should be here soon. The ships are usually on time in the spring weather, unless there's a storm.* The silhouette of a liner came into view like a phantom coming out of a fog. As it drew closer, he saw faint figures standing along the railing of the ship, but he couldn't tell which were the ones he was there to welcome.

He waited impatiently until it docked, watching the passengers crowded on the deck. Then he saw his brother, Zeke, accompanied by a short woman in a broad-brimmed hat, clutching her coat tightly around her. *That must be Addy. Boy, he sure married a doll.*

As the ship's crew tied up to the pier, Josh saw the couple hurry toward the ramp being lowered to the boardwalk. Zeke had grabbed the woman's hand and was looking around as he strode down the gangplank until he spotted Josh's wave and returned it.

Josh wove his way through other people greeting passengers and gave Zeke a bear hug. "Good to see you again, big brother! It's been too long."

"Josh, you haven't changed a bit. Still have that blue-eyed baby face." The brothers laughed and slapped each other on the back.

Josh turned to Addy. "This must be the infamous Adeline Rose, who brought Majestic Studio to its knees." He took her hand and kissed it. "You will be our first star on the stage of the Golden North."

Addy gave Josh one of her biggest smiles, her brown eyes sparkling. "Pleased to meet you. Zeke and I are happy to help you with the theater."

Josh led them to his truck, where they loaded their trunks in the back after retrieving them from the ship's off-loading area. The three of them squeezed into the front seat, with Addy sandwiched in the middle. She gazed around as they went up the streets. "I thought Alaska would be all ice and snow, but it's pretty here. It's not as warm as California, though."

Josh grinned. "It will get warmer in summer, with the sun being out most of the day. At least that's what they tell me. I've only been here since last fall."

Josh stopped the truck and, following his lead, the two newcomers piled out of the vehicle as he waited for their reactions.

Addy's horror was evident as she looked at the huge ramshackle building before her. She glanced wide-eyed at Zeke, and he turned an equally dumbfounded gaze at his brother, stabbing a finger toward the gray wood monstrosity with the peeling white paint. "This is what you bought? Are you crazy?"

"Wait until you really see her. She's been closed and boarded for ten years. Of course, she needs some work, but it'll be worth it."

"Well, I certainly hope so!" Addy's reply was followed by a groan. Holding on to Zeke's arm, she looked pleadingly at Josh. "May we go somewhere to sit down? My legs are still pitching with the ship, and I'm tired."

Josh led the way. "I've fixed up the apartment in the back for you two. We can talk there."

The heavy mist turned to rain and Addy started to shiver. "How peculiar for a mid-May day. Well, I guess I should have expected as much up here in Alaska, but it's going to take a lot of getting used to, for a Californian." They sloshed around the building on a road that felt like wet oatmeal underfoot, and Josh opened a gray door at the back.

In the small parlor, Josh had whitewashed the walls and put a few braided rugs on the bare wooden floor. Now he lit two hurricane lamps on the wall. Their light cast a yellow glow around the room. "I'm sorry we don't have electricity yet. This building was closed in 1911, and Juneau didn't get its power plant until 1914."

Zeke's mouth dropped. "You mean we have to completely wire the whole place? Impossible! It will cost a fortune to get this theater going."

Addy sat on one of the old parlor chairs with a disgusted expression. The crates and boxes they'd sent ahead from Los Angeles were piled up in every corner. "At least we have heat." Addy pointed to a large radiator coil popping busily by the window.

Josh nodded. "It's an old gas furnace I connected up first thing. The nights were very cool here even in September. Would you like to see the rest of the building?"

"Where are you staying?" Zeke asked.

"I fixed up one of the rooms upstairs."

"Was this an inn, too?"

"Uh, no." Josh tried to avoid meeting their eyes.

Addy and Zeke glanced at each other, then back at Josh. "You mean...a cat house?"

Josh grinned. "The finest in the territory. Come on."

He led them to a door on the far end of the parlor. Through it was an office. A large maple rolltop desk dominated the center of the room and a vault stood on the far wall. Bookcases and file cabinets lined the rest of the walls, with a few chairs placed here and there, for good measure.

From there, they stepped into the former barroom. It looked like something from a haunted house. The large mahogany bar, with its badly cracked mirrors, broken glass shelves and all, held at least an inch of dust and dirt. Long gray cobwebs connected the chandeliers with the floor and festooned the small tables and chairs that lay crazily around the room. A smell of mold emanated from certain areas of the baseboards, and a strong odor of stale cigar smoke hung everywhere. Without comment, they picked their way gingerly to the swinging double doors on the other side.

A small lobby brought them to the theater, with its red-and-gold wallpaper peeling and flaking off. Broken cherub gaslights lined the sides down to the stage.

As they walked down the aisle, Addy pointed to small round spots on the walls. "What caused those holes, do you know?"

"Those are from bullets."

Addy swayed and looked pale. "What?"

"That was just the way miners showed appreciation for a good performance."

Suddenly the piano on stage burst into ragtime music. While Josh and Addy stopped to talk, Zeke had gone up and sat himself at the old upright.

Addy came up behind him and put her hands on his shoulders. "I didn't know you could play piano. That sounds horrible."

Zeke turned with a smile. "Don't shoot the piano player. He's doing the best he can. This old gem is way out of tune. The first thing I'm going to do is fix that. Working at Majestic Studios as a gofer, I never got a chance to play, and Nathan and I couldn't afford a piano, even if there'd been room for one in our little apartment."

4

"Did you learn at home?"

"Heavens, no. Our Baptist preacher father considered music the devil's work. I learned from one of my schoolteachers on the sly."

Josh went around the piano and picked up a banjo. "The same way I learned to play this thing." He sat down and launched into "By the Sea" while Addy and Zeke added the harmony. Zeke got up and whirled Addy around in a big showy dance routine; ending up on one knee with her on the other. All three then arose and bowed to the phantom audience.

Zeke looked at his watch. "It's almost six-thirty. Is there a place to eat nearby? The first thing I want to do, even before tuning that piano, is eat."

Josh nodded. "There's Millie's, down a block. That's where I've been going, since the kitchen isn't running yet."

"That's the first thing *I'm* going to fix." Addy placed her hand on Josh's shoulder firmly. "We don't have the money to keep eating at a restaurant."

Josh shook his head. "Millie's isn't that expensive. Come on." He grinned at both of them. "If you two keep doing first things, we won't have time to get anything done."

Zeke thumped him on the head.

Outside, Addy looked around, completely awestruck again with the mountains. "Oh, Josh, with the clouds lifting a bit, I can see Juneau is surrounded with beautiful scenery." The territorial capitol was nestled on a shelf between the sea and Mt. Juneau. "And what strikes me is the green, so different from California. It seems like every open land space is bathed in plants."

Josh nodded and looked up. Sea birds floated lazily above the town and up to the cliffs of the mountain. The breeze from the ocean brought the salty fish smell with the odor of oil from the wharfs.

He felt at home here and hoped Zeke and Addy would, too.

A bald eagle soared off the cliffs, and Addy tugged on Zeke's sleeve. "Oh, look! I've never seen an eagle outside of a zoo before."

Josh smiled. "They have lots of wildlife around here. We'll have to take a hike outside Juneau one of these days."

"If we ever get some time," Zeke put in. "We have a lot of work to do."

"Here's the place." Josh opened a door and ushered them in.

Millie's was a simple but cheery eatery in a storefront off the street. Around them were plain white walls with paintings of flowers along them, topped by a tin ceiling whose decorative squares added an elegant touch. The place glowed colorfully with red gingham curtains at the front windows and yellow oilcloth on the tables.

A smiling middle-aged woman looked up from the counter. "Josh, come on in. I'll be with you in a moment."

They found an unoccupied table and sat down as the woman brought them three menus. Josh made the introductions. "Millie, this is my brother, Zeke, and his wife, Addy. This is Millie, the owner of this establishment and my favorite waitress."

"Millie?" Zeke raised his eyebrows.

Millie waved her hand. "Oh, shoot, we're not formal around here. First names are fine. Hell, Addy, you can even speak right to me with your order. We don't stand on ceremony hereabouts."

Addy looked shocked but amused as well at this offhand dismissal of the usual social custom of letting her escort order for her. "What's good tonight?"

"Miner's Stew with buttermilk biscuits."

"What's in it?"

"Meat, potatoes, onions, carrots, and a lot of gravy."

They all agreed on that, with hot coffee. Within minutes, a bowl of steaming stew appeared in front of each of them, smelling delicious. It took the chill off the rainy day.

Addy took a spoonful of the stew. "This is tasty. What kind of meat is this?"

"Caribou." Millie smiled at her reaction. "They're as common as cattle up here." With that, she went back to the kitchen.

Addy made a sad face. "Caribou are like Santa's reindeer, but it does taste good."

"You two met at Majestic Studios, didn't you?" Josh abandoned his bowl of stew long enough to ask.

Addy nodded. "I was working as Nora Steele's double at the time. I was even under contract as a lead, before the scandal."

"We heard about the collapse of the studio even up here. Was it true the mob was making bootleg on the grounds?"

"Yes, I saw it," Zeke put in. "I was working in shipping, with the crates the film was sent to the theaters in. When a board came loose on one of those crates, I could see it had a false bottom, packed with straw, and a bottle rolled out. I sniffed the liquid and knew it was liquor. When I got curious and looked in a back room, lo and behold they had set up a still. So I alerted the police. That's how we got in trouble with the gangsters. Addy almost got killed. So we got out of there as soon as we could."

Josh glanced at Addy. "That's why the bullet holes bothered you so much."

She looked down. "I was never so frightened in my life. I hope we're far enough away that they won't try to get revenge on us."

Zeke put his hand on hers. "I think they were glad to see us go."

They ended their meal with a big piece of Millie's freshly baked apple pie for each of them before they headed back to the old building that was now their home.

The three of them sat talking in the apartment parlor after Josh made sure the new arrivals knew where everything was, including his room upstairs. As the brothers caught up on their years apart from each other, Josh finally commented to Zeke, "Tomorrow we can look at our monies and decide what to do first on the building. I have the plans upstairs, and I'll study them again tonight while you two get settled in." He stood and picked up the ledger. "See you in the morning." He left by the office door.

Josh eased himself down in the chair behind the desk and opened the ledger. That water heater installation was expensive, but it was something they needed. He took a quick look at the funds they had left. *Well, it's enough to get started, but we're going to need help.* He was putting the ledger in the drawer when he heard the scream of metal from the apartment.

What was—and then he realized it must have been the bed springs. *They certainly are settling in.* He smiled as he rose and headed to the restaurant. As he carefully closed the door behind him, there was a whole symphony of "screes" and "thunks" coming from the other room.

The evening sun lit his way upstairs to the hallway of the little rooms above the theater. Josh's enclave faced west, so he could hold as much of the daylight as possible for as long as he could. He'd learned to treasure sunlight over the long, dark winter, even though he didn't get depressed by the lack of it.

God, it's good to have Zeke here. He'd always looked up to his older brother, who had often saved him from a brutal beating from their father. He didn't realized how much he'd been sheltered until his brother left home.

From the letters he'd received from Zeke, he knew Addy had a strict but loving family, but Zeke hadn't written much about their experiences with the gangsters. This evening's conversation had given Josh a small glimpse of what had driven his brother and Addy to leave California. *She is an incredibly brave girl—it's amazing what she went through to bring justice against the Giovanni family. Zeke said she almost died. They need to make a success of this new life here just as much as I do.*

Josh spread out the plans and took inventory on what they would need, until finally his drooping eyelids wouldn't let him continue. He snuggled into bed with happy thoughts surrounding him.

Chapter 2

Next morning, Josh brought the building plans downstairs with him and deposited them on the desk in the office before listening at the apartment door to hear if his brother and Addy were up yet. He heard nothing but Zeke's snores. Josh sighed and sat in the big office chair at the desk, swinging his feet up on the top next to the typewriter while he put his arms behind his head. *I hope they're up soon,* he thought when he heard his stomach growl.

Suddenly there was a shriek from Addy and curses from Zeke, along with a violent metal screech. Josh's feet flew off the desk, and he threw open the door of the apartment. "Are you all right?" he exclaimed as he rushed in, startling Addy further— and himself as he saw a little more of Addy than he'd expected.

Cheeks burning, he quickly turned his back to the room even as Addy dropped behind the bed, dragging the quilt with her.

She must have uncovered Zeke as she did so, because he added more blue words from his repertoire as he jumped out of bed, accompanied by a few more metal screeches. "What the hell is going on here?" From the corner of his eye Josh saw him grab his robe.

Addy wrapped the quilt around herself and got up slowly, while the two brothers waited. "I—I saw a..." She gulped. "I saw a...mouse on my pillow."

Eyebrows raised, Josh turned to look at Zeke over his shoulder.

"Why didn't you just brush it off the bed? You're

bigger than it is," Zeke said, shrugging into his robe and tying the belt with a jerk.

Addy shivered. "I hate mice!"

Josh stepped out the door, his color still high. "Well, since everyone is all right, I'll wait in the office, and we can go to breakfast when you're ready."

"A mouse," Josh heard Zeke mutter to himself as the door closed. "She can stand up to gangsters, but she's afraid of a damn mouse."

The three of them walked to Millie's in relative silence. Millie greeted them with a smile as they took a table. "Well, how was your first day in Juneau?"

Zeke shook his head. "A challenge. That building needs a lot of work."

Addy spoke up. "Do you have any ideas on how to get rid of mice?"

Millie nodded. "Old buildings like the theater probably have quite a colony of them. After you've finished your breakfast, we'll go out back here. We have some cats that keep the mice out of our food storage, and I can let you have one."

"I don't know." Josh looked doubtful. "We're going to be working on the building quite a bit. A cat might get in the way."

"Nah, cats keep to themselves pretty much, and all of ours are good mousers."

Addy looked expectantly at Zeke and Josh. "I'll take care of it."

The brothers reluctantly agreed.

Millie pulled the pencil from behind her ear and took her order pad out of her apron pocket. "All right, what would you like for breakfast?"

They ordered griddle cakes and sausage, with stewed rhubarb on the side. While they were eating, Zeke looked at his brother. "Josh, can I borrow your truck? I want to buy a box spring for the bed."

Josh tried to hide a grin. "Now, why would you want to do that?" Then he relented. "Yes, that bed is pretty noisy, isn't it? Sure, you can." He was silent for a moment. "That one-note aria went on for quite some time last night."

Addy blushed.

Zeke scowled at his brother's comment. "Just keep your dirty thoughts to yourself," he shot back.

Their meal over, the brothers went back with Addy to the rear of the restaurant, led by Millie, who called one of the girls to take her tables for a few minutes. Millie opened the food storage room attached to the building and came out with a colorful calico cat.

"Here, this is Chloe. She's only a little over a year old now, but she was well taught by her mother, who is one of our best mousers."

Addy cuddled the creature that purred in her arms. "I've never had a cat before. How do I take care of her?"

Millie smiled. "Cats are pretty easy. I give them half a can of sardines every day and a saucer of milk. You got to keep them a little hungry, though, so they'll hunt. And keep her inside the building for a few days, or she will try to come back here. After that, she'll know to stay with you." Millie went back into the storage room and brought out four cans of sardines. "This will get you started. You can buy more at the cannery. Oh, and leave a dish of water out for her."

"Thank you, Millie," Addy said, scratching Chloe's ears. "Can I give you anything for her?"

"Pshaw." Millie waved her hand. "Just save me a seat in the front row when you get the old theater going again."

Addy and the brothers said their goodbyes and took the cat home. She and Josh had everything set up for Chloe by the time Zeke came back from the mercantile store with the box springs.

"Chloe seems a little nervous in her new home," Addy informed him. "She follows me around everywhere I go."

Zeke grinned. "It's going to take a few days for her to relax. We had some barn cats when I was a child, but never any in the house." He scratched Chloe under the chin, and she purred happily.

The next day, Josh finished hooking up the gas stove in the apartment's kitchen while Addy fixed up the icebox to ready it for the first weekly delivery of ice, which she had arranged for Mondays.

Chloe roamed around the building for a while, then turned up after dinner Sunday night. Addy sat on the couch in the parlor, sewing, while Zeke and Josh went over their funds. At Addy's sharp intake of breath they both looked up. Chloe had laid a dead mouse at her feet.

"Praise her, Addy, don't scream. She has accepted you, and that is her offering," Zeke said quickly.

Addy looked uneasily at the cat and scratched her back. When Chloe had gone away again, Addy pointed to the little corpse. "Could one of you dispose of this?"

Zeke gallantly bowed before he picked up the mouse by the tail and threw it out the door.

Addy shook her head. "I thought she would eat them."

Josh chuckled. "Most cats share with their owners once in a while."

After the block of ice came for the refrigerator on Monday morning, Addy made out a list and went shopping to stock up on food staples. When she returned, Zeke and Josh helped her store all the food and put dishes and utensils in the cupboards. She made some tea when they were finished, to go with their lunch.

Suddenly, tears rolled down Addy's cheeks. "Fixing up the kitchen made me realize how much I miss my family." She sighed. "All those special dinners in Aunt Jen's home... I guess this is what it feels like to be homesick. But there's no changing it, I suppose."

Zeke put his hand over hers. "We'll make this into a home. Anywhere you are is home to me."

Josh nodded. "I felt homesick myself when I first came here, but putting my mind to this building, I didn't have time to feel sorry for myself."

That afternoon, they started stripping the walls in the theater. The brothers had hired roofers to work on the old building so rain damage wouldn't hamper the remodeling of the interior. The large room rang with hammer blows from outside, and Addy was complaining about that as she soaked the wallpaper with a terrible-smelling solution.

Suddenly, a booming voice trumpeted from the entrance door, "Joshua, my friend! I'm back to help you!"

A big bear of a man, with a bushy black beard, strode down the aisle, a small Indian woman in tow. Josh jumped down from his ladder on the stage, where he had been taking the gaslights off either side of the proscenium, and met the stranger with a delighted shout, slapping him on the back as he greeted him.

"Ivan! Thank you for coming. We've started on the theater, as you can see, and we could sure use your assistance. Zeke, Addy, come over here."

Zeke was on the far side of the room pulling up the aisle carpeting. He straightened up and came to stand next to Addy, and Josh put his arms around their shoulders. "Ivan Nikolaevich, I want you to meet my brother and his wife, Zeke and Addy."

Ivan shook their hands, and Addy was clearly fascinated to see her hand disappear in his huge grasp. "I'm pleased to meet you," he exclaimed. "I've brought my wife to help, as well. This is Kata. She is a Tlingit woman from the island across the harbor. She's back from helping her sister with her babies in Douglas." Then, speaking to the petite woman, he said, "This is Josh. I told you about him."

Kata looked shyly at them and turned to Ivan. "They are all *cheechako*?"

"Yes, my dear."

Addy glanced from one to the other. "What is *cheechako*?"

Ivan laughed. "That is the word for newcomers. Did you move here from Indiana, too?"

Zeke spoke up. "I lived there originally, but Addy is from California. We moved from Los Angeles."

"Ah! The other golden state. Well, we will all work together on this theater and make it glow again, eh?" He gave a hearty chuckle and went up to the stage with Josh.

Kata approached Addy shyly as Zeke went back to work. "May I do something to help?"

Addy handed her the scraper. "You can strip some of the wallpaper I've already soaked."

While they worked, Kata kept glancing at her. Finally, the girls took a break and Addy poured Kata some hot tea in the apartment.

"Addy, may I ask you something?" Kata gazed at her cup.

"What do you want to know?"

"Are you a native, too?"

Addy stared at her, puzzled. "What do you mean?"

"You are dark—your hair, skin and eyes—like an Indian."

Addy smiled. "No, I'm half Mexican. My father married an American."

Kata took a sip of tea. "My people up here are

trying to get citizenship in the territory, so we can have a say on what becomes of us. We were here even before Ivan's family came and settled from Russia. When Alaska was purchased by the American government, they granted his ancestors citizenship, but they still haven't given it to our people."

Addy nodded. "The Mexicans in California have problems with the government, too. I really didn't get involved in that, because I lived with my mother's family after my parents were killed in the San Francisco earthquake. I was six years old." A look of sorrow crossed Addy's face, but she quickly changed the subject. "Where are you from?"

"I was born in Angoon, which is on the southwest side of the island across the harbor. I'm part of the Kootznoowoo tribe. That means, 'fortress of bears.' My mother named me after a legend about a man named Kats who married a bear that took the form of a woman. Kata is the woman's form of that name."

"So this is where you went," Josh said, when he found the two in the apartment. They both turned to see him standing with Zeke and Ivan by the doorway from the office.

Addy waved them over. "We were just taking a break, and Kata and I were getting acquainted. Have some tea?"

The men each took a cup and sat down.

Josh had brought in the accounting book from the office. "We need to buy some new wallpaper and carpeting for the theater. We also have to look into electrical wiring." He was silent for a moment as he studied the figures. "We need to bring more money in."

Addy looked up. "Millie told me she needs some help at the restaurant."

He shook his head. "We need more than a

waitress' salary to pay for this."

Zeke spoke up. "This is the territorial capital. Maybe we can get someone to back us or have some kind of fundraiser for the arts. A lot of the mine owners and other company heads live here. They like cultural things."

Ivan stroked his beard. "I know Mayor Robertson. Maybe he can help."

Addy jumped up. "We could have a party or a ball and show people what we are planning to do. If we get the stage ready and the piano tuned, we can perform a couple of numbers."

Josh frowned. "That will take several weeks to be ready for that."

Ivan hit his fist in his other hand. "In the meantime, we can go to the newspaper, put up notices around town, and send invitations to the government people and the company owners."

Josh scratched his head. "It may work. We can give it the old college try."

Zeke nodded. "If we can get backers, that will help. Addy and I planned to get jobs when we arrived here, but fixing up this building is a job in itself."

The next few weeks saw a flurry of activity to get the building renovated. They had contractors working on the outside and on the wiring, while the two couples and Josh threw themselves into the interior cleaning and redecorating.

Chapter 3

Addy and Kata were painting the trim on the lobby when an elegantly dressed woman entered. Her golden-blonde bobbed hair was topped by a fashionable hat that matched the white silk fabric of her suit. She eyed the two women with an air of superiority. With a red kerchief tied at the nape of her neck to keep the paint out of her hair, and dressed in Zeke's old shirt and a pair of overalls rolled up at the ankles, Addy wasn't the height of fashion.

"Girl!" the woman pointed at Addy. "Can you tell me where I can find one of the Shafer brothers?"

Addy felt a stab of anger at the tone of voice. "What do you want?" Addy tried to look calm.

The woman glared at her. "Well, I don't think it's any of your business."

Just then, Zeke walked in. "Can I help you with anything? I'm Zeke Shafer."

Instantly the stranger was all smiles. "Hello, I'm Gladys Pembrook. I might be interested in investing in your theater. My husband was a mine owner, and he left me his estate. I'd like to see this place turned into a legitimate establishment." She turned her gaze to Addy. "Maybe you can find a better class of workers, with my help."

Addy bristled. "Excuse me?"

Zeke cleared his throat. "Mrs. Pembrook, may I introduce my wife, Addy Shafer?"

Surprise written across her face, the newcomer made no apology. "Well! It's a natural mistake. I didn't realize you had married a native person."

Addy stood by the frame of the lobby door, paintbrush in hand, trying to decide whether to aim it high or low. Zeke, seeing Addy's expression, steered Mrs. Pembrook through the door to the office.

"Wait in here and I'll get my brother." He came back to the lobby. "Sweetheart, please take a deep breath. We do need the money." He gave her a hug and went to find Josh.

As Addy began slapping another coat of paint on the trim, Kata stopped what she was doing and went over to her. "I didn't know you'd be treated like that."

Addy bit back an angry sob. "I was hoping we'd left behind all those types when we moved from Los Angeles. Now I understand what you told me before."

Kata shook her head. "I guess prejudiced people are everywhere."

****

Josh gritted his teeth as he and Zeke went to the office. Zeke had told him what had gone on in the lobby. If Gladys Pembrook was to be a backer, Josh hoped she wouldn't stay so unfriendly to Addy.

He saw that Gladys had settled into one of the chairs by the desk and was pulling out a cigarette holder. She smiled sweetly at Zeke. "Do you have an ashtray?"

Zeke looked at Josh, and Josh took one down from the top of the filing cabinet. He handed it to her. "This was here when I purchased the building."

She lit the end of the cigarette. "Don't you smoke?" She blew out the match and flipped it into the glass dish.

Both men shook their heads as Zeke put his hand on Josh's shoulder. "This is my brother, Josh Shafer."

She took Josh's hand and then released it.

"Delighted. You can call me Gladys." She leaned back in her chair as Zeke settled himself behind the desk and Josh perched on the edge of its neatly organized surface. "I was so happy when I heard this theater would open again. The others in this city are not so grand. Tell me what you want to do with it."

Josh leaned forward. "We want to open the stage for vaudeville and legitimate theater, for one thing. And we're going to construct a retractable motion picture screen and put a projection booth by the lobby."

"Besides that, we want to make the old bar into a restaurant and a place for dances," Zeke put in.

Gladys smiled. "Well, that all sounds quite interesting. I'm prepared to advance ten grand, if you'll let me take care of your publicity and fundraising." She flicked the ashes into the tray. "You see, I know all the influential people in this city, and I know where the money is."

Zeke shifted back in his chair. "We appreciate your generous offer. Why do you want to help us?"

"My late husband and I were patrons of the arts." She gave him a slow smile. "And now I have an opportunity to work on improving culture here and making new allies."

The brothers looked at each other. Josh rubbed his forehead. "What do you think?"

Zeke nodded. "I think we can give her a chance to help us."

Gladys stubbed out her cigarette in the ashtray and put the holder away in her pocketbook. She stood to leave. "Good. I'll get started on fundraising plans right away. I'll have them okayed by you before I execute them."

Josh slid off the desk. "We'll see you out."

Mrs. Pembrook once again swept into the lobby, flanked by the brothers. "I'm going to enjoy doing business with you." She shook Josh's hand, but held

Zeke's for a moment longer after shaking it as she smiled sweetly at him.

She passed by Addy and patted Addy on the head. With a look that could only be described as a sneer, Mrs. Pembrook said, "So-o nice to have met you, dear." Addy spit on the floor after Mrs. Pembrook went out the door.

She turned and gave the brothers a look that shot daggers. "Zeke, Josh, in the office right now!" Once there, she slammed the door. "How could you do business with that—person!" she blurted out. "Did you see how she treated me?"

Zeke came over and put his arms around her. "Addy, please. Mrs. Pembrook wants to back us with ten thousand dollars. That will pay for the rest of the work. Also, she wants to arrange fundraisers with the people she knows in the community."

She trembled. "I don't know if it's enough for putting up with a gold-plated bitch like that."

Josh took a deep breath. "Sometimes you have to do unpleasant things to reach the goal. If we can put up with her for a while, we won't need her once we start making money."

She looked at Zeke. "She wants more than to back the theater. Her eyes were like a cat's trying to find its next meal. Mrs. Pembrook put a big red circle on you."

Zeke laughed. "I'll be very careful, darling."

"That doesn't make me feel any better."

Later, Josh helped Zeke finish tuning the piano on stage. He had the front off and turned the string pegs while Josh tried the keys.

"I think I've got it," he said as he leaned on the top. "Play something."

"How about 'In the Good Old Summertime'?"

"Sure."

He started playing. "It sounds right. Swell! You did it."

As Zeke was putting the piano back together, Addy came in with some tea on a tray. "I thought you two would like something before we call it a night." She set the tray down on a small table near the instrument.

Josh helped himself to a cup, and she took one over to Zeke, her face unreadable. Zeke took his cup and set it on the bench. "Addy, I know what's bothering you about Mrs. Pembrook." He put his arm around her. "You know I'm not interested in her, not in the least, but with her help, we can get this old theater going again."

She pursed her lips. "I just hate kowtowing to these elite types. Why do the hateful people seem to be the ones with the money? If we ever become rich, I'm never going to act like that."

He kissed her on the nose. "That's why I love you."

Josh took his cup with him up the aisle of the theater. "And this is where I make my exit." He smiled as he realized the two lovebirds hadn't heard him.

Chapter 4

Muriel Giovanni cuddled her two-day-old daughter as the lace curtains billowed in the lush Los Angeles summer air. A warm glow went through her, looking at the baby in her arms. *I never knew motherhood could be like this. Oh, Jenny, my sweet child.* A pink bassinet stood between her bed and her cousin Addy's old bed in the room where they had grown up. The young widow wavered between missing her husband and hating his family, who had taught him that killing was honorable. Tony had been so good to her, but it was hard to believe she had fallen into the trap of thinking like they did. *Well, he'll never see his daughter, thanks to them. He walked into that police trap with them and was one of the first ones shot.* A knock at the door broke into her thoughts. "Come in."

Her father opened the door. The look in Henry Carter's dark eyes revealed his concern. "Muriel, you've received a letter from the Giovannis," he said, handing her an envelope.

Muriel stared at it for a moment and then, with a quick glance at her father, opened it. As she read, her stomach tightened and she began to shake. "It's from Tony's Uncle Aldo. He wants me and Jenny to come and live with Tony's mother, Sofia." She looked up. "How did he know she was born? We didn't tell anyone."

Her father's mouth formed a straight line under his mustache. "He must have taken over the Giovanni operations, and I'm sure they still have people in the government on their payroll. They probably have someone in the county records office."

Tears formed in her eyes. She couldn't let the Giovannis take Jenny. "What can I do? I never want to see those people again, even if Jenny *is* Sofia's grandchild. I don't want them to get their hands on her."

With a sigh, her father sat on the wooden chair at the vanity. "There is a way, but it will come as quite a sacrifice to all of us. We could send both of you to Alaska, to be with the Shafers."

"I don't want to be a burden to them. Where would we stay?"

He rubbed his chin. "In Adeline's last letter, she mentioned they have several bedrooms above the theater." He rose and went to the door to call downstairs, "Jen, come up here to Muriel's room."

They heard running feet on the staircase and Muriel's mother rushed in. "What's the matter? Are Muriel and the baby all right?"

As her husband told her about the letter from the Giovannis, her light brown eyes grew wider. "What can we do?" she asked.

"Could you write a letter to Adeline and ask if Muriel and the baby could live at the theater there?"

Her mother sat on the side of the bed and took Muriel in her arms. "Oh, my! So far? Are you sure that's the only way?"

"I don't know, but Jenny is as much a Giovanni as she is a Carter. They might be able to take Muriel to court, and they probably have judges on their payroll, too. It would be harder for them to do that if she was out of the state."

Jen Carter gently took the bundle from Muriel's arms and kissed the tiny forehead. "Oh, why does everything have to be so complicated?" After a moment of rocking, she gave the baby back to Muriel and stood up. "I'll get to work on a letter right away."

Muriel echoed her mother's sentiment. She

hated the thought of being so far away from most of her family—but part of her was happy that she would be able to see Addy again. They had always been as close as sisters.

Chapter 5

It was one of Juneau's rare sunny and warm August days. Josh, Zeke and Ivan were working on the restaurant area when Addy came running in from the post office with a letter. "Zeke, Muriel had her baby! She named her Jenelle, after Aunt Jen."

"Isn't Muriel your cousin, the one who was married to the mob family?" Josh asked.

"Uh-huh, and Muriel wants to know if she can come up here and help. She's worried about her late husband's family trying to get the child."

Zeke took the letter and glanced at it, but Josh could see Zeke was thinking more than reading. "She worked in shipping, so she knows how to get along with business. I wonder if she could handle booking acts and motion pictures?"

Josh nodded. "We're going to have to start booking soon, to open next May. Addy, write back to her about it. Maybe she can start booking there. Tell her we're wide open."

Zeke stopped her as she headed for the apartment to compose her letter. "You know, now that we have the electrical wiring in, we need someone who is good with lights and sound. James should be seventeen by now. Do you think your uncle would let him come, as well?"

"I can ask. I'm sure James would love that." She added to Josh, "He built his own radios."

"Good. That's a recommendation for him. We need to get a staff together, and those two are a good start. Now, can you think of someone who can run a restaurant?"

Zeke nudged Addy. "What about Mrs. Hutton? I'm sure we could pay her better than what she gets as a housemother at a dormitory. And her food was delicious."

"Okay, I'll write to her, too. And we'll need a resident cast. Let's see, there's Anne and her husband, Ray, and there's Roxie, and Nathan and Babs. I'll write to them all."

Josh cleared his throat. "When you write, make it clear we can't pay wages yet. All we can offer them is room and board, before we open."

She nodded. "I think they'll understand."

Addy went into the office and closed the door. A few minutes later she returned, her eyes dark with concern. "Zeke, if I extend an offer to so many people, do you think the mob could find us?"

Zeke took a deep breath and looked at Josh. "What do you think?"

Josh turned to Addy. "Go ahead and send the letters. We need workers. If it does attract attention, we'll deal with it."

"You don't understand what these people can do." Fear was written large on Addy's face.

Zeke shook his head. "Addy, we can't live under a rock for the rest of our lives. Write to them."

She went slowly back to the office.

While Addy was making another trip to the post office to mail her letters, Ivan and Kata arrived for the day. Ivan went directly to finish up in the restaurant, but Kata brought a garment bag into the office where Josh and Zeke were going over the ledger. "Josh, I've finished the linen suit for you."

Josh inspected the garment. "That looks great, Kata!"

"Why don't you try it on?"

Zeke waved toward the apartment. "You can go in there."

Josh came back to admiring looks from Zeke and

Kata. "This fits swell—ow!"

Kata inspected the right shoulder seam, where Josh's hand had flown with his exclamation, and pulled out the offending straight pin. "I'm sorry, I thought I got them all." Just then, Addy returned to the office and sucked in her breath.

"That looks wonderful!" Addy gave it a critical eye. "Where did you get it?"

He smiled. "Kata made it. She wants to do the costuming for the theater. What do you think?"

Addy examined the suit closely. "I can't tell that from store-bought clothing. Where did you learn to sew like that?"

Kata laughed. "My mother saved up during the gold rush and bought a sewing machine. She was a dressmaker for the wealthier women in Juneau. She taught me how to do it, but when the mercantile started getting in pre-made wear, our business declined."

Josh chimed in. "I asked her to make an ice cream suit for our fundraising performance. I figured if it came out well we'd ask her to make one for Zeke, too, and a costume for you."

Addy put her hands on her hips. "When is the fundraiser?"

"Next month. Gladys Pembrook is organizing it."

Addy's hackles went up. "Why is *she* organizing it? I could've handled it. And why wasn't I told about this sooner?"

Zeke and Josh glanced at each other. Josh felt the blood drain from his face. "I guess we forgot. Gladys mentioned it when she talked to us in the office."

Throwing her hands into the air, Addy steamed, "Gladys, Gladys, Gladys! Both of you jump when she snaps her fingers."

Zeke put his hands on her shoulders. "Calm down. Gladys made the fundraiser—and her being the organizer of it—one of the conditions for giving us the money. She knows who to invite and how to put on a gala. None of us has ever done anything like this."

Addy sputtered under her breath. "Why does it have to be Gladys? She is the most aggravating person I've ever met! Now we have to rely on her?" Addy gritted her teeth. "I'll be in the apartment." The door slammed behind her.

****

Addy plunked herself down on the couch, and Chloe immediately jumped into her lap. As Addy scratched Chloe's ears, the cat started to purr, ignoring Addy's agitation. "Chloe, I smell a rat, and it isn't the sort of rat you can catch. I have bad feelings about Gladys Pembrook, but she has the money, damn it." She looked at the framed picture of her parents and little brother, a photograph taken only a few months before they died in the San Francisco earthquake. "Papa, Mama, what can I do? If we get the theater going, I have to be nice to that woman, even though she barely acknowledges I exist. She has to be at least forty years old, but she's after Zeke, and..."

She heard a knock at the door from the office. "Addy, may I come in?"

"Yes, Kata." Addy deliberately sounded more cheerful than she felt.

Kata entered with pictures, paper and tape measure. She pulled a pencil out of her hair. "I want you to choose what clothes you want me to make, and I need your measurements."

Addy put Chloe down and shuffled through the pictures Kata handed her. There was one with a white mutton-sleeve blouse and a red nineties-style skirt cut off below the knee. "That should go with the ice cream suits the men have."

Kata nodded. "I think so, too. Stand up and I'll

make this fast."

Addy stood still while Kata took the measurements. "What do you think I should do about Gladys Pembrook?"

Kata looked at her thoughtfully. "She's a thorn under the blanket. I guess it's a matter of how much you want this theater to succeed. Unfortunately, she has the money and the contacts you need to get it going. It's a little like my people and the Americans. We've had to put up with a lot, but we've gotten jobs and a better life because of it." She stopped for a moment. "I'm sorry if that offends you. You and the Shafer brothers don't seem to treat me like a lower animal."

"I can't speak for them, but having been treated that way myself, I try to judge everyone fairly."

Kata stood up and put her paper and pencils away. "There, I'm done. I'll have the outfits for you and Zeke ready in a couple of weeks."

****

Josh and Zeke were in the office, going over sheet music, when Addy came in after seeing Kata and Ivan off. Zeke looked up and patted a chair beside him. "Come here and help us decide what numbers to do."

Josh handed her some of the music. "Here are some new ones I picked up at the mercantile. They told me these have been popular over the past year."

They shuffled through the stack, finally deciding on five numbers for the fundraiser: "Ain't We Got Fun," "Swanee," "Whispering," "You're the Cream in My Coffee," and "Charleston." They thought that much singing and dancing would be enough of a sample, and then Josh would give a brief explanation of what else they were going to do with the theater.

Zeke glanced at Addy. "Gladys is going to have the posters and programs printed up."

Addy clamped down on her back teeth. "Oh?"

Zeke put his arm around her. "I know how you feel about her, but she seems to want to help make us a success. I'm sure after the fundraiser she'll warm to you. You have more talent than the two of us brothers combined."

"Singing and dancing isn't what she's after, and you know it."

He shook his head. "She won't get anywhere with that, and *you* know it."

She pursed her lips. "A woman like that is going to pull out all the stops, and she wouldn't like to lose." Then she glared at them. "Why haven't I been included in your little tête-à-têtes with Gladys? Aren't I part of this partnership?"

Zeke and Josh looked at each other. "Sorry, Addy. We haven't left you out on purpose." Josh felt a little flustered. "It seems like every time Gladys comes over, you're out somewhere."

Zeke thumbed the music sheets a couple of times. "Maybe the next time Gladys wants to bring in some ideas, we can make sure Addy is here."

Addy smirked. "Well, I can get my two cents' worth in." They went back to the sheet music.

Gladys showed up a few days later with the printer for the newspaper, Elmer McKneely. He did posters, notices and invitations for extra money. Zeke and Josh sat him down at the desk in the office while Addy brought more chairs from the apartment.

Gladys set her elegant body on one of the chairs next to the desk and lit a cigarette. "That's good of you, dear, and now you may leave." She blew a stream of smoke into Addy's face.

Zeke cleared his throat. "Mrs. Pembrook—"

"I told you to call me Gladys," she interrupted.

"Gladys, Addy is involved with this as much as Josh and me. She's put her money in this, as well."

Gladys looked daggers at Addy. "Very well, if

you insist."

Mr. McKneely took out an inked sample of the invitation. "This is what Mrs. Pembrook and I came up with. All we need is your approval." There was a professional line drawing of two men on a stage, one man playing the piano and the other a banjo. The printer read aloud the words, "Come to the fundraiser to help the old Golden North Theater shine again. Joshua and Ezekiel Shafer have transformed the building into an entertainment palace and restaurant that Juneau can be proud of. You can see a sample of their talent and dreams for the place on..." He handed the invitation to Josh. "I can fill in the date and time when it's decided."

Addy steamed, and Zeke was visibly upset. "Why isn't there a mention of Addy in there?" He slammed his hand on the desk. "We are forever grateful to you, because of your generous backing, Gladys, but you have treated Addy very badly. She is not only an equal partner in this, financially, she is also our premiere star, and she is our Art Director. She has appeared on stage and in motion pictures. She doesn't deserve this treatment!"

Gladys turned a critical eye on Addy. "You've appeared in motion pictures? What kind?"

Addy looked her straight in the face. "I was a lead player at Majestic Studios. What are you insinuating?"

Josh felt lightheaded as Gladys stared stonily at Addy. She seemed to be going through some internal turmoil for a moment. "Well, isn't that interesting. I'm sorry, dear, I didn't realize you were so—talented."

Addy's jaw muscles twitched, but she didn't say anything. Josh wanted to see where Zeke was going with this.

Zeke took the invitation from Josh and gave it back to Mr. McKneely. "I want you to add a woman singer in this picture and include Adeline's name along with ours."

Mr. McKneely nervously looked at Gladys Pembrook, and she nodded before announcing, "I think our business here is finished for the time being." She shook hands with Josh and Zeke, giving Addy a sideways glance. "We'll be back to discuss the program in a couple of weeks—with the *three* of you."

"Bitch," Addy said under her breath after Gladys and McKneely left the room.

Josh looked at his brother. "Damn, Zeke, you almost blew us out of the water."

Zeke glared back. "I won't stand by and let her run down Addy like that. I know we need the money and the contacts, but I'm not going to sacrifice my wife to do it!"

Josh was silent for a moment. "You're right. I hope we can find someone else to back us, someone who isn't so judgmental."

Chapter 6

For the next week they went to work on the restaurant with Ivan and Kata, setting up a kitchen and food storage area where the liquor supply used to be. The large bar, where Josh especially put in a lot of elbow grease, became a diner-style counter, with booths and tables elsewhere around the old dance floor. A small stage at the back of the room would be for live music. They planned a north woods décor showcasing rough-hewn logs and wood on the walls, with a few deer and moose heads. The lighting was wagon-wheel chandeliers, and every table would have a candle.

Toward the end of the week, they had an unusual caller. At a knock on the swinging double doors, all of them turned to see a small man in a pinstripe suit and derby hat stepping in. He looked around nervously. "Are any of the Shafer brothers here?"

Zeke stepped down off the ladder where he had been putting bulbs in the lighting fixtures. "I'm Zeke Shafer. May I help you?"

The man glanced around again. "Do you have a place where we can talk?"

"Yes, come with me." And Zeke ushered him into the office and closed the door.

Everyone glanced at each other and shrugged, going back to what they had been doing. Suddenly, they heard a shout and a wail. The door to the office flew open, and Zeke had the man by the scruff of the neck and the seat of his pants. When the pair went through the double doors, everyone ran over to see

Zeke bodily throw his visitor out the front door and lock it. He walked past the group of stunned people and climbed up the ladder again.

Eyes wide, Addy called up to him, "What was that all about?"

"He wanted to sell us bootleg." Zeke calmly went back to working on the chandelier.

"Oh my, you mean those gangsters are up here, too?"

He looked down at her. "I don't think he knew about the connection in Los Angeles. He just saw an opportunity to sell. I'm not worried about it."

Josh leaned over the bar. "I hope you're right." *This just keeps getting better and better. I'm sure glad Zeke was here to deal with that fellow.* He went back to work.

A week before the date set for the fundraiser, Josh and Zeke were working on the ledger in the office when Addy rushed in from the post office. "Zeke, Josh, I've got letters back!" She gave a couple to Zeke and opened two others.

Addy waved one letter in the air and shouted happily to the brothers, "Muriel booked a premier vaudeville troop for the opening and ordered Chaplin's new motion picture, *"The Kid."* She's going to work on the bookings there yet, until she leaves, but she and James will be moving up here in two weeks. Hurrah!"

Josh checked the calendar. "Let's see. This is the end of September. We have time to get the five other rooms upstairs ready. Your cousin has a baby? We can give her the largest of the rooms."

Zeke nodded. "Should work out just right. Nathan and Babs are coming, as well as Mrs. Hutton. She says she will be here in mid-November to set up the restaurant kitchen."

Addy took a quick read of her other letter. "Anne and Ray are coming, but Roxie won't be here until

June. She's getting married, and she says, 'Wait till you see who it is.'"

Josh smiled. "Well, it looks like we have a staff. They can stay here until they find someplace else to live after we get rolling."

Zeke turned to Addy. "While you were gone, Gladys stopped by. She's bringing over a newspaper reporter from the *Daily Empire* for a story on the fundraiser in..." He looked at his watch. "About fifteen minutes now."

Addy's mouth and the corner of her eye twitched visibly. She took a deep breath and went into the apartment.

Gladys sailed in with the reporter before Addy emerged for the meeting. The reporter was just shaking Zeke's hand when Josh heard Addy open the door in time to hear the reporter say, "It's nice to meet you, Mr. Shafer. Gladys has nothing but the best to say about you. I haven't seen her this sweet on anyone for a long time."

Josh saw Addy clutch at the knob. Gladys glanced at her with a half-smile, and Zeke flew to Addy's side. "Mr. Louis, may I present my wife, Adeline?"

Mr. Louis looked embarrassed. "Oh, I'm sorry. I didn't know you were married. Gladys didn't tell me." He regarded Gladys, and she shrugged.

"It never came up. I'm sorry, dear." Gladys dripped honey.

Zeke and Josh gave most of the interview. They told about their background and why they wanted to bring the old theater back to life. The reporter asked Addy a few questions about her background, but she answered in few words.

After Gladys and Mr. Louis left, Addy picked up one of the chairs and threw it at the door to the restaurant before bursting into tears.

Josh stared. "What the—"

Zeke went to hold her. "Addy?"

"I have to get out of here!" she sobbed before running out of the office, calling back, "I have to go for a walk!"

****

It was fall in Juneau, and a heavy mist hung darkly over the harbor. The chill went to Addy's very bones. She angrily brushed away the tears from her face and found herself in front of Millie's. The lunchtime crowd had thinned out, so Addy went in and slipped onto one of the stools at the counter.

Millie came over with a concerned look. "What's wrong, Addy?"

Addy took a nickel out of her pocket. "A cup of coffee, please."

Millie brought over a steaming cup. "What's upset you so, honey?"

Stirring some cream into it from the little ceramic ewer on the counter, Addy sighed. "I'm trying not to let Gladys Pembrook get to me, and I'm mad at myself for letting her. If that makes any sense. Because of her, my nerves have been on edge, and I seem to be weepy all the time."

Millie looked closely at her. "Hmm, there might be something more, but that's not for me to say."

"She keeps trying to get Zeke's attention."

"Has he given you any reason to doubt him?"

Addy stared at her cup. "No, but he keeps being civil to her because she is putting up so much money. And I have to admit, if it wasn't for her backing, we wouldn't have been able to get the theater going again, at least not nearly so soon."

"Well, both those boys are handsome, but Gladys is old enough to be their mother. I don't usually spread the dirt, but Gladys has been known to flirt with younger men, even while her husband was still alive. She thinks her money will get her anything." She put her hand under Addy's chin and made her

37

look up. "You're a beautiful young woman, Addy. That's one of the things you have over Gladys."

Addy smiled. "Thank you, Millie." She put a penny tip on the counter. "I think I'll go home now."

****

That evening, Josh, Zeke and Addy put in their usual two hours of rehearsal. Addy had purchased a tambourine to add rhythm to the banjo-piano combination. Now, a few days before their debut, Josh was sure they knew every word, note and dance step on their program. The times Ivan and Kata listened to them in the theater, they applauded and cheered.

Josh got up and put the banjo back in its case. "I think I'll call it a night. I'm starting to see elves in the theater. Goodnight, you two."

The next morning, Josh and Zeke were going over the backstage of the theater. Zeke turned to him. "Josh, I'm worried about Addy. I've never seen her this melancholy before. Gladys is really bothering her."

Josh looked at him thoughtfully. "I know she's been crying at odd times. I've heard her."

Zeke shook his head. "Maybe she's still homesick. Having Muriel here might be a good thing for her."

Spotting something white on the floor by the piano, Josh picked it up. "Hey, what's this?" He held it out to Zeke with a grin. "It seems to be a woman's drawers!"

Zeke yanked the material out of Josh's hands. "I told you to keep your dirty thoughts to yourself!"

"You keep handing me all this ammunition." Josh chuckled as Zeke took the offending garment back to the apartment.

Chapter 7

Muriel clamped a hand over her hat as the sea breeze threatened to take it from her. From the deck of the ship that had brought them from Seattle, she watched Juneau come into view. The trip by train from Los Angeles and then by ship had not been an easy one, and she was glad her parents had decided to come with her and Jenny and James. Taking care of a baby was hard; she never could have done this traveling without help. Fortunately, the rocking of the train and the ship seemed to soothe the infant most of the time. Her parents said they wanted to help her settle in, but she knew they missed Addy as much as she did and were looking forward to seeing her again.

Next to Muriel stood her mother, holding Jenny, who was cooing with the rocking motion of the water. James leaned over the railing, excitement written all over him at this wonderful adventure. Her father stood behind them, stoic as ever.

Muriel squinted through the mist toward the docks. "I see them!" She started waving frantically.

Addy and Zeke waved back and made their way to the ramp area. As the ship slowed, the crew threw the heavy ropes to the dock workers to secure the liner.

Muriel and her family hurried to the gangway, and she flew into Addy's arms. The cousins held each other tight, tears streaming down their faces.

Addy pulled back and cupped Muriel's cheeks. "You look wonderful! Oh, I've missed you so. I'm glad you all could come. I'm sorry Grandpa and Grandma didn't."

Muriel held Addy's hands. "They're watching Casey, Buster and Maggie. There was no way they could all come, but they all send their love." Muriel took the bundle from her mother's arms and handed it to Addy. "This is Jenny, your new cousin."

Addy's eyes softened as she smiled at the little one. "She's beautiful! Look, Zeke." Zeke stroked Jenny's cheek with his finger before Addy gave her back to Muriel and greeted the rest of her family.

Zeke embraced Muriel with one arm in greeting, being careful of the baby. "It's good to see you again. Thank you for starting the bookings. We don't have telephone service here, so we have to rely on the telegraph."

Muriel nodded. "I know. That's why I have a list of addresses we can use."

Zeke drew a handsome young man over to them. "Muriel, this is my brother, Josh."

She drew in her breath for a moment as she studied the sparkling blue eyes. She could tell they were brothers, but where Zeke wore a serious expression, Josh radiated good humor.

He swept his hat off his head and took her hand. "A pleasure to meet you, Muriel."

She felt her face grow warm. "Good to meet you, too."

"And this must be your little one." Josh grinned at the baby. "She's a cutie. We have your room ready for the both of you."

She let go of his hand. "Thank you. We appreciate all you've done for us."

Suddenly serious, he looked at her steadily. "You're part of the team now. We need all the help we can get for starting this theater."

Zeke and Addy were encouraging everyone to head toward what Muriel discovered was Josh's truck, with some of their trunks on it. Next to it was another loaded truck and a seemingly mismatched couple, Mutt and Jeff style, introduced by Josh as Ivan and Kata.

Behind the trucks was a handsome surrey with enough room for six people. Zeke climbed in on the driver's side and picked up the reins. "We borrowed this from a neighbor. Most people still have good old horse power instead of autos."

Zeke gave a hand up to Addy, who settled beside him, and Josh helped the others onto the cushioned seats. Her mother held Jenny as Josh boosted Muriel up to the seat. She smiled a thank you and Josh tipped his hat with a gallant flourish that made Addy and Zeke exchange a look as he slapped the reins for the two dapple horses to go.

Muriel found herself quite enchanted with the little city nestled into the hillside. The pine and hemlock trees dripped moisture constantly to the green below even as mists rose from the ground. The mountain Muriel had seen from the ship appeared to rise from the sea with Juneau perched on a shelf at its base, while the surrounding ranges encased the area like a fortress.

Soon, they pulled up to a large building with scaffolding around three sides. Zeke stopped the horses at the back by a large door with the words "Stage Entrance" painted on it. "This is it, folks. The Golden North Theater, our home."

The two trucks had already arrived, and Josh and Ivan busily unloaded the trunks and took them inside. Zeke helped everyone off the surrey, then swung up into the driver's seat again. "I have to return this rig to the neighbors. I'll be right back."

Addy took them all on a tour of the building, ending up in Muriel's room on the second floor, a corner room with two big windows that had a view all the way to the harbor.

"This is a beautiful room! I think Jenny and I

will be very comfortable here." Muriel took the baby from her mother and laid the sleeping infant in the crib Josh had just finished setting up.

James had a smaller room down the hall, next to Josh's. Muriel's parents would stay in the room across the hall.

The tour completed, everyone drew up chairs in her parents' room so Muriel could listen if Jenny woke up. Muriel had noticed her father didn't say much on the tour, but now he turned to her. "I can see the Shafer brothers have made impressive improvements to this old building."

Addy grinned. "You should have seen it when we first arrived. We're halfway finished now."

Zeke chimed in, "Addy has done quite a bit of work, as well."

Muriel's father shook his head. "Fortunately, Adeline has never been the delicate lady." Addy narrowed her eyes at him. "You should have this finished in a few months. Why are you waiting until May to open?"

Josh waved his hand. "That's when the docks open up. Winter is a slow time in Juneau. People tend to hole up during the cold weather here. We get sightseers when it warms up, so it made sense to open then."

Addy grasped her aunt's hands, bringing out a smile. "How long are you and Uncle staying?"

"We plan to stay for a couple of weeks to help Muriel and James get settled and have a good visit with you. Maybe we can give you a hand, too."

They talked until little Jenny woke, and then they all went down to the dinner that Kata had prepared for them.

The next morning, Muriel and Josh were in the office, going over the ledger, when they heard a knock on the door. At Josh's "Yes?" Kata opened the door.

"I told Addy yesterday I had her costume ready, and she said to bring it by when I came in."

Josh waved his hand. "Go on through. She's waiting for you in the apartment."

When Kata disappeared through the door, Josh leaned over Muriel, seated at the desk. His closeness distracted her, and she tingled every time his arm brushed her.

Suddenly, there was a quick knock on the door and Gladys swept in, bringing responses to the invitations for the fundraiser. Josh made the necessary introductions, and Gladys was shaking Muriel's hand as Addy and Kata came in. "Nice to meet you, dear. It's hard to believe you're related to Aggie."

Addy stood stony still.

"Her name is Addy," Muriel corrected firmly, "and yes, we most definitely are related." Addy had already told Muriel all about Gladys.

Gladys turned and gave Addy a half-smile. "Sorry, darling. I can never get that straight."

Muriel shook her head slightly.

Just then Muriel's parents returned from a walking tour of the neighborhood, and her father said, "This is a charming little city. You must take a walk with us, Muriel."

Gladys turned an interested eye in his direction. "Who is this?"

Once Josh had introduced them, she smiled. "Well, Muriel's parents! How sweet of you to come up with your daughter. Of course you want to make sure she'll be treated right."

Addy made a low sound in her throat.

With a glance at Addy, Henry Carter turned to Gladys. "We have no concern about how our daughter will be treated. My wife and I wanted to see how the rest of our family was, madam."

Gladys frowned, as if her comment hadn't

43

elicited the proper response. "Well. I see. Josh, here is a list of the people who are coming. I'm going to the caterers to plan the food and drink, since the kitchen isn't ready yet. They also will decorate the lobby and restaurant, since we want it done right. Ta!" Gladys disappeared as fast as she'd appeared only seconds ago.

Addy steamed. "That woman is so aggravating, I want to scream! Now she's telling us we can't do anything right."

Muriel put her arm around Addy. "I see what you mean. It's terrible you have to put up with that."

Josh leaned his hands on the desk. "Addy, as soon as we're on our own, you won't have to put up with her, I promise."

Muriel's mother shook her head. "Some people don't realize what they say reflects on them. That's a very unpleasant woman."

Her father turned toward the door. "We're going to Millie's now. That walk brought out my appetite, the air here is so brisk. Anyone care to join us?"

The others declined, and Mr. and Mrs. Carter went on their way.

Addy waved her hand. "Come on, Kata, let's see if the men need any help in the theater."

That evening, Addy, Zeke and Josh put on a dress rehearsal for a critical group: Muriel, her parents, James, Ivan and Kata. Their performance was met with a standing ovation.

Jenelle Carter hugged Addy. "If that doesn't convince Juneau you'll bring entertainment to them, I don't know what will."

Her husband nodded. "You have quite an enterprise here. You all must be commended for the work you've put into this."

Too soon, the weeks had gone by, and Muriel's parents were at the docks to go home. The white passenger ship creaked at its moorings as the sea birds sailed overhead, calling to each other. Mr. Carter clapped his hand on Zeke's shoulder. "I can help with the bookings on the telephone, if you wish."

Zeke smiled. "That would be swell. It's not easy to get a fast response by telegraph."

Muriel's mother had a hard time tearing herself from little Jenny. "I can't stand the thought that all of you are so far away." She sniffed as she handed the baby back to Muriel. "I hate what the Giovannis have done to us."

Her father grasped Zeke's hand. "Take care of them all, Mr. Shafer. I'll be forever in your debt."

"You know I will, sir. Have a safe trip home."

Addy threw her arms around her aunt. "Give my love to everyone. I miss them so."

Aunt Jen brushed the windblown hair out of Addy's eyes. "I will, dear."

The little group of Addy, Zeke, James and Muriel watched the ship until the fall mists made it disappear as though by a magician's sleight of hand. Addy pulled her coat tighter around herself and gave Zeke a hug. "Let's all go home." They turned toward the trucks.

At the theater, James went to help Ivan with the spotlights while the other three headed toward the office. There they found Gladys chatting with Josh.

She turned a critical eye on Addy. "You know, dear, the fundraiser is just days away. Do you have something suitable to wear at the reception?"

Breezing by her and into the apartment with a brief, "Just a moment," Addy came back with a blue satin dress she hadn't managed to return to the wardrobe department before Majestic Studios closed down. It was floor length, Grecian-style, and very elegant. "Will this do?" she asked icily.

Gladys was taken aback, but recovered quickly.

"My, I didn't think you had something like that. Sorry, honey."

"She doesn't look sorry," Addy said to Muriel under her breath as Gladys sauntered out.

Chapter 8

The night of the fundraiser, Josh, Zeke and Addy greeted a flow of people at the theater entrance. Muriel had decided to stay upstairs with Jenny, but she wished them all well.

Gladys appeared from the restaurant, where she had been directing the caterers. She wore the latest fashion fad, an Egyptian-style multi-colored silk gown and a jewel-encrusted headband with a large pink-dyed ostrich feather. Josh thought Gladys definitely was trying to outshine Addy's ice blue satin. With her was a young man and an attractive girl. Behind them was a tall thin girl, hunched over, looking at the floor.

"Darlings," she said as she rested her gaze on the two brothers, "this is my son, Manfred, and his intended, Lettie." Manfred had a look of perpetual boredom, and Lettie was his paper doll. Gladys made a gesture in the thin girl's direction. "And this disappointment is my daughter, Amelia." Josh's heart went out to the girl at such an introduction, and Amelia looked like she wanted to disappear. Gladys waved her hand toward the three Shafers. "This is Josh, Zeke and Ada."

From between gritted teeth Addy said, "Addy. My name is Addy."

Manfred barely acknowledged them, and Amelia didn't even look up. Gladys glared at her daughter. "Don't you have any manners at all? I'm ashamed of you."

Amelia winced and said in a small voice, "Hello, pleased to meet you." Then she gave them a feeble attempt at a smile.

Addy held out her hand and took Amelia's warmly. "I'm happy to meet you, dear. Thank you for coming."

Gladys glared at Addy and then beamed at her son. "Manfred just became a junior lawyer in a firm. I'm so proud of him. An intellectual like his father." With that, she swept off to greet the arriving social lights of Alaska and point them toward the Shafers.

They met the new territorial governor, Scott Bone, and his family, who had just moved into the territorial mansion a few blocks away. Mayor R. E. Robertson, who had set the ball rolling in getting the city government behind the theater after Ivan talked to him, mentioned how glad he was to find someone to take over the business. They were even graced with the presence of a former judge and delegate to Congress, James Wickersham. He was happy to see more culture evolving in the old gold rush capital.

Josh was in awe of the important people who came to support their venture. They spent the next hour hobnobbing with the elite of Juneau before Josh saw Zeke nudge Addy and point to his watch. She nodded, and Josh joined them as they all disappeared backstage, where they had hastily set up the dressing rooms a few days ago.

Kata was in Addy's room to help her with dressing and makeup. The plan was for Addy to put on the red-fringed dress first, and then Kata secured the breakaway skirt and blouse over it. The blouse was tied at the back of the neck and the skirt had one hook at the waistband. All Addy had to do was go behind the curtain by the piano, whip the outer costume off, and be back on stage in seconds.

After makeup, Addy put on the jeweled headband that was part of the dance outfit, and then a large stylish hat of the turn of the century went over her short bob.

Josh and Zeke rapped on the door when it was time to go on stage. As Kata opened the door to the dressing room and the brothers stepped in, Addy stood up and looked at herself in the mirror. "You did a wonderful job on this, Kata."

Her seamstress smiled. "You really look like a star tonight."

Suddenly, Addy turned pale and leaned against the chair. "I guess my nerves are getting to me. I feel a little lightheaded." Zeke made her sit for a moment until the feeling went away.

"Are you going to be all right?" Zeke asked.

She took a deep breath. "It's show time. I'll be fine."

The stage wasn't yet completely renovated, so they were going to perform in front of the curtain. They waited in the wing until Gladys, on stage to quiet the people in the theater for the beginning of the performance, made their introduction.

"Attention, everyone! I guess you noticed our hosts disappeared a while ago. Well, they want to give you a short sample of their talents. Then after a few numbers, Mr. Josh Shafer will explain what they plan for us in the future." She turned toward the wing and held up her hand. "Now here he is with his brother Zeke and Zeke's wife."

Addy puffed out her cheeks and her hands formed into fists at her side.

Before he sat down at the piano, Zeke introduced her to the crowd: "My wife's name is Addy, folks, and we're happy to be here." There was applause as Josh picked up his banjo, and Zeke helped Addy to sit on top of the upright, then seated himself on the bench. There was one second of breathless silence, and then they launched into a lively version of "Ain't We Got Fun," each one taking various verses.

Ivan worked the spotlight and for the second

number trained it on Josh as he did a solo of "Swanee" with some grand picking on the banjo. Addy's tambourine and Zeke's piano filled in accompaniment.

Zeke's song "Whispering" was slower and more romantic. During his performance, he smiled at Addy, seemingly directing the words to her. Then he got up and lifted her off the piano, and she did the saucy "You're the Cream in my Coffee" while she tapped the time on the tambourine. Then she disappeared around the piano and through the curtain.

Josh and Zeke did the introduction and started singing "Charleston" as Addy reappeared in her red fringed dress, dancing the popular new dance. For the last verse, she grabbed Josh and, while Zeke played the piano and sang, Addy and Josh danced together. At the end, the theater erupted in cheers. The three on stage held hands and gave a deep bow.

When the applause had died down, Josh stepped to the front and shushed the crowd.

"Thank you!" Josh started. "I hope you liked our sample." The audience applauded again. "Now, this is what we plan to do in the Golden North Theater. We will have a regular cast to put on shows for you, but we will bring in vaudeville troupes for your entertainment, too. As we build our theater up, we can put on plays straight from Broadway. Also on order is a screen and projector, so we will be able to bring you the latest motion pictures from the studios. Not only that, but the old bar is being made into a restaurant, with space for dancing. All we ask is for your support. Thank you, again."

Gladys took over the stage again as Josh, Zeke and Addy went back to the wings. Josh noticed Addy staggering a bit, and when they reached the dressing rooms, she literally collapsed into Zeke's arms. He put her on the cushioned couch in the hall and Kata, alerted, got a wet towel to put on her face. Addy stirred and groaned as Zeke hovered and then knelt on the floor beside her. "What happened, Addy?" He held tightly to her hand.

"I don't know. I've been getting dizzy spells today. Must be nerves." She sat up with the towel to her forehead. "I'm feeling better now."

Zeke looked concerned. "You've never had nerves about performing before. I think you ought to see a doctor. Kata, who's a local doctor around here?"

"Dr. Lindsay has an office three blocks from here. I've been to him before."

Addy shook her head. "I'm all right."

Zeke frowned. "I just want to make sure. We don't know how this change of climate is affecting you."

"I'll go with you tomorrow morning," Kata offered. "He opens his office at nine o'clock. I'll be here at a quarter to."

Addy sighed. "All right. Just to make you two happy, I'll go."

Just then James came in and whispered something to Josh. He had been in the wings, watching as Gladys encouraged donations to help with the theater's refurbishing. Josh grinned, rubbing his hands together. "James says he thinks we have several thousand dollars in support, thanks to our efforts tonight. I think that's more than enough to finish up the building and have some left over for hiring traveling shows."

James looked at Addy. "How are you feeling?"

She made a face as she sat up. "Better, but my two nursemaids want me to see a doctor."

"Well, I agree with them. We can't lose our star attraction. You were quite a hit out there."

With Zeke on one side and Josh on the other, Addy went out to the lobby with them to thank their benefactors, James trailing behind to once again

watch the crowd from the wings.
****

Muriel knew Addy felt a little queasy the next morning, but neither of them let on to Zeke. By the time Kata arrived, Addy said she felt much better. Josh, James and Ivan had already left for the docks to pick up the motion picture projector and screen, which would take two trucks to transport. Muriel gave Addy a critical eye and an "interesting" when Zeke told her how Addy had fainted after the show, Muriel put Jenny in her buggy and decided to walk along with Addy and Kata. "A stroll in the crisp fall air was just what we all need."

It was a rare sunny day and the trees were in a blaze of glory. "This is amazing! I've never seen leaves change like this." Wildflowers still clung to the side of the mountain and added to the palette. The sky was a rich blue, and the harbor water sparkled with the sun. "Why are so many people out shopping today, do you think?"

"They scurry around like the squirrels do, taking advantage of good weather to prepare for winter," Kata replied.

"And I've never experienced a real winter." Muriel looked worried. "How should we be getting ready for it, do you think?"

With a sidelong look, Addy asked, "Kata, would you help me and Muriel with what to get for winter? We've never lived in a cold climate, and we don't know what all to do."

Kata smiled. "First, warm clothing. We can go to the mercantile. They have some winter things in stock, but they will have more in a few weeks. We'll go then. I'll show you what you need. Ivan can take James. Will Zeke need help?"

"He lived in Indiana, and I think they had winter there. Anyway, Josh has been through winter here. He should be able to help Zeke."

They had arrived at their destination, a flight of covered stairs leading to a door on the second floor of a building with a law office in the storefront on the first floor. The sign on the wall read, "Dr. Dwight Lindsay, one flight up." Muriel trailed behind them, carrying Jenny. There was an elderly lady in the waiting room and a young nurse sitting at a desk by the interior door.

The nurse smiled at Kata. "How are you, Mrs. Nikolaevich? Are you here to see the doctor?"

"No. I brought my friend, Mrs. Addy Shafer, to see him."

The nurse turned to Addy. "You're one of the people fixing up the old theater, aren't you?"

Addy smiled. "Yes, I am. I'd like to have a checkup, please."

"You can see the doctor after Mrs. Andrews. Please have a seat." With a look at Muriel, she asked pleasantly, "Are you here to see the doctor, too?"

Muriel shook her head. "No, but I will come another time and bring my baby in for a checkup."

They all took seats on the old caned wooden chairs. The sunlight streamed through the two curtained windows. An aged building smell was all around them, mixing with the alcohol scent of a medical office.

When Addy was called into the office, Muriel glanced at Kata. "What exactly happened last night? Zeke told me she had fainted, but he didn't go into detail. You were there."

Kata related to her what she had seen. "I think there's something more than nerves."

Muriel nodded. "I remember feeling lightheaded when I first became with child."

"My sister, who just had twins, was the same way."

The girls chatted while Jenny happily played with her rattle. When the door to the inner office opened, they gathered their things and rose as Addy came into the waiting room. The nurse looked up. "Mrs. Shafer, be back next week at this time."

Addy nodded and went down the stairs with Kata and Muriel. As Muriel tucked Jenny back into the waiting buggy, Kata asked, "Does the doctor have any idea what's wrong?"

"A few ideas, but he said he'll know when the tests come back. He doesn't believe it's anything serious."

Kata studied her critically. "Hmm, I see. Well, I'm going to the mercantile to get some material. I'm going to make some standard costumes for the theater, since I have all of your measurements." She paused for a moment, as if she was waiting for Addy to say something, then shrugged. "See you tomorrow."

Muriel and Addy started toward the theater. Muriel took a deep breath. "Dear, I do know what those symptoms sound like. Are you afraid of being with child now?"

Addy was silent and pulled her coat tighter against the chilly fall breeze. "I've been under some stress lately. That's probably what it is." But Muriel noticed a concerned expression on her face.

"Addy?"

"I don't want to think about that now!" she snapped, thrusting her hands in her pockets.

Chapter 9

As they reached the front entrance of the theater, Muriel heard a bicycle stop behind them, and both girls turned to see a Western Union messenger boy approaching with an envelope. He tipped his hat to Addy. "'Scuse me, ma'am, are you Mrs. Adeline Shafer?"

She nodded. "Yes."

"I have a telegram here for you."

"Thank you." She gave the boy a quarter.

He tipped his hat and left, and she opened the message. Almost immediately she gave a cry and handed the small yellow paper to Muriel, who read:

MURIEL JAMES AND ADELINE STOP GRANDFATHER DIED YESTERDAY STOP THOUGHT YOU SHOULD KNOW STOP FATHER AND UNCLE

Tears flowing, the cousins leaned against each other for several minutes, mourning. Their beloved grandpa, who was like another father to them, was gone.

"I need to find Zeke." Addy went into the building and headed for the office, dashing away the wetness from her eyes. Muriel followed and was taking Jenny out of her buggy in the lobby as Addy threw open the office door, leaned against the jamb, and managed to get out, "Zeke?" before sobs overtook her.

Zeke leaped up from the desk and went to her, saying, "Sweetheart, what's wrong?"

"Grandpa...Grandpa...died." She handed him the telegram.

He put his arms around her and held her tight. "Oh, Addy, I'm so sorry."

Muriel, following Addy, heard the door from the apartment open. She couldn't see who was there because the office door was in the way, but she could hear the voice from the other side of the room: "Zeke, honey, where are you? Let me show you what a real woman is like."

I know that voice, and Addy doesn't need the aggravation right now.

As Zeke turned, Gladys was behind him, clad only in a robe tied loosely around her waist. Her bosoms were visible on either side of the deep vee of the blue satin lingerie.

"What the hell are you doing? I thought you wanted to use our apartment to freshen up," he barked.

One look at his face told Muriel he didn't know anything about Gladys' plans.

"Oh, I see the little wife is back. I thought you were out for the morning," Gladys sneered.

Addy's pressure cooker temper blew. A sound came out of her that was like the bellow of an angry bull. "How dare you!" Her hands clutched into claws.

For the first time, Gladys had the decency to look scared. Addy flew at her and grabbed the lapels of the robe. She swung the slightly taller woman around toward the door.

"Addy," Zeke cautioned, but she turned a glare on him.

Gladys had apparently never been in a fight, because she had trouble loosening Addy's grip. Addy pinned one of Gladys' arms behind her back and marched her to the front door of the theater, where she pushed Gladys bodily out the door and locked it. Addy flew past a stunned Muriel and Zeke into the apartment, returned with Gladys' clothes mashed into a ball, and ran with them to the lobby door, where she threw it all into the street next to Gladys.

Muriel, watching in horror through the lobby window, saw that Gladys had recovered enough to try to get back into the building, clawing at Addy, but Addy pinned Gladys' arm again. This time she whipped off the sash of the robe, throwing that into the street, as well, whereupon Gladys made an attempt to slug Addy, but Addy grabbed Gladys' arm and threw her against the wall. When Gladys took a handful of Addy's hair and pulled, Addy took Gladys in a choke hold.

Just then Josh, James and Ivan arrived with the trucks of projection equipment and were met with the naked spectacle of Gladys, her robe flapping in the breeze. James turned red and ran inside, while the other two gaped momentarily at the fight. By this time Zeke had come out and managed to pull Addy off Gladys.

Gladys closed the robe around herself as Ivan and Josh ran up. "What the hell is going on here?" Josh yelled.

Gladys turned a furious eye on all of them. "Forget any more backing from me until you get this wildcat out of here!"

Addy struggled against Zeke's hold. "You're the one making plays on a man that doesn't want you!"

"Thank you for your help, but Addy stays," Josh said, his jaw set.

"I will make sure no one else backs you," Gladys hissed.

"And I will let everyone know what a pitiful woman you are," Zeke stated firmly.

Gladys huffed. She gathered her clothes and marched to her automobile, an expensive REO. "You'll regret this!" she shouted before she drove away.

Josh looked bemused. "I hope no one stops her, since she's wearing just a robe. Now that's something she'll regret."

Ivan turned to the Shafers. "I wouldn't worry. You got contributions from the fundraiser, eh? And I heard many good things about all of you in town."

Josh looked concerned. "But can she talk everyone into not supporting us?"

Ivan stroked his heavy beard and chuckled. "You'll find townspeople who will love the story of this day about Gladys. She just *thinks* she runs society."

****

Addy still trembled, and Zeke cupped her chin. "Sweetheart, are you all right?"

A small sound came out of her throat, and she looked at Zeke with tears in her eyes. "This has been a terrible day!" She wriggled out of his grasp and ran to the apartment, where she threw herself on the bed and sobbed into the pillow. She felt Zeke sit beside her.

"I love you, darling. Please talk to me." He rubbed her back.

Somehow, he always found the right thing to say. She turned to sit on the edge of the bed next to him, and he handed her a handkerchief, his other arm around her. She dabbed her eyes and sniffed. "I'm sorry for losing my temper, but I couldn't take that woman anymore."

He held her tight against him, resting his chin on the top of her head. "Addy, I should've done or said something before this, but I was afraid of losing our backing. I shouldn't have put the theater first. I'm sorry." He was silent for a moment. "I'm also sorry about the loss of your grandfather. I respected Mr. Applegate, and I know what he meant to you."

"There's something else I haven't told you." Addy took a deep breath. "I was going to wait until I knew for sure, but the doctor said I might be with child."

It took a moment for Zeke to absorb the information, and then a huge smile broke out on his face, and he gave her a squeeze. "A baby? You're going to have a baby? That's wonderful news!"

She looked at him, aghast. "You don't think this is a bad time? We have so much to do, and money is tight now, and..."

Zeke laughed. "Other theater people have managed. Hell, a lot of vaudeville performers have their whole families travel with them. Haven't you heard the term, 'born in a trunk'?"

Her heart swelled with love for this man. She laced her fingers with his. "I love you so much. We can do this. I know it."

He had a concerned set to his face. "Let's get one thing clear. If you are with our child, I want you to promise me there will be no more fighting." He waited a moment. "Addy?"

"I can't help it. Sometimes I get so angry, I have trouble controlling myself."

"I mean it. You have to learn to check your emotions now. You have to be responsible for your conduct."

"All right, I promise." She smiled to herself. "But you have to admit, I got the better of Gladys." They laughed.

****

Muriel stood back against the far wall of the lobby holding Jenny. She could see why Addy was so upset about Gladys. *That woman could be hateful. The very idea! To make a play for Zeke right under Addy's nose? Could she be mentally a little unstable?* Muriel wondered.

Josh came to her with concern written on his face. "Muriel, did you see what happened?"

She nodded and related to him what had happened with Gladys before he got there. Then as she remembered the telegram, she started crying. "I haven't told James yet of Grandpa's passing."

Josh gently lifted Jenny from her arms. "Why don't you ask Zeke and Addy to join you in the office, and I'll send James in. I'll take Jenny upstairs for you." She saw the mist in his eyes.

Muriel hurried to the office and knocked on the office door. "Could the two of you come in so we can tell James about Grandpa?"

Addy and Zeke came in a few seconds later, and Addy picked up the telegram just as James opened the office door, glancing at them all. "What is it? What's wrong?"

Addy drew a ragged sigh and handed him the telegram. "It's from your father. Grandpa died."

James read the telegram then crumpled it, tears shining in his eyes. "No, it can't be! He looked so healthy when we left!"

Zeke hurried to put his arm around James' shoulders. "Addy and Muriel will wire your father to get some flowers from all of us. I'll wire money for that."

Muriel kissed his cheek. "Thank you. I think I'll write a letter to Grandma."

Addy nodded. "James, you can write, too. We can send all the messages together."

With a squeeze to James' hand, Muriel started upstairs. She came upon Josh standing over the crib watching Jenny sleep. He turned and gave Muriel a hug. His arms felt so good around her that for a second her breath caught.

He cupped her chin. "If you need to talk, I'm a willing listener."

She smiled as a tear trickled down her cheek. "Thank you. You have been so good to Jenny and me. We kind of barged in on you here."

His sunny smile came back. "Nonsense! One job I hated was the bookwork. I'm so happy you took that over. But, I'd better get back to work before

Ivan comes to get me."

Muriel took some stationery to the desk and sat to write. Before she dipped the pen into the ink, she glanced at the door Josh had disappeared through...and smiled.

****

A week went by, and Muriel wanted some coffee from the urn they'd set up in the restaurant bar for all the workers. She heard the lobby doors open and caught a glimpse of Addy passing by. Knowing she had come from her doctor's appointment, Muriel hurried to follow as Addy entered the theater. Zeke was helping James wire the spotlights, and Addy sidled up to him and whispered in his ear.

Zeke whooped and spun her around in his arms. James, Ivan and Josh hurried over. "What happened?" Josh put his hand on Zeke's shoulder.

"Addy's with child!" Zeke beamed.

Addy turned red and fled past Muriel, through the office and into the apartment, with Zeke following close behind.

Muriel was close enough to hear Addy say, "You told everyone in there! Now they know we—" She gulped. "That we—do that." Muriel suppressed a giggle.

"We're married. Of course we do that." Zeke sounded flabbergasted.

Muriel knocked. "Addy! I want to tell you both congratulations!"

From the other side of the door, Muriel heard, "Thanks to you, Zeke, now everyone knows."

The next few days, in the throes of morning sickness, Addy was relegated to the office to help Muriel with the bookkeeping. Zeke would not allow her to actively work on the upstairs rooms. He said the four of them could do it, and Muriel knew Addy hated that she could only listen to the activity above her.

The times in the office gave Muriel a chance to discuss with Addy what was ahead, however. They had some sisterly heart-to-heart talks that seemed to put Addy's mind more at ease about being with child.

As the days in late October got shorter, colder, and darker, Muriel felt a certain amount of depression. She could still smile with Jenny, and the prospect of a shopping trip gave her a definite lift of spirit. Finally, she and Addy were going with Kata to the mercantile to pick out winter clothes.

Kata steered her down to the long underwear. "Might as well start you out with the first layer." She chuckled. She picked up what looked like a ladies' version of a union suit.

Addy took it. "One piece? How do you—" She blushed.

Kata turned it to the back. "There's buttons here on a flap that goes down."

Muriel shook her head. "The legs will show below the hem of my skirt."

"That's the next item. You'll freeze in silk stockings. Now, this is what you have to wear." She held up thick knitted stockings that would go all the way up to the top of Muriel's thighs. "And a pair of boots for your feet."

Addy and Muriel gave each other an incredulous glance. Muriel wrinkled her nose in distaste, and Addy nodded. So far, she didn't think these Alaskan fashions were very flattering.

They went to the outerwear and found dresses and ladies' suits of tightly woven wool. Addy selected a couple of loose-fitting ones for herself and admired the flattering colors Muriel chose.

The store had some lovely Eskimo parkas for sale, with attached hoods and fur trimming. Muriel tried one on and found it soft and warm. Heavily knitted cap, mittens and scarf completed the outfit.

"I'm going to feel like I'm wearing my whole wardrobe." She sighed.

Shaking her head, Kata grinned. "Believe me, you two Californians will appreciate your whole wardrobe when the winds howl and the snow flies."

Kata showed Muriel heavier buntings for babies and helped her pick out a few for Jenny.

Addy and Muriel put their purchases on their business tab and carried their bundles back to the theater.

****

Josh breathed in the fresh painted scent of the upstairs rooms and was amazed at how far they had come in half a year. *This building will be ready to go in the spring. I never thought we could do it.* His thoughts were interrupted by the sound of someone running up the steps.

Addy burst into the room where they were working. "Josh, Zeke! Here's a letter from Mrs. Hutton. She'll be here in a week, and the dear woman wants to set up the restaurant kitchen herself. Will you get a room fixed for her next?"

"Sure. That's swell," said Josh. "Maybe we can get the kitchen going in time to have a New Year's Eve party for our patrons."

"That's a wonderful idea! It will keep our name alive in the town." Addy bounced on the balls of her feet in excitement. "We have the addresses of our regular contributors. They could be sent invitations the first part of December." She turned to Ivan and Kata. "Do you know of any bands around here that we could hire for a party?"

Ivan glanced at Kata. "Uncle Nickolai and some friends play weddings around here. They are good, and they can play anything, old or new. What do you think, Kata?"

"They played for our wedding, and they know some native music, too."

Josh nodded. "See if you can get them for us. Addy, when Mrs. Hutton arrives, you can work out a menu with her."

"Aye-aye, Cap'n!" Addy saluted and went happily back to the office.

Chapter 10

Muriel and Addy waited at the harbor for the cruise ship carrying Mrs. Hutton to come in. Josh and Zeke were stationed at the unloading dock to pick up her trunks. The waters were unusually calm for October, and the rising sun peeked through a sea mist that was beginning to burn off.

"It's a good thing she's coming now," Muriel said. "Josh told me this will be the last of the passenger ships until spring. Freighters sometimes carry passengers, he said, but that wouldn't be nearly as comfortable."

Addy shaded her eyes. "Here it comes." She pointed to a liner traveling up the channel.

The wind ruffled Muriel's hair and carried the smell of the sea and of oil to her nose. "Addy, are you sure you're up to this? You said you were sick this morning."

Addy smiled. "It seems the fresh air has cleared it up. Anyway, the morning sickness doesn't come as often now."

Muriel grimaced at a blast of cold wind. "This fresh air is chilly."

"I'm fine. This coat Kata helped me find is perfect."

The liner was secured at the dock and, with a clang, the gangplank was put into place. The cousins were already looking among the passengers for the large fiftyish woman. Suddenly there she was, Cora Hutton, carrying a black satchel, picking her way carefully down the ramp.

"Mrs. Hutton!" Addy called and started running

toward her, dodging the other passengers.

Mrs. Hutton set down her satchel and gathered the young woman into an embrace. "Addy! It's so good to see you again. I'm happy you asked me to help you. I was having trouble finding any work in Hollywood. Seems like anyone who worked for Majestic was looked on with suspicion, because of the scandal."

Addy glanced at Muriel, who stood back, not knowing what her reception would be. "Mrs. Hutton, this is my cousin, Muriel."

Mrs. Hutton pursed her lips. "Yes, I remember you from Addy's wedding. You were the one who married the gangster's son, am I right?"

Muriel took a breath. "Yes. And before you ask, I'm the one who almost killed Zeke. That part of me is gone. I know I hurt a lot of people, and I regret it."

Mrs. Hutton put her arms around Muriel. "If Addy and Zeke can forgive you, I can, too."

Addy headed toward the waiting room. "Let's all get some coffee while Zeke and Josh find your trunks."

They took their coffees to one of the wooden tables. Mrs. Hutton took a careful sip of the hot liquid. "Well, you two look positively radiant. Things going smoothly for you?"

Muriel shrugged. "Yes and no. The theater is coming right along, but we've had a few problems along the way. For instance, a man tried to sell us bootleg, but Zeke dispatched him right away."

Mrs. Hutton sighed. "I guess you can't get away from that, even up here."

Addy studied her cup. "I'm also with child."

"That's good."

Addy pursed her lips. "I don't know if it's a good thing or not. Oh, I want to have children, but I think the timing's bad."

Mrs. Hutton smiled. "Children never seem to

come at a good time, but may I offer my congratulations? I know you and Zeke will work something out. It's good that you have your cousins up here with you. The more support you have, the better."

Addy put her hand on Muriel's. "Well, Muriel seems to do all right with Jenny. I think I worry too much. I'm glad you wanted to take on the restaurant."

"I'm happy to help you all out with setting it up. For me, it'll be nice to work where I won't be looked on as a potential rum runner." She took a sip of coffee. "I'll tell you, I've always wanted to run a restaurant. I'm very excited about this chance to work with all of you. After what we all have been through with the mob, starting out fresh up here sounds wonderful."

"That must be the reason everyone I asked is coming up to help us. All of them except Roxie are arriving in March, and she will be here in June." Addy paused a moment. "We're hoping to have the kitchen up and running by the end of the year so we can have a New Year's ball to thank our contributors. You'll have to tell us what you think, after you see the place."

Just then Zeke came in and greeted Mrs. Hutton before making introductions to Ivan, James and Josh, who accompanied him.

Mrs. Hutton nodded to each of them. "Pleased to meet you, Ivan. James, I remember you from the wedding. Josh, I swear, you look a lot like your brother." Her eyes shifted from one face to the other.

Addy laughed. "And they are surprisingly talented. I didn't even know that Zeke could play the piano. And Josh plays the banjo."

Mrs. Hutton stood and put her arms around both brothers. "Now, that is something I must hear." She gave them each a pat on the shoulder, then turned toward the door. "I'm anxious to get started."

As the trucks pulled up in front of the theater, Mrs. Hutton marveled at the large building. "How much had to be done to this?"

"Quite a bit," Josh said. "It was a gray shabby heap when I first got here. There's still a lot to do, but it looks better."

As soon as Mrs. Hutton had settled into her room upstairs, she came down to the restaurant kitchen to inspect what she needed to do. She found the brothers and Muriel ready to show her around, and Addy came in just then with Kata, who had met Mrs. Hutton on her arrival at the theater.

They all trouped into what was to be Mrs. Hutton's domain and looked around silently. Finally that good woman put a hand to her chest and said, "Oh, my," with some dismay.

The old gas stove was almost rusted through the top from years of a leaky roof and neglect. The porcelain kitchen sink was a filthy mess of soap scum and ten years of collected dirt. The large icebox had loose panels on the back. Suddenly, a mouse flew across the floor with Chloe in hot pursuit, startling the quiet group and breaking the spell of gloom.

With a forced little laugh, Mrs. Hutton remarked to Muriel, "This is going to take some time and work. Do you have enough in your ledger to do this?"

Muriel glanced at Josh.

Josh nodded. "Muriel said we have fifteen hundred to work with, from all our contributions. The important question is, will it be ready in time for New Year's?"

Mrs. Hutton rolled up her sleeves, her reserves of energy coming to the surface. "I'm up to the challenge. Are you?"

Josh went to get Ivan and James to help clear

the disaster, while Muriel set about scrubbing the sink. Addy, forbidden by Zeke to do any heavy lifting, was given the job of going through the drawers and seeing what could be salvaged of the old utensils.

At dinnertime, they all treated Mrs. Hutton to a meal at Millie's and introduced her to the proprietress when Millie came over to take their order.

As she delivered their meals, Millie gave a sidelong glance at Josh. "I've got some news, if you want it," and looked at Mrs. Hutton.

"Anything you say is safe with her," Josh said.

"Mmm, well, I found out Gladys doesn't have as much sway with the elite as she thought she did. She was spreading dirt about Addy around town, but apparently there were other stories going about Gladys setting her hat for Zeke. Everyone knows how she goes after the young men. Anyway, you folks made such a good impression on the upper crust that she couldn't get anyone to go against you." Millie chuckled. "Looks like the only one who's sorry is her."

Zeke gave a sigh. "Thank goodness that all we've worked for didn't go up in smoke because of her."

Millie shook her head. "That woman needs to be taken down a peg or two. Well, enjoy your meal."

Mrs. Hutton dug into her Miner's Stew and tried a mouthful. "Mmm, this tastes good. What kind of meat is this?"

Muriel giggled. "It's caribou. How do you like it?"

"Tastes a lot like the venison we used to get. I could work with this at the restaurant." From then on, throughout the meal and as they walked back to the theater afterwards, Mrs. Hutton made little comments, asked questions, and sometimes seemed to be thinking out loud. Muriel could tell she was already working on new things to try.

A few days later, Muriel was going over the accounts with Josh in the office. Baby Jenny slept in a cot Ivan had made for her and set in the corner. "See, you can work and be a mother at the same time," he had said with his customary grin.

A knock at the door made them both look up to see Zeke come in with Gladys. Muriel and Josh glanced at each other, and Josh took a breath. "Gladys?"

Gladys twisted the ties on her purse. "I want to apologize to all of you for my behavior. I would like to back the theater again, if you'll let me."

Muriel locked eyes with Zeke, and he asked, "Will you apologize to Addy?"

Gladys ground her teeth and nodded.

He went to the door. "Addy is sorting canned goods for the restaurant. I'll go get her."

When Addy followed Zeke into the office, her eyes narrowed as she spotted Gladys standing before the desk. Muriel clasped Josh's hand, waiting for Addy to explode. Muriel gave Addy a warning expression meant to stave off the wave of anger she knew was possible from her cousin, and Zeke held up his hand. "Remember your promise, Addy. Will you listen to what she has to say?"

Addy swallowed hard and said, "All right."

With a sigh, Gladys started talking in a tight voice. "Addy, I'm sorry for trying to lure your husband. I know now that it's futile. What I want is to work with all of you to open this theater. I would like to back it again. Would you please give me another chance?"

Muriel knew Gladys just wanted to get back in the good graces of the community, but Addy looked at Josh and Zeke. "If she's willing to behave herself, I'll go with any decision you make." She turned and went back to her pantry work, while Muriel silently congratulated her for not flying off the handle.

Later, when they all were at lunch, Zeke came up behind Addy and gave her a quick kiss before he sat next to her. "Josh and I decided Gladys could come back and work for us, on the condition that she remains businesslike and professional." He put his arm around her. "I was very proud of you today. You held your temper and heard her out."

Addy shook her head and set her fork down. "I'm not happy about her coming back, but I'll give her another chance. Maybe holding a grudge isn't a good thing, either."

Zeke smiled. "That's the girl I love." And he began work on his meal, joining in the general conversation about the day's accomplishments and laughter over the various oddities that had occurred.

Muriel said to Josh, "Isn't Mrs. Hutton a marvel, to be able to prepare meals for us out of the provisions stocked so far?"

"Mm-hm, I guess!" He swallowed the last bite from his plate. "Between the two of you, the sink and every other surface in the kitchen has been scrubbed within an inch of its life. Ivan is a genius to be able to fix that old gas stove and hook it up so it works now."

"The icebox is still out of order, but with the weather so cold it isn't hard to make do with that little unheated room by the back door, and the pantry is almost full, and not overrun by mice anymore, thanks to Chloe."

"Oh, yes." Josh chuckled. "Chloe and her mice. You can't beat what she does for Mrs. Hutton with her continual presentation of those conquered mice, laid out with such great ceremony on the kitchen mat."

With an answering laugh, Muriel let her eyes meet his for a long moment that held more than thoughts of mice.

That evening after dinner, Addy took Muriel's hand. "I don't know what to do about my feelings for Gladys. I wish your mother were here. I need a woman's advice for this problem."

Muriel thought a moment. "Maybe you could talk to Mrs. Hutton."

Addy hugged her. "That's a wonderful idea. Thank you. Are you going up to your room already? It's not late, but I'm tired from getting that pantry in order, and it's still not done." Muriel agreed with her, and with good-nights said, they parted for their respective rooms.

The next day, on a break from completing the stocking of the pantry in the restaurant, Muriel, Mrs. Hutton, Kata and Addy all sat down with their midmorning cups of hot coffee at the big table now installed in the middle of the restaurant kitchen. Muriel was exclaiming over how cold the days were getting and how thrilled she was to see the light dusting of snow over everything outdoors. She'd never been in snow before, and the flakes seemed so magical, floating in the air.

Addy nodded in agreement with her but then turned to Mrs. Hutton.

"Mrs. Hutton—" Addy began.

"Addy, you can call me Cora, now that we're working together."

"Okay, then, Cora, I have a problem with Gladys coming back. She seems to be very businesslike right now, but can a leopard really change its spots?"

Cora shook her head. "You need all the financial backing you can get. Kata here needs material for stock costumes, you've been designing a variety of scenic backdrops, and the men have been putting the finishing touches on the projection booth and the retractable screen. All of this takes not only time but money. Sometimes you have to sleep with the enemy to get what you want."

"Sort of like a high-priced whore." Addy snorted.

Kata nodded. "A lot like what my people have to do to get along with most Americans."

Cora smiled. "Watch, Kata. The Indians are very close now to getting full citizenship. I hope someday they also get the respect they deserve."

Muriel glanced at Cora. "You sound like you know what you're talking about."

"While I lived in the Arizona Territory, I saw the squalor the Navajo and Hopi lived in. I always thought they got a raw deal from the government. They're human beings just like everyone else."

Chapter 11

It was the first week in December. Gladys had spent it in the office, putting invitations to the New Year's ball into envelopes for Muriel to post. As Josh bolted the new projector to the floor in the finished projection room, his mind ran through all that had been done so far by the crew who had come together to get the theater going.

The crew, and Muriel. He felt the tingling he always experienced when he thought about Muriel, but he tried to ignore it and concentrate on the job at hand. The men had been working all day at setting up the large projection screen and getting the light from the projector lined up on it. When they finally broke for the day, Cora had an appetizing meal ready, aided in getting it on the table by Addy and Muriel, who had left pantry and office only a short time before. Afterwards, Josh and Zeke went outside with James to check on the wiring, but Zeke and James looked up into the sky and watched, fascinated, as the Northern Lights danced above.

"We should let the girls see this." Zeke motioned for Josh to follow him.

Muriel and Addy were finishing up the dinner dishes when Zeke and Josh came in. "Put on your coats—you have to see this."

Addy and Muriel slipped into their fur-lined parkas and went out behind the theater with the two brothers. Muriel took a sharp breath as she looked up into the clear cold sky. It looked like it was on fire! Multi-colored ribbons of light played around in the arctic air. "Oh, Josh, is Juneau on fire? What is that?" She gripped his hand in fear.

He put his arm around her. "Shh, don't be afraid. It's called the Northern Lights. It has something to do with the sun. I've heard it only happens way up here in the north."

They stood there for some time, watching the fascinating play of light above them, before they were interrupted by the sound of angry voices raised in argument, coming from the other side of the building, around by the stage door.

"Mother, have you gone insane? Why are you giving these people so much of our money?" The voice was Manfred's.

Gladys' voice was clear in the silence. "*Our* money? Since when do you have a say? I can do with the money however I want! Giving to charities is one of the things I do."

"This isn't a charity, Mother. You're wasting Father's fortune on theater people."

"How do you think you're going to stop me?"

"I have several ideas. You'd better watch your step. I've been to our lawyer's office, and Mr. Conner is furious with you. He and I are thinking about committing you as incompetent."

"Are you threatening me?"

Josh heard Jenny cry from her cradle inside just then, and Muriel left the group to take care of the baby while the others went around the corner of the building.

"Is there a problem here?" Zeke gave Gladys and her son a stern look.

Manfred glared at them. "Yes, there is. You're conning Mother out of her money!"

"She's backing us of her own free will!" Josh said, angrily.

Manfred grabbed his mother by the shoulders and shook her. "One way or another, I'm going to stop this!" Suddenly letting go of her, he stomped to his Stutz-Bearcat and roared away.

Gladys gathered her wits about her. "I'm sorry you had to see that. I was leaving for the evening when he drove up and confronted me. I think I'll go home now."

Josh was concerned. "Are you sure you'll be all right?"

She nodded. "I love my son, but he won't control me. I have final say on what I do. Goodnight." She hurried to her auto and drove away.

"Well, isn't that interesting? She spoke so well of her son, but he treats her like dirt under his feet," Addy said.

"Her family seems to have a lot of problems." Josh shook his head. "I imagine she's spoiled him so much, he feels entitled to treat her that way. I guess it would be wise to keep our noses out of it."

She looked at both brothers. "Why on earth did you let her come back here?"

Josh glanced at Zeke. "I think you ought to tell her why. I'm going to turn in. Come on, James."

Addy put her hands on her hips. "Stay here, Josh. You're as much a part of this as he is." James slipped through the stage door as she turned to Zeke. "Well?"

Zeke put his arm around her. "Calm down first."

She glanced from one to the other and folded her hands in front of her. "All right, I'm calm. Now, tell me, why did you take her back?"

"Two reasons," he began. "She was very sorry for what she tried to do and apologized to all of us, asking for another chance. Now, if it was because she couldn't turn the community against us and that was hurting her standing, I don't know, but we said we'd give her one more chance. She's been working well and hasn't given us any more trouble. She has been all business since then."

"And the other reason?"

Zeke pointed at her nose. "You."

Addy looked puzzled. "Me? What about me?"

"It's time you controlled your temper a little. Putting past hurts behind you and offering a person a chance to start over again is the right thing to do. If Gladys tries anything again, she's gone for good."

Josh nodded. "Addy, you can't live on hate and anger. Our father was like that. He lost Zeke and me because he wanted to force us to do what he wanted and he beat us if we didn't."

An expression of hurt and frustration crossed her face. "I couldn't do that! I'm not like that."

Zeke squeezed her tight. "Dear, may I remind you about the fight with Gladys? And before that, the few scuffles you've had since I've known you?"

Addy pursed her lips. "Well, I've never thought of that as abuse. I think of that as self-defense." She sighed. "Keeping my temper is hard to do, but I don't want to be angry all the time. I've got to learn how to forgive. Especially with the baby coming. I want it to grow up right."

He kissed her. "That's my girl. I'll help you any way I can." He nuzzled her hair. "Now, come with me to our bed," he said with a playful but seductive leer.

"This *is* where I make my exit." Josh quickly headed into the building.

****

A few days later, Muriel was passing through the lobby when she saw a bundled figure standing outside the doors, shivering in the cold. She opened the door and found Gladys' daughter Amelia there. "Why are you out in the weather? Come inside," Muriel said with concern.

Amelia looked at her shyly. "Mother told me to wait out here for her."

"Nonsense! You'll catch your death out there." Muriel grabbed her arm and pulled her into the lobby. "You can wait for her here."

"Mrs. Giovanni, I—"

"Call me Muriel."

Amelia chewed her bottom lip nervously. "Muriel, she'll be upset with me."

"Tell her it was my fault."

Amelia looked around. "What is that wonderful smell?"

Muriel laughed. "Cora Hutton, our restaurant manager, is trying out some recipes for the New Year's Eve party. Come with me to the kitchen. You can sample some."

"But Mother—"

"Your mother is in the office. We can see the door from there. Come on!" She moved the reluctant girl ahead of her.

Cora looked up as the two came into her domain. "Ah, my laboratory rats have arrived. Who is this young lady, Muriel?"

"This is Amelia Pembrook, Gladys' daughter. Amelia, meet our chef extraordinaire." She gave a stage wave in Cora's direction.

Cora held out a plate full of small sausages on toothpicks, islands in a creamy sauce. "This is smoked caribou in horseradish."

They each tried a bite. Muriel closed her eyes as she savored the mouthful. "This is delicious."

Amelia nodded. "This *is* good." She looked at a plate of small cakes, some of which were already decorated with small dollops, bows, or flowers of multicolored frosting. "Those are beautiful!"

Cora smiled. "These are my petits fours that I was frosting."

Amelia picked up the red cloth frosting cone. "May I try to do one?"

The chef nodded. "Be my guest."

Amelia took one of the plain white iced cakes and carefully made a red rose on top, squeezing the cone as the petals formed on the top of the cake. Then she took the green frosting cone and added leaves in the four corners, flipping the tips of them up artistically. She looked up with a satisfied smile.

Cora gave it her critical eye. "You did that very well. How would you like a job helping me with the pastries for the party?"

Amelia looked at the floor. "I, I don't know. I would have to ask—"

"Amelia!" came a shout from behind them. "I thought I told you to wait outside!" Gladys stormed into the kitchen.

Muriel pursed her lips. "I asked her to come in. It was cold out there."

Cora stood in front of Gladys. "I'd like Amelia to help me with the pastries for the party. She has a real talent for decorating."

Gladys studied Cora for a moment. "Well, I guess..." She turned to Amelia. "As long as you don't bungle this like you do everything else. You can come back tomorrow. Right now, come on. We're going home."

As Amelia silently retrieved her coat and followed her mother out the door, Cora crossed her arms and tapped her foot. "I swear that's an unhappy woman, and she seems to want to make everyone else miserable, too. I don't think she likes anything."

Addy had come in from the meeting with Gladys and watched the retreating figures. "Oh, put a bow on Zeke and give him to her. She'd be giddy."

Cora shook her head. "I don't think so. A woman like that loves the chase. You fighting for your husband made him more attractive to her. If she ever got him, she'd lose interest and set out for her next conquest."

Muriel meanwhile resolved that she must help Amelia gain some self-confidence. The poor child would never get it from her mother, with that treatment.

The days before Christmas found both Muriel and Addy sullen and homesick. The almost constant darkness and cold was getting to them. Juneau had no more than three or four hours of daylight at this time of year, and the cousins had never felt such freezing temperatures before. Muriel glanced at the unopened crate in the corner of the office and thought about Christmases past. She deeply missed the rest of her family in California, and the shipment of their presents to them in that crate only made it worse. The girls had sent their gifts in November, to make sure they got to California on time. Native Alaskan goods and foods made up most of the shipment. Recent photographs of the family and the building were included, as well.

Addy had confided to Muriel that Zeke was adamant about not letting her help with any of the construction of the backstage or with hanging the heavy curtains. She was over her morning sickness and felt strong, but he didn't want anything to happen to her or the baby, so she was still helping with the bookkeeping, where she claimed she felt like an office lackey. Muriel knew Addy found more solace with helping Cora in the restaurant kitchen.

Muriel was brooding over these thoughts in the office and watching Josh as he went through the files, when Cora and Kata came in.

"Where's Addy?" Cora folded her arms across her chest.

Muriel nodded toward the apartment door. "She's been in there for an hour."

Kata pointed toward Muriel's parka and boots. "You both need to come shopping with us."

Josh glanced Muriel's way. "I could watch Jenny for you."

That did sound good to Muriel. "Thank you,

Josh, but Addy's a hard one to move when she gets into one of these moods."

Cora looked her in the eye. "I have the gift of persuasion."

Muriel smiled. "Indeed you do." She knocked on the apartment door, and at Addy's response they went in.

Cora, Muriel and Kata stood in front of Addy. Cora made a gesture toward Addy's parka. "Get your coat and boots on. We're going shopping at the mercantile."

Addy sighed. "You go ahead. It's too dark and dreary out there. Besides, it snowed yesterday."

The three others looked at each other. Cora grabbed Addy's boots and Kata took her parka from the hook. "We need to get Christmas started here, and you need to stop brooding," Cora said as she helped Addy with her boots.

Addy looked at Muriel. "If you want to go, I'll watch Jenny."

Muriel shook her head. "Josh is in the office and said he'd watch her. I'm homesick, too. We need to do something."

Addy gave her a wan smile. "All right. Let me go get my pocketbook."

Outside, the cold air crackled around them as they walked the three blocks to the mercantile, the snow crunching under their boots. The full moon shone off the snow in glittering sparkles and made light enough on their way to where the downtown shimmered in its street decorations and the colored lights in business windows added a rainbow effect to the snow. The Salvation Army bell rang merrily on the street corner. Muriel almost felt cheerful as they went into the store. She knew she wouldn't have the money to buy expensive presents like she did when she was married to Tony, but she would make do.

The mercantile wasn't dressed up as fancy as

the department stores they remembered in Los Angeles, but all three floors were buzzing with shoppers finding their treasures, and busy clerks shot small money boxes along high cables, getting change from the mysterious offices above. The garlands and tinsel worked their magic, and as the four split up to choose gifts on their own, Muriel and Addy smiled at each other and dove into the busy crowd.

Chapter 12

Josh was going over the books at the desk when Zeke poked his head through the office door from the restaurant. "Hey, Josh, are the girls gone?"

Josh looked up. "I just heard the apartment door close. Why?"

Zeke came in with an impish smile and a small tree in his hand. "I'm going to surprise Addy while she's out. I'm decorating the parlor. Want to help?"

Josh glanced at Jenny. "I told Muriel I'd watch the baby." He considered the sleeping infant. "If we leave the door open, I could hear her from there."

Zeke put the tree on the parlor table and started decorating while Josh got the stepladder and set about hanging the garland. Chloe eyed them curiously from her perch on the bookshelves.

Josh looked down at Zeke trimming the tree. "If there are any decorations left, may I put some in Muriel's room? It would probably make her a little less homesick. Both she and Addy have been pretty down lately."

The corners of Zeke's mouth edged up. "You have been Mr. Sunshine since Muriel got here. What's going on between you two?"

Josh grinned and flushed. "Nothing. It's just that Muriel and Jenny have reminded me there's something more than this damned theater. I guess up till then I was pretty obsessive about this building. Now that it's almost finished, I've found a kindred spirit in Muriel."

Zeke chuckled to himself as Chloe jumped onto the table and stretched out a paw to gently tap a glass ball and sniff it. "Little brother, you were always a sucker for flashing brown eyes."

Josh tried to glare at him, but it came out as a smile.

****

Muriel found a book of popular tunes for Zeke, so he wouldn't have to juggle sheet music all the time. She bought Josh a new fedora to replace his old battered one. Ivan loved to smoke a pipe, so she picked up some tobacco she thought he would enjoy. When she saw dates and figs from California, she pounced—Kata had never tasted them; she would introduce her to them. James would receive one of the latest books on popular electronics. Muriel found a fur muff for Addy and a silver Christmas rattle for Jenny. For Cora, she bought a beautiful native shawl. She ran into Addy at the cashiers.

Addy laughed and picked up a catnip ball. "Can't forget my Chloe."

Muriel's spirit soared as she met the other ladies with their packages at the front door, and she could see that Addy was feeling much happier, too. They sang "God Rest Ye Merry, Gentlemen" as they walked back to the theater.

Kata put her purchases in the back of Ivan's truck and turned just as he came out of the building, greeting her with a bear hug. As the two of them left, Cora went to the main entrance of the theater and up the staircase to her room. Addy had already disappeared into her apartment, and Muriel, feeling a rush of concern at not seeing Josh and Jenny in the office, followed her.

Addy had left the door standing open, and as she entered behind her Muriel could see why. Her breath caught. There were candles lit around the room. Garland and tinsel were everywhere. She smelled the sweet pine fragrance and saw Addy, just as much in awe, setting down her packages. Zeke, and

Josh holding Jenny, stood by the lovely small tree perched on the parlor table. Glittering glass ornaments and small electric lights were woven together with strings of cranberries and popcorn. On the top, with one of the lights shining through it, was a homemade gold paper star.

Zeke grinned at Addy. "Merry Christmas, darling."

"Zeke, when did you have the time to make all these decorations?"

He laughed. "On breaks from working on the building. I wanted to surprise you."

"Well, you did, but Christmas is still a few days away."

"With all this night and cold around here, we needed something to cheer the place up. Don't you agree?"

Addy flew into Zeke's arms. "You're wonderful to come in from the cold to. I love you so." They kissed in the glow of the warm holiday light.

Muriel quickly turned her attention to Josh and Jenny. As Josh rang a tiny brass bell, the baby giggled. Muriel smiled at the scene, and then met Josh's gaze. His look was so intense, it took her breath away.

Suddenly, they heard paper rip.

Addy flew to her packages, forgotten by the door, and found Chloe had claimed the catnip ball. "Naughty kitty! That was your present!"

Zeke chuckled as Addy inspected the hole in the paper. "Let her have it. Then put your packages in the wardrobe. That will keep her from opening anything else. Now come on, I made some stew and biscuits for dinner, while you were out. Josh and Muriel, why don't you stay, too. I've made enough."

Addy looked at him, astonished. "I didn't know you could cook."

Josh chuckled. "He's a man of many talents."

Zeke laughed in response. "Nathan and I didn't starve when we shared that bachelor apartment in Hollywood. We had to learn to fix meals."

"Do you have any more talents I don't know about?"

He kissed her. "I'll let you in on them a little at a time."

They all sat at the kitchen table, and Zeke served the meal. Later, they laughed at Chloe's antics as she played with the catnip ball. Suddenly, Addy put her hand to her belly. "Oh, Zeke, I think I felt the baby move!"

He tenderly put his hand over hers. "And a Merry Christmas to you too, little one." Zeke put his arm around Addy and they sat there, contented, in a domestic tableau.

With a quick glance at each other, Muriel and Josh rose, and Muriel took Jenny. "I should put her to bed. Thank you, Zeke, for the delicious stew."

Zeke saw them to the office door. "Goodnight to both of you."

They went upstairs to Muriel's room and she gasped as she opened the door and saw the garlands and tinsel decorating her walls and window. "Josh, did you do this?"

He half-smiled. "You needed some cheering up, too."

She reached up and kissed him on the cheek. "Thank you."

Josh flushed and backed toward his room. "You're welcome. Merry Chris—er, goodnight."

A warm glow for him radiated over her as she readied Jenny for bed.

****

Muriel came into the restaurant with her arms full of packages to set under the tree. Everyone had agreed to celebrate together on Christmas Eve. Kata and Ivan wanted to spend the next day with their respective families, splitting the day between them, while the others simply wanted a day of rest. Josh and Muriel had helped Cora decorate the restaurant in holiday finery the day before their celebration, and Muriel and Addy helped her fix the meal in the big kitchen. There would be plenty of leftovers to feast on, at their leisure, the following day.

The decorations would stay up until after the New Year's Eve ball.

A lovely ceiling-high balsam tree decorated with lights, tinsel and glass ornaments dominated one corner of the restaurant. The tree glittered brightly when its lights were on. Garlands of pine and holly scalloped their way around the walls near the ceiling and wound around the wagon wheel lights. Even the moose head sported a red-and-white Santa hat.

Josh and Zeke had put three of the tables together for their special meal, and Muriel spread them with snowy white tablecloths before she set in place and lit two festive candelabras as Cora, Addy and Kata started loading the surface with food. The men carried in more presents and placed them under the tree.

Cora smiled. "Well, it looks like we have the three wise men here."

"More like the three wise guys." Addy giggled.

"There goes your present," Zeke said, as he buried it behind the tree.

Everyone took a place around the table. Jenny sat on Muriel's lap, happily grabbing everything she could reach. When everyone was seated, Josh stood and raised his glass of ginger ale. The others followed suit. "Here's to loving friends and family. We're truly blessed to be here together after this trying but productive year. God bless us all, from the ones we lost to the ones who are yet to be." He raised his glass toward Addy and sat.

Then they dug into a savory meal of caribou

roast and Yorkshire pudding. Baked potatoes, carrots and onions were laid out in bowls. Mounds of fluffy white rolls, still warm from the oven, soaked up the gravy and butter. Corn, pickle and beet relishes that Cora had canned before her journey to Alaska added a touch of California sunshine.

After the dessert of mince pie that Cora and the girls had labored over, they took their chairs to the tree to open presents. Muriel tingled with excitement as she always did at this time of year. Christmas was her favorite holiday. She had always loved getting presents, but since she had gotten older she reveled in watching people's delight when they opened gifts she had selected for them.

Halfway through exchanging presents, they heard a knock at the front door, and Josh went to see who it was.

Addy was opening Kata's gift to her as Josh ushered in Gladys, Amelia and an unknown young man. *What's she doing here uninvited? And how does Addy feel about Gladys' intrusion?* But Muriel needn't have worried. With only a vague nod to the interlopers, Addy continued to open the present. She pulled out a Tlingit fishing spear. It was about five feet long, its handle intricately carved with various symbols, including fish, and the large bone tip was shaped like a raven's beak.

"That's one of several spears that have been in my family for years," Kata explained. "I want you to have it, because you Shafers have been so kind to me. Just be careful how you handle it—the bone blade is razor sharp. It represents Raven, who, in our beliefs, created the people and the land. The handle is a charm to draw fish to you."

"Kata, I can't accept this from you. It's a family heirloom." Addy tried to hand it back to her.

Kata shook her head. "We have several. You have been a friend to me, and I want you to have it, to say thank you."

Addy moved her hand lovingly over the surface. "It will go on top of the bookcase in our apartment. Thank you so much."

The visitors had stood silently with Josh, watching and listening, but finally Gladys spoke up. "We were on our way to my son's house, and Amelia wanted to stop to give you something. Come on, child, hurry up."

Amelia looked at her mother, and it seemed there was some internal conflict going on in the daughter. "Before I do, I'd like to introduce my escort, Lester Marcel." She made the introductions around.

Muriel studied his face. *For some reason, he looks familiar to me.* She nodded to the dark-haired gentleman.

Amelia opened her satchel and pulled out a metal apple peeler. "I know Mrs. Hutton mentioned that she wished she hadn't left her apple peeler in Los Angeles, so I thought I would give you one as a thank-you gift for accepting my help."

Cora took the peeler and gave Amelia a kiss on the cheek. "Thank you, honey. A Merry Christmas to you."

Gladys waved her hand. "Come on, let's go. Merry Christmas to you all," she said briskly as she hurried out of the room.

Cora shook her head. "That Gladys is as sour as they come. That's the first time I've ever seen Amelia stand up to her like that, to introduce the young man, and did you see how Gladys glared the whole time?"

Addy nodded. "Gladys is a rude, domineering woman."

Zeke put his arm around her. "Dear, it's Christmas."

She sniffed. "Well, I hope she gets visited by

three ghosts tonight."

Zeke looked puzzled.

"It worked for Scrooge, didn't it? If I remember correctly, he went from 'bah, humbug' to a warm loving person."

Everyone laughed, and Zeke dug out her present from behind the tree. "Here, open this, darling."

Addy tore off the paper and showed everyone a framed tintype picture of a handsome young man in a Union uniform. He held a rifle on his shoulder, and on his chest was a sharpshooter medal. Addy teared up. "Oh, look, it's Grandpa," she managed to say. "How did you get this?"

Zeke pulled a folded paper out of his pocket. "I wrote to your grandma and said I wanted to give you something to remember your grandpa by, this Christmas. She sent this letter with it." He opened the paper and read:

> *Dear Adeline,*
>
> *Zeke sent a letter, telling me how much you missed your grandpa and asking if I could send something special for you. Here is the picture that he made for me before he went off to war. I kept this picture by my bed all the time he was gone, so it would be the first and last thing I would see every day. I want you to have it. He loved you very much, Addy, and prayed for you every night. Some of his sparkle left when you moved away.*
>
> *I miss you very much, too. We know there is a baby on the way and we rejoice with you. May you and your family have a rich full life such as I have been blessed with.*
>
> *With much love,*
> *Grandma*

Addy buried her face in her hands as he read the letter. "Oh, Zeke, thank you. This means more to me than you know. I was so sad that I didn't have any memento of him." She stood and embraced Zeke.

After a minute, he stepped back and gave her his handkerchief. "You're welcome," he said softly. He turned to Muriel and James with two more packages. "Your grandma sent these for the two of you."

Muriel opened the gift, and her eyes misted over as she read the similar note that came with it. "Oh, Addy, James, look at this." She held up a family portrait that must have been taken in the 1880s. There was a much younger version of Grandpa and Grandma Applegate, seated, with three solemn children standing behind them. They were in front of a garden wall backdrop, and Grandpa and Grandma were seated on a faux garden bench with a couple of potted plants next to them. Muriel pointed to the boy, who looked a lot like James. "In Grandma's letter, she says this is a picture they had in their bedroom. She tells me that's Uncle James, who was killed in the Spanish-American War. He was thirteen here." Her finger moved to the two little girls, whose long curls hung down nearly to the bouquet of flowers they each held. "That's your mother, Addy. She was nine here, and my mother was seven." She handed it to Addy, who smiled through her tears.

James opened his gift and took a breath. He looked at his note. "Grandma sent me all of grandpa's war metals. She put them in a shadow box." He held it up for all to see. "Look, here's the medal Grandpa is wearing in the photograph, Addy."

Cora looked at the pictures. "I met Mr. Applegate at your wedding, and I thought he was a good-looking man, even in his late seventies."

Kata nodded. "And how wonderful he served the Union during that time."

Ivan studied the metals. "He was a

sharpshooter, eh? Your family must have been very proud."

James smiled. "He was a brave man, from what I've heard, but he never wanted to go into detail about the war. He said it wasn't at all like the romantic notion most people think it is. He still had nightmares about it."

To change to a happier subject, Josh went to the swinging doors. "Let's go into the theater and sing carols." He turned on the lights and they all trooped to the piano. Zeke played a few chords, and then they sang, "Oh, Come All Ye Faithful," their voices blending together. They went through several songs they all knew, ending with "Silent Night."

It was getting late and everyone decided to call it a night, each wishing all the others a Merry Christmas. Ivan and Kata put their presents in their truck and waved as they drove off down the street. James and Cora bade goodnight as they went upstairs to their respective rooms, while Muriel and Josh helped carry Addy and Zeke's presents into the apartment.

On the way, Addy lovingly picked up the picture of Grandpa, carrying it to the bookshelf. Zeke placed the fishing spear on the top of the bookcase, propping it up for display, while Addy carefully set the picture next to the portrait of her parents and brother, lost in the earthquake those years ago.

"There now," she said quietly. "They're all watching over us."

Muriel hugged her cousin, knowing the depths of her emotion. "Goodnight and Merry Christmas to you both. We can go to church together in the morning."

Josh and Zeke glanced at each other. "We'll take care of things here," Josh said, looking at the toe of his shoe.

Muriel and Addy sighed and smiled knowingly

at each other.

Josh carried the sleeping baby upstairs. Once he had laid Jenny in the crib and turned to go, Muriel put a hand on his arm. "Thank you for the help with Jenny."

"I don't mind. She's a good baby." He hesitated and gave a short cough. "Goodnight, Muriel." He turned back to her as he was opening the door, as if he wanted to say something else, but then he just nodded and headed to his room.

Chapter 13

The night of the New Year's ball, Muriel had just taken the guest book from the bookshelf in the office when Addy opened the door to the apartment. "Muriel, could you help me with this dress?"

"Of course, honey, but what's wrong?" Muriel asked as she came over to her. Her cousin was trembling, and she never got pre-party jitters.

Addy was silent for a moment. "I was thinking back to last year, when John was killed."

Muriel's stomach knotted. The party last New Year's Eve at the Giovanni home weighed heavily on her mind, as well. It was at that party Addy's co-star was killed by Muriel's husband, Tony Giovanni, because John had raped Addy. She shuddered. That was the way his family took care of everyone who wronged them and theirs. Well, Tony and his father had been killed by the police. That was over and done with, she hoped.

Muriel chided herself as she fastened the back buttons and tied the sash on Addy's pale pink satin gown. That was a year ago, and nothing had occurred for her to think the mob had followed them to Alaska. Her dress arranged, Addy sat and looked at herself in the vanity mirror as she brushed her short curly bob. "I think you're thinking the same thing that I am. Are we really out of their grasp? Is Alaska far enough away?"

Addy was echoing Muriel's own fears. "Well, they haven't tried anything—yet."

Addy stood and checked herself in the mirror. "Muriel, could you loosen the sash?" Muriel retied it.

"There, that's a little more comfortable. The folds make my stomach less visible." Her hand ran down the growing bump and she turned to the side. "I'm anxious to meet this little one." She and Muriel looked up as Zeke and Josh came in from the office.

"Are you two ready?" Zeke's breath caught on the words. "Addy, you look beautiful."

Josh grinned. "Muriel is quite a picture, as well."

The girls took in the dashing figures the brothers made in their tuxedos. "You both look pretty swell yourselves." Addy took Zeke's arm. "Come on, let's go dazzle our guests."

Josh offered Muriel his arm, and they strolled into the restaurant, where they had worked all day to set up the stage for the band. Addy, Muriel, Amelia and Kata had helped Cora decorate and lay out the hors d'oeuvres and refreshments, and Cora had made her wonderful mock champagne punch from apple cider and ginger ale. Sheriff Amos Darcy was going to be there, so nothing was spiked. If alcohol showed up, it wouldn't be their fault. James had helped with preparations and was in and out of the kitchen all day, but, shy as ever, he'd volunteered to watch Jenny so Muriel could enjoy the festivities.

Ivan's Uncle Nick and his twelve-piece band had just finished setting up on the removable stage when the guests started to file in. Josh fielded a lot of attention from the young ladies who came with their families, while his eyes were always searching Muriel out.

Muriel was glad she'd saved this organdy gown of pale blue from her time in the Giovanni family. She was in charge of the guest book, stationed in front of the restaurant doors, and many of the young male patrons hovered around her.

Gladys, one of the first through the door, stared

disapprovingly as Amelia helped set up the food. Amelia's young man, Lester, stood watching near by. Muriel still thought he looked very familiar. *I wonder if he worked in Los Angeles for a while? I don't know why I think I know him.*

Nick's band got the party started with "Tiger Rag" and "Darktown Strutter's Ball." Muriel, her guestbook duties finished, danced with several of the gentlemen, and during one of the sessions she saw Manfred and Gladys arguing in the corner. Manfred took Gladys' arm and tried to move her toward the doors to the lobby, but she resisted. When Josh went over and said something to them, Manfred grabbed Lettie, his fiancée, and stormed out.

Muriel bit her lip. She knew Addy had come to tolerate Gladys since her apology, but the way the woman dealt with her children still bothered both of them. Manfred was an arrogant boor, and Amelia was criticized for everything.

****

The band took a break, and Josh was in the middle of a deep conversation with Muriel when Addy motioned him to the door of the office. He reluctantly followed her, with Muriel in tow.

"What happened out there with Gladys and Manfred?" Addy closed the door behind them.

"He threatened a court action over the inheritance if she didn't cease giving money to the theater."

"Maybe we should convince her to back off. We don't need to drain her, and we're getting quite a bit of contribution from others now."

Josh nodded. "That's what I told her, but she stubbornly refused to listen to me or to her son."

A knock on the door made them jump and Zeke walked in. "Well, well. Should I be jealous?" He hadn't seen Muriel standing quietly at the side.

"The jig is up, darling. You have to tell him our

secret." Josh swept Addy into an elaborate embrace, and she thumped him on the head. "You're insane!" Addy turned to Zeke. "I wanted to know what was going on between Gladys and her son."

"Ah. Josh already told me. Now, as hosts and hostesses, we'd better get back to the party."

Josh straightened his tie. "Yes, I have a dance scheduled with Muriel."

Addy laughed as he took Muriel's hand and led her out. "I guess we're finished here."

****

As Addy turned after shutting the door, Zeke made a sweeping bow in front of her, saying, "May I have the next dance with my enchanting other half? I made a special request." He held out his arm to her.

She gave him a pixie smile. "Charmed, I'm sure."

When the band started playing "Whispering" he spun her onto the dance floor, softly singing the words as he guided her around. Colors were a blur around them as Addy gazed at his handsome face.

The music stopped and he gave her a kiss. "Thank you, darling. We should mingle, but you're mine after midnight."

Addy danced a few more dances with guests, but she was starting to feel dizzy. *Maybe if I go into the apartment and rest for a few minutes, I'll feel better.* She disappeared through the office door and, from there, into the apartment. As she put her feet up, Chloe was there, meowing, beside her. She picked the cat up and nuzzled her. "What's wrong, sweetie? You seem upset about something. Is all that noise bothering you?" Addy stroked the little animal, who seemed soothed and soon settled down.

****

Muriel tightened her fingers around Josh's arm as she led him from the dance floor and into the kitchen. "I have to talk to you, and I don't want to be interrupted this time."

His eyes turned serious. "What is it?"

"I was going to tell you, and then Addy waved us into the office. The fight between Gladys and her son reminded me. I was at the courthouse the other day and overheard a conversation between Manfred and someone I think was his lawyer. Anyway, the man told Manfred he had to prevent his mother spending the estate, and she should be stopped one way or another."

Josh looked at her steadily. "This was out in public?"

"No. I was walking past an office door and recognized Manfred's voice."

"When did you hear his voice? You were upstairs during the fundraiser."

"But I heard the fight he and his mother had at the stage door, remember."

He wiped his hand slowly over his mouth. "We should definitely ask her again to drop the backing. He may be thinking of bringing legal action against us." He clasped her hand in his. "Come on, let's get back to the party. We'll do something about this first thing tomorrow."

Returning from the kitchen, Muriel and Josh passed Amelia, sitting with Lester at one of the tables by the wall. Muriel couldn't help but notice several long red scratches on Amelia's arm. "Oh, honey, did you get hurt?"

Amelia looked down and took out her handkerchief and dabbed at the blood. Her face was pale and drawn.

Lester spoke up. "That happened when her brooch loosened. The pin must have scratched her arm." He seemed to be tending her, so Muriel and Josh took to the dance floor once again.

Fifteen minutes later, Muriel saw Addy come

through the office door. She paused in front of the restaurant's decorative mirror only long enough to smooth her hair before rejoining the festivities.

She was getting some punch, assisted by Muriel, when Zeke came up behind her. "What happened to you?"

"I went to the apartment to put my feet up. I was feeling dizzy."

Turning her so he could look in her face, he voiced his concern. "Are you all right?"

"Just a little tired, that's all."

It was almost midnight, and everyone was on the floor for the last dance. As soon as they heard the church bells begin to peal out midnight, the band launched into "Auld Lang Syne." Zeke kissed Addy deeply as the cheers and whistles went on for a few minutes, while Josh and Muriel exchanged a deep and silent gaze.

Josh and Zeke were helping to hand out coats from the cloakroom when they heard a scream from outside, behind the theater. Everyone ran in that direction. Muriel saw the banker's wife, Mrs. Taber, sobbing in her husband's arms as Sheriff Darcy moved through the crowd to where the Tabers stood.

"All right, stand back, everybody!" Darcy shouted. He looked for all the world like a prospector who just happened to get a tin star. His build was imposing and his face not quite clean shaven.

Everyone still at the party had crowded out into the cold night to see what had upset Mrs. Taber so badly. For Muriel, one glimpse of the crumpled heap by the back wall was enough. Her mind flew to last year's studio party and the death of Addy's co-star. Muriel reached for Addy's arm and found she was also shaking.

Darcy took out his flashlight and shone it at the heap. There was blood in a scarlet trail across the back of the wall and pooling on the ground. He turned the body, and Muriel gasped, sickened to the core. It was Gladys' gray-blue face in the light, with a grotesquely swollen tongue. The azure blue gown was a dark purple where the blood soaked it, and protruding from the middle of her chest was a fish spear. *Was that the one Kata gave Addy as a Christmas present?* Zeke caught Addy as she swooned.

Back in the apartment, Zeke held a cold cloth on Addy's face as she lay on the couch. He kept saying, "Addy, Addy!" Finally she moaned and opened her eyes. As she focused, Josh escorted Dr. Lindsey in.

The doctor nodded. "Good, she's awake."

"I need to ask her some questions," came a gruff voice from behind him, and Sheriff Darcy came into view.

Zeke angrily turned around. "Could you give her some time? I don't want her getting upset."

The doctor put his hand on Zeke's arm and glanced at the sheriff. "Amos, Mrs. Shafer is with child."

Addy sat up, gingerly. "That's all right. I'm okay."

"Mr. Shafer, I want the rest of you to leave the room." Darcy moved a chair next to the couch and got out his notepad.

Addy held on to Muriel's hand. "Can Muriel stay?"

The sheriff hesitated. "In light of your condition, she may be more of a help than your husband."

Zeke glared at him, but Dr. Lindsey clapped Zeke on the shoulder and motioned toward the door. Josh followed them out.

When they all had gone, Darcy turned to Addy. "What do you know about what happened tonight?"

Addy shook her head. "Just what everyone else saw."

"When did you last see Mrs. Pembrook?"

"The last time I remember is when she was fighting with her son at the other side of the room. I couldn't hear what they were saying. Manfred and Lettie, his fiancée, left after Josh went over there. I asked Josh what happened a few minutes later, in the office."

"The fishing spear. I understand it was a present to you from Mrs. Nikolaevich. Is that correct?"

"She gave us one, but...Was that spear ours?"

"Mr. Shafer identified it. Where did you keep it?"

"It was on top of the bookcase in the parlor."

The sheriff stepped over to the bookcase. Muriel watched as he took the step stool and carefully looked on top. He got down and opened the door to the office. "Has anyone disturbed the top of the bookcase since we came in?"

Muriel heard several nos.

He turned to Addy. "Did you know it was missing?"

"No, sir."

"Were you at the party the whole time?"

"No, I was feeling dizzy a little while ago and came in here to put my feet up for a few minutes."

"What time was that?"

"I don't know exactly, but it must have been between eleven-thirty and midnight."

"Did anyone see you?"

"No, sir." Muriel squeezed Addy's hand. *Does he think Addy killed her?*

Sheriff Darcy called everyone back into the apartment. "I don't want anyone touching the bookcase before I can see if there's any evidence." He stepped back up and made some notes. The sheriff looked at Addy seriously. "It was known that there was a lot of anger between Mrs. Pembrook and yourself, leading to a fight in front of the theater."

Addy paled and started to tremble again. Now Muriel knew the sheriff suspected her. "She apologized, and we gave her another chance. We've been civil with each other since then."

The sheriff put his hand on her shoulder. "I think I've got enough for this evening. I'm asking you to stay in Juneau, Mrs. Shafer."

Addy sighed deeply. "I plan to."

Darcy tipped his hat, said, "Goodnight," and left the apartment.

Muriel left her seat and went to Josh, who took her arm worriedly as he and his brother came in, while Zeke sat on the couch next to Addy. "My God, this has been a hell of a night," he said.

Tears came to Addy's eyes. "Hold me," she pleaded. Zeke put his arms around her, and she cried out her misery onto his shoulder. "He thinks I did it."

Zeke pulled back and looked at her sadly. "I'm on the list, too. He found a crumpled note in her hand, seemingly from me."

"When did he question you?"

"Before you came to. He isn't finished with suspects yet. Seems like there was a long list of people that didn't like her, including her own family."

Josh came alert. "What was in the note? Did you see it?"

"It was a typewritten note asking Gladys to meet me in back of the theater."

Addy looked down. "I really feel sorry for her. It's horrible, how she died."

Muriel kissed her cousin on the cheek. "Why don't you two get some rest."

Josh nodded. "We can clean up tomorrow."

Muriel and Josh left the doctor to do a brief checkup on Addy, but Muriel was sure she wouldn't get much sleep tonight.

****

The next day, Josh came in to a somber group around the table in the restaurant. Eight people who had put so much work into a dream sat on the brink of a very large chasm.

Josh rubbed his eyes. "I know this sounds terrible after what happened to Gladys, but how is this going to affect us? I can't see how we can open in May, after this."

Cora passed around sweet rolls. "It wasn't your fault. Other places have been scenes of murders, and they still carried on."

Zeke shook his head. "That's true, but the owners probably weren't suspects in those cases. Cora, if you and Ivan and Kata want to pull out now, we'll understand."

Ivan spoke up. "We'll stay by all of you. Gladys was backing you. Why would you possibly want to kill her, eh?"

"Well, someone tried to set us up. They carefully planned this whole thing out."

Cora took a sip of her coffee. "I'm certainly not pulling out now. You and Addy have already paid your dues in Los Angeles, with those gangsters. I, for one, aim to do anything necessary to prove you're innocent."

Kata glanced at Ivan. "Maybe I should ask Sarah to help us."

Addy set down her sweet roll. "Sarah?"

"My cousin, Sarah Lakat. She works as a detective with our local police and does some private business on the side. I like Amos Darcy, but sometimes he tries to get cases done quickly and, the way it looks, you and Zeke are high on his list, along with Manfred and Amelia."

Zeke stood up. "When can she come?"

"She lives across the channel in Douglas, but she has been working in Juneau to help finish cases against the Treadwell Mine flood-out a few years ago. I can bring her in tomorrow. She will want to examine Gladys' body at the coroner's office."

Midmorning, Josh was working at the filing cabinet while Muriel balanced the ledger. Muriel looked up from her task. "Do you think Addy or Zeke will be found guilty of murder?"

He pulled a folder out of the drawer. "Muriel, if there's an investigation, I'm sure they'll be found innocent. I know they've been set up somehow, not only with the note but with the fishing spear being used as the murder weapon."

"But who would want to do this to them?"

"Oh, who knows? Let's give Sarah a chance to clear them."

Muriel felt a fear that went all the way down her spine. They seemed to jump from one crisis to another. Would they have no peace, even here? Josh came over and put his hand on her shoulder. It felt reassuring and warm.

Chapter 14

Sarah Lakat turned the knob of the door to the coroner's office and walked in confidently. Coroner Elmer Stanton looked up from his desk. "Sarah, what brings you in today?"

"I want to see Gladys Pembrook's body." Sarah tapped the top of his desk with her fingernail.

Elmer's mouth pressed in a straight line underneath his handlebar mustache. "The sheriff's office took the case. Amos made it known to me to keep the police force out of it."

Sarah sighed and sat on the corner of his desk. She knew there was a power struggle between the police and the sheriff's department over who was the law in Juneau. It would help if they would work together, but they guarded their territory jealously. "I'm not here on behalf of the police. I was asked to do some investigating on my own."

"I'll have to go next door and tell Amos."

She smiled. "Fine. And tell him to bring his notes with him," she called after Elmer as the door closed. Sarah swung her legs and looked at her watch. "Let's see. Ten, nine, eight—"

The outer door opened with a bang. "What the hell is going on here?"

She grinned at the agitated, whiskery face in front of her. "Sheriff! Very good. You made it over here in less time than usual."

The sheriff's ruddy face seemed to take on an umber tone. "Lakat! What are you doing here? I told Elmer this was my case! I don't want the police nosing in on it."

"Calm down, Amos, you'll blow a blood vessel. I'm not here for the police department. I was asked to personally investigate for a client. In fact, I'm offering to work with you. I wouldn't dream of usurping your authority." She winked at him.

Amos stared at her. "Lakat, for a Tlingit woman, you sure use some high-falutin' words. Who is your client?"

She gave him a half-smile. "Now, you know I don't have to tell you, but I think, with both of us working together, we can solve this."

His face a turmoil of indecision, Amos nevertheless went to the front door and motioned to the man still standing outside. "Elmer, take us into the back."

The coroner came in slowly and looked at them. He eyed Amos cautiously. "Both of you?"

Amos jerked his thumb in the direction of the morgue. Sarah didn't know how to react. The sheriff didn't usually give in so easily, no matter what manipulations she used.

The small room built onto the end of the building, like an ice house, had several smaller chambers that looked like walk-in refrigerators at its edges. Elmer opened the first one, and Sarah and Amos went inside while Elmer stood by the door. Their warm breaths raised clouds of steam in the cold.

On the wooden table was Gladys' sheeted body. Amos pulled the sheet down to the wound in Gladys' chest, a smooth cut between the ribs and into the heart. "Where is the murder weapon?" Sarah turned to look at Elmer.

Elmer disappeared and returned with the fish spear. "This was in her chest when she was found."

Sarah scanned the bone blade and held it next to the wound. "Amos, this isn't what killed her."

Amos studied both her face and the comparison

of blade and wound before he nodded. "Go on."

"That bone blade isn't wide enough to make this cut, and the blade isn't long enough to penetrate the heart, for one thing. Besides that, there's bruising around her neck like she was choked first, then stabbed."

"That's what I thought, too. It looks like a frame-up for some reason. It's possible someone wanted to get rid of Gladys and took the opportunity of blaming the well-known bad blood between her and Mrs. Shafer."

She shook her head. "By the angle of the cut, the killer knew where to aim for the heart."

Amos raised an eyebrow. "Lucky shot?"

"Possibly. Or a professional." She handed the spear to Elmer. "Let's go into the office. I'm freezing in here." They made their way to the front, where Sarah turned to Amos. "Did you bring your notes with you?"

Amos tugged on his mustache and cleared his throat. "No, I was going to bodily throw you out of here."

She smirked. "What made you change your mind?"

"You have a good mind, for a woman, and your cousin is a friend of the Shafers. You might be able to get some inside information from her. I suggest that we still consider Mrs. Shafer a suspect. That might lull the real killer into making a mistake."

"What makes you think Mrs. Shafer didn't do it?"

"I checked on top of the bookcase where the spear was taken, and there were several spots of fresh blood. Mrs. Shafer didn't have any cuts or scratches on her hands or arms. The blood might have been left by the killer."

"Sheriff, for a man, you're very devious. Your mother did a good job."

Amos frowned and headed for the door. "I'll show you the notes, but the police department is not involved, understand?"

"Understood." Sarah saluted and followed him out the door.

****

Muriel led Kata and Sarah through the lobby. Sarah was a little taller than Kata but with the same chiseled Tlingit features and raven black hair. Her hair was pulled back into a tight bun, and as she removed her parka Muriel could see she was dressed in the uniform of the police department, a charcoal gray shirt and black wool skirt. Her dark brown eyes seemed to take in everything around her and process it, but there was warmth there, as well.

The Shafer brothers, along with Addy, James, Cora, and Ivan, were waiting for them at a long table in the restaurant. The men stood as Kata led her cousin in, and Josh immediately offered Sarah his hand. "You must be Sarah Lakat." He made introductions around the table, and Muriel watched Sarah studying them all one by one.

"I'm a sergeant with the Juneau police department. Kata told me what happened, and Sheriff Darcy briefed me at the coroner's. He wanted the sheriff's department to handle this, but I convinced him we would probably do better working together, with me as a private investigator. He showed me the notes he took last night. May I go over them with you?"

Josh looked around. "Should some of us leave?"

She shook her head. "These were statements you all made without knowing what the others said. It doesn't matter if you hear them now."

Sarah went over Addy's statement first. "Is this correct?"

Addy nodded.

Sarah glanced at Zeke. "Mr. Shafer, were the

doors to the apartment locked?"

"The outside door was, but the office door was not."

"So the only people who would have had access to the apartment were the ones at the party?"

Zeke rubbed his chin. "I suppose so."

"Did you write a note on your typewriter asking Mrs. Pembrook to meet you in back of the theater?"

"No."

Sarah turned next to Josh and asked him about the argument between Gladys and her son. He confirmed what he'd told the sheriff. "Did any of you notice anybody leaving, then coming back?"

Muriel shook her head. "There were a lot of people here. I know I couldn't tell you if anyone left for a few minutes. I didn't even notice that Gladys was missing."

Sarah glanced at her notes. "Mrs. Giovanni, you said you heard an argument between Mr. Pembrook and his lawyer at the courthouse. Could you tell me what you heard?"

Muriel related the conversation she remembered, and Addy looked at Zeke, a concerned look on her face.

Sarah tapped the notebook with her pencil. "This brings some new things to light." She turned back to Zeke. "Could you type this on your typewriter: Gladys, would you meet me in back of the theater? Zeke."

He registered surprise, but did as he was told. Muriel didn't know what to think. Sarah was all business and showed no emotion one way or the other. Given what Muriel knew of Kata, she was inclined to trust this cousin despite her unusual methods.

When Zeke handed Sarah the paper, she gestured at both him and Addy. "Was there anyone in the office or in your apartment during the party, besides the few minutes Mrs. Shafer rested?"

"Just our cat, Chloe."

Sarah smiled and nodded. "Thank you all for your cooperation."

Kata was amused. "Sarah, how did you get around Amos like that? He usually wants to work on cases himself."

Sarah raised an eyebrow. "I have my ways. Good afternoon, all."

As Kata returned from seeing Sarah to the door, Addy turned to Muriel. "You didn't tell me about that discussion between Manfred and Mr. Conner."

"I didn't get a chance to, we were so busy setting up for the party. I told Josh after we were in the office. And of course after the party Gladys' murder took over my thoughts."

Zeke stood. "Muriel, with Gladys' backing ended, how do our finances look?"

"Not too bad right now. We got in the money for the advertisements on our new curtain. So we're set for now. I'm hoping advance sales for the opening night tickets will help. That will start in March." She stole a glance at Josh.

Cora sighed. "I don't know what this will do to Amelia. That young lady is as fragile as they come. I was hoping I could give her some confidence."

They all sat in silence. Finally, Josh stood up. "I, for one, want to thank you all for standing with us in this crisis. As long as we're united, I think we can pull through this. Now, I've got a couple of things I need to check on." He quietly went through the double doors. James followed.

Ivan and Kata took their leave, and Cora went back to the kitchen. Addy and Zeke were headed toward their apartment door when Addy turned back to Muriel. "Would you like to join us? I was going to heat some water for tea."

When the tea was ready, they all sat around the

apartment's small dining table.

Chloe jumped onto Addy's lap, and Addy scratched the little cat. "Who would try to frame us, and why?"

Zeke shook his head. "I don't know, but it seems all the evidence points to you or me."

Addy sighed. "Are we ever going to find any peace?"

Zeke didn't answer but brushed a tear off her cheek.

Muriel felt miserable. "Why, oh, why did this have to happen? Gladys died so horribly, and I feel awful about that. We've worked so hard to make this theater go, and now everything is collapsing around us. Most of all, I feel sorry for Josh. He put his heart and soul in this."

Zeke glanced at her. "I agree. We try to do the right thing and get kicked in the teeth every time. First the gangsters, and now this. We must have been born under an unlucky star. Come on, let's all go to Millie's for dinner."

They set out on their way. The stars in the unusually clear sky sparkled like distant fires, and the smell of wood smoke interlaced with the smell of the harbor. Muriel felt the chill of the winter air and shivered. How she longed for warmer weather.

There were many people at Millie's. As the little group from the theater walked in, the room went silent. Muriel could feel the tension in the air. Millie came up to them with a concerned look on her face. "Could I talk to all of you out back?"

They went with her to the kitchen door of the building. Zeke glanced around. "What's wrong, Millie?"

"There's rumbling going on around town against you folks. Gladys wasn't very popular, but she was one of ours. All of you are still considered outsiders and—" She nervously brushed off her apron. "Well,

I'm asking you, for now, please don't come here for a while. Just until things cool down a little." She took a breath. "Look, I don't think any of you did it, but—"

Zeke nodded. "I know. It's bad for business."

With a quick nod, Millie turned away and went back inside. Muriel felt walls crashing in on them. Addy and Zeke looked at each other, the steam from their breaths causing a deep fog between them.

Addy had been clutching his arm, and now she squeezed it hard in her desperation. "What are we going to do? We need the good will of the townsfolk for the theater to be a success."

He retrieved his arm and put it protectively around her. "We'll think of something. I hate to have to tell this to Josh, though. Come on, let's go home."

Muriel bit her lip. "Zeke, let me tell Josh what happened."

He nodded, and they all turned to go.

Tears of misery froze to her face as they made their way back to the big white building.

****

Muriel's heart went out to Josh. He looked the picture of despair, his head in his hands and his elbows leaning on the desk as Muriel told him what had happened at Millie's. Slowly he raised his head. "Well, that's it, isn't it? Muriel, I'm sorry you had to come into this. You seem to have traded one problem for another."

Muriel caressed his shoulders. "I'm sure Sarah and Amos can find out what really happened. When they do, the townspeople will come around."

"We may not be here by that time." He straightened and threw his hands up. "I really wanted to prove to myself that my father was wrong, that I could make something of my life. Well—" One hand slammed down on the ledger.

Muriel's chest tightened. He could be right about having to leave. She didn't want to think it, but her eyes swam with tears. How could he blame himself, though? He had worked so hard.

Josh looked at her through the mist in his own eyes. He stood and took her in a gentle embrace, then pulled back quickly. "I'm—I didn't mean to—"

Muriel put her fingers on his lips. "Don't apologize." She drew him toward her again, and they gazed at each other for a moment before she put her hand on the back of his neck and kissed him.

Chapter 15

Sarah strode into Manfred Pembrook's inner sanctum in the territorial courthouse building. An attractive blonde receptionist greeted her. "May I help you?"

Sarah showed her private detective license. "I'm Detective Lakat. I would like to talk to Mr. Manfred Pembrook. This is about his mother's death."

The receptionist hesitated a moment, her red nails tapping on the desk. "I'll see if he's in." She rapped on one of the doors and went inside. When she came out, her rosebud lips were in a straight line. "He said he already gave his statement. You are to leave."

Irritated at such a brush-off, Sarah pushed past the protesting receptionist and opened the door to Manfred's office. "Mr. Pembrook, new things have come to light, and I want to ask you about them."

He looked at her icily. "I gave Sheriff Darcy my information. That should be good enough. I don't have to put up with a nosy Indian woman asking questions."

Sarah bit back a bitter retort. It wouldn't work on this stuffed shirt anyway. "I wanted to ask about an argument you had with Mr. Adrian Conner—your lawyer, I assume—on the twenty-ninth of December."

Manfred Pembrook's eyes grew wide. "How did you know about that?"

"That's not important. Did he tell you your mother should be stopped from backing the theater *one way or another*?"

His hand struck the desk with a resounding

smack. "Are you insinuating I killed her?"

Sarah gazed steadily at him. "Am I?"

His face turned umber. "Get out of here, you Eskimo witch. How dare you!"

She flipped her notebook closed. "Thank you, Mr. Pembrook, you answered my question." Sarah left him steaming as she quietly closed the door.

Outside, the frosty cold sleet stung her face as she made her way to the sheriff's office. She hoped he'd had some luck at Mr. Conner's office, but she had certainly found out that the argument took place. Could Manfred have found it in his gut to kill his mother over money? Sarah had never thought he had much of a spine, but inheritance had driven a lot of people to desperate acts before this.

The sheriff nearly ran into Sarah from the opposite direction in front of the door of his office. He looked at her, his mustache a frozen fringe on his face. "Lakat! Good. Come in and tell me what you found out."

They shrugged out of their wet parkas and hung them over the radiator coil. The steam from the warmth had an odor not unlike a wet dog.

Seeing that one of the deputies had put a pot of coffee on the woodstove, the sheriff turned to Sarah as she settled in an armchair on the other side of his desk. "Coffee?"

Sarah smiled. "If you have a clean mug."

He huffed and pulled a mug off a hook. She thought she heard him mutter, "Women," under his breath.

Sarah warmed her hands on the ceramic mug as Amos settled himself in his chair behind the desk. Taking a light sip, she looked at him expectantly. "How did you do with Mr. Conner?"

A choke came from Amos. "Nothing. He cited lawyer-client privilege and said he didn't have to tell me anything." He blew on the coffee and some of the melting sleet from his mustache sprayed over his desk. "I told him this was a murder investigation, and he better tell me something soon or I'd have his carcass hung out for the wolves."

Sarah chuckled. "How diplomatic of you, Amos."

"Did you get anything out of Pembrook?"

"He was insulted I even asked, but his reaction spoke volumes. I found out the argument took place as Mrs. Giovanni overheard. He accused me of thinking he killed his mother."

"Do you think he did?"

"I find anything is possible when it comes to money, but I've never thought he had it in him." She tapped her cup. "Has anyone talked to Amelia Pembrook?"

Amos checked his notes. "Just at the theater after the murder. She and her escort, Lester Marcel, were there at the party. Amelia seemed to be in a nervous state, but that's the way the young lady usually is."

Sarah shook her head. "Thanks to the way her mother treated her, she has never handled social situations well. This Mr. Marcel is the first man to escort her anywhere, to my knowledge."

"When I talked to him that night, he said he was here from Trenton, New Jersey, on business. He's staying at the hotel."

"Is he still here?"

"I asked him to stay in town until the investigation was finished. He wasn't real happy about that."

Sarah hesitated. "It looks like Mrs. Pembrook might have fixed him up with her daughter. Did you ask what kind of business he was here for? Was it for the Pembrooks?"

Amos rubbed his chin. "He said he was a salesman wanting to open a market here in Alaska." He paused for a moment. "Lakat, why don't you pay

Miss Pembrook a visit, and I'll do the same for Mr. Marcel. What did you find out about the typewritten note?"

"It wasn't from the theater office typewriter." She showed him the crumpled original note and the one she'd had Zeke type. "See, on the original, there's a slight space in the middle of the 'm' that doesn't appear on the other one."

Amos nodded. "Let's see if we can find the typewriter, then, as well."

At that moment, there was a knock on the door and a deputy came in. "Sir, you received a telegram from the Hall of Records in New Jersey."

"Speak of the devil." Amos took the envelope from him. "Lakat, this says they have no record of a Lester Marcel in Trenton. Interesting."

****

His father came toward Josh with a sneer. "You're worthless! You'll never amount to anything. Your brother ran from me, and you will, too. God will bring down his wrath on these sons of mine."

Josh's eyes snapped open to pitch blackness. He was lying in bed soaked with sweat, and despair flooded his mind. *Why did I ever think I could get away with this? The theater is dead, and I should never have started this.* With anger bubbling, he ran down the stairs and into the kitchen, where he found one of Cora's meat cleavers.

Still half-asleep, Josh strode into the theater and gazed at their new advertising curtain, received and hung only two days ago. Yes, it had cost a whopping two hundred dollars, but the colorful banner mocked him. He dragged a ladder to the center of the stage, intent on destroying the monstrosity that no one would ever see anyway.

He was startled from his purpose by a sharp voice from the back. "Josh, what the hell are you doing?"

Josh looked back to see his brother hurrying to the stage. "It's over, Zeke. All we've worked for—it's destroyed." A desperate feeling washed over him, and he swung wildly at the curtain, chopping a foot-long rip through the heavy fabric. "Father was right. We aren't worth a hill of beans."

Zeke ran up on stage and put his hand on the ladder. "You come down right now, or I'll pull you over."

"No!" And Josh made a move to work at the tear again.

"I mean it!" Zeke gave the ladder a gentle shove.

Josh grabbed the top to steady himself. "All right, all right, I'll come." He climbed down and stared at Zeke. Josh's hands shook.

Zeke reached out. "Give me the cleaver."

Josh studied it for a moment, then sighed and handed it over. In a sudden movement, he collapsed into a cross-legged squat on the floor of the stage, his head drooping. "I didn't think that anything like this would happen. I didn't plan for any of this. Father was right. I didn't know what I was doing."

Zeke flipped the cleaver to the end of the stage and sat himself next to his brother, his arm around Josh's shoulders. "You're still hearing Father chide you, aren't you? To him, none of us could do anything right. But we'll get through this, one way or another."

"And there's another thing, Zeke, I think I'm falling in love with Muriel. I think she feels the same. But she and Jenny deserve more than a failure. She's been through a lot with that gangster family—"

Zeke shook him hard. "You're not a failure! I wouldn't have joined you up here if you were. We just have a rough patch we have to get through, and we'll do it together."

A moment more of silence, and then Josh sighed

deeply. He stood, yanking Zeke up with him. "Okay, big brother, we'll continue on."

Zeke patted Josh's back and looked up at the tear in the curtain. "I think Kata could fix that up." He retrieved the cleaver from the far side of the stage. "I'll put this back. You go to bed."

Josh nodded and headed up the aisle.

****

Sarah climbed the steps to the handsome mansion at the end of the road. Unlike most of the wooden houses hastily put up in Juneau, this was fieldstone. Its massive, marble-columned porch alone could have held Sarah's entire family home. She turned the bell next to the heavy oak door and waited until a formally dressed man opened it.

"May I help you, ma'am?" he asked after a slight bow.

"I'm Detective Lakat, working with Sheriff Darcy on the murder case. Is Miss Pembrook at home? I would like to ask her a few questions."

He waved her into the hall. "Wait here." She watched him go upstairs. Her gaze took in the green-and-silver velvet wallpaper, the crystal sconces along the walls interspersed with paintings and shelves on which huddled exotic knick-knacks—small native items, English Wedgewood china, Oriental dolls. Thick black velvet drapes, heavy with fringes, hid the two side rooms. In the center of the room, a large potted plant dominated the middle of a round of green-cushioned seats, and by the door stood a calling card plate on a small table. Sarah smiled. No one used calling cards much anymore.

Her musings were broken by a middle-aged woman with henna-colored hair huffing down the stairs. "Miss Lakat? I'm Miss Martha Davis, Miss Pembrook's aunt. I'm sorry, but my niece is indisposed. She is ill, and I'm tending to her."

Sarah set her jaw. "Miss Davis, I need to ask her

a few things that are very important to the investigation. I won't keep her long. If she's awake, please take me to her."

Miss Davis' mouth set in a straight line, but she nodded curtly and headed upstairs with Sarah behind her. They paused in front of one of the doors while Miss Davis turned to Sarah. "Wait here." She went in, closing the door behind her. A minute later, she opened it again. "She will see you now."

Amelia Pembrook was in bed, her body supported by many pillows. She looked flushed, and her right arm lay on a cushion. The arm was very swollen, and festering wounds were airing out.

Sarah took the chair next to her bed. "Miss Pembrook, what's wrong with your arm?"

Amelia answered slowly. "I was scratched at the party, and it got infected. Dr. Lindsey cleaned it out today." Her words were slurred, and Sarah was sure the girl had been given some sort of narcotic.

"Can you tell me where you met Mr. Marcel?"

"Les? I met him at my brother's place. Manny said he was in Juneau on business and asked if Les could be my escort while he was in town."

"Do you know what kind of business he's in?"

She shook her head. "He said it was too complicated to explain to a woman."

Sarah coughed to cover her snort. "How did you get scratched at the party?"

Amelia drew in a breath and hesitated for a moment. "A glass—yes, a glass broke, and I got scratched picking up the shards."

Sarah looked at her arm. "The scratches are on the top of your arm."

Amelia stared bleary-eyed and shrugged.

Sarah stood. "I'll let you rest now. Thank you for your time, Miss Pembrook." She turned to the aunt. "And thank you, too, Miss Davis. I can find my own way out."

As Sarah headed back to the sheriff's office, her mind was taking in the information. There was blood found on the top of the bookcase where the fish spear had been. Amelia had the only visible wound from the party, and Sarah didn't believe the story of the broken glass. *I think I'll stop over to Dr. Lindsey's office before I see Amos.*

Sarah sat in one of the wooden chairs in the doctor's office to wait until he finished with a patient. He came in and greeted her warmly, then sat down behind his desk.

"Miss Lakat, what can I do for you?"

Sarah leaned forward in her chair. "Doctor, I was over at the Pembrooks' this morning to see Amelia and ask her a few questions on the investigation. She said that you were over there, cleaning out those infected scratches on her arm. How did she get them?"

He sat back and steepled his fingers. "She said she didn't remember."

"What do you think?"

"It looked to me like a cat clawed and bit her. She had a bit of a fever, as well."

"Thank you, Dr. Lindsey." Sarah stood to go.

He rose as well. "Miss Lakat, please keep this off the record. I really shouldn't be discussing my patients with you, but I want to help. I think the Shafers are being unfairly judged in this town."

Sarah nodded. "I agree. I know how much work they've put into the theater. I want to help them, as well. Good day, Doctor."

She hurried to Amos' office. *Amelia lied to me. Why?*

****

Muriel's throat tightened as she and Addy watched Zeke show Kata the foot-long rip at the top of the expensive advertising curtain. *Poor Josh, what he must be going through, that he would do this.*

Kata climbed the ladder to inspect the tear more closely. "I think with some thick thread and a large needle I could fix it. Could you take it down tomorrow?"

Zeke nodded. "We'll spread it out on the stage so you can get at the rip easily. Has anyone seen Josh this morning?"

Muriel took a deep breath. "He took Jenny for a walk. Do you think I should be worried?"

"No. He probably wanted to take his mind off things. I managed to calm him down."

They heard the lobby doors open, and Muriel hurried up the aisle, arriving at the lobby just as Josh took Jenny out of the buggy and raised her over his head playfully. The baby giggled, and Muriel sighed in relief—he certainly looked like he was all right.

He turned as she approached. "You came from in there, the theater?"

Muriel nodded and laid her hand on his arm.

"Can the curtain be fixed?"

"Kata said she could repair it." She looked into his eyes. "Are *you* going to be—?"

"Repairable? I don't know. Zeke wants me to go on, so I might as well see how this turns out. I hate to let the rest of you down."

Her mouth went into a tight line. "This isn't your fault. None of us asked for this. We have to leave this in God's hands." She gazed into eyes that had lost their sparkle, and she wished she knew how to cheer him up.

"Let's go into the office. I want to check the ledger." Josh started toward the door.

Muriel grabbed his arm and took Jenny from him. "No. Let's go to the kitchen and see what Cora has to eat this morning."

"I'm not really—"

"You have to eat." She guided him to the other door.

As they opened it, the sharp, warm aroma of cinnamon rolls recently taken from the oven hit them. Cora wiped her hands on a towel as she looked up. "Ah, some customers, I see. Sit at one of the tables, and I'll bring you some rolls and coffee." She chucked Jenny under her chin. "And a bowl of warm applesauce for you, my pet."

Josh brought Jenny's high chair over to a table in the dining room, and, as Muriel tied the baby in with a dishtowel so she wouldn't slide out, Cora brought out the tray she'd prepared for them. Josh insisted on feeding Jenny as Muriel enjoyed the warm sweet bread, and she watched him with a glow. "You really don't mind being with Jenny, do you?"

He flushed slightly. "I guess she helps take my mind off our troubles. I had eight younger brothers and sisters at home, so I'm used to this."

Muriel put her hand over his in a comforting gesture, and he smiled and had started to speak when he was interrupted by sounds of activity in the lobby, followed by the entrance into the restaurant of the rest of the theater staff, along with the sheriff and Detective Lakat. Addy went into the kitchen and brought out Cora, and they all carried chairs over and sat with Josh and Muriel.

The sheriff cleared his throat. "Folks, there is information I have to check with you. First, did any of you see an injury on Miss Pembrook the night of the party?"

There was silence for a moment or two before Muriel spoke up. "I remember seeing scratches on her arm. They looked quite fresh, and I asked her about them."

Amos rubbed his chin. "Did she say how she got them?"

Muriel looked at Josh. "Didn't Mr. Marcel say she got scratched by her brooch?"

Josh nodded. "Muriel offered to help, but Miss Pembrook just shook her head and dabbed at the blood with her handkerchief."

The sheriff wrote down a note on his pad. "Mrs. Shafer, you have a cat, don't you?"

Addy looked puzzled. "Yes, I do."

"Where was the cat on the night of the party?"

"She was in our apartment."

He tapped his pencil on the paper. "Did she get out of the apartment at any time during the party?"

Addy bit her lip. "No, sir, I believe she was there the whole time."

Amos and Sarah glanced at each other. "Are you certain of this?" Sarah asked.

"Yes. She was there when we left at the beginning of the evening, and when I went in to lie down for a few minutes she was there with me."

Amos flipped the notepad shut. "Thank you all."

Cora shifted her feet. "You don't think that child killed her mother, do you?"

"As of now, I'm not ruling anything out. We're trying to get as many of the details as we can." He tipped his hat. "Good day to all of you."

Muriel caught the look between Sarah and Kata before Sarah and Amos departed.

****

Sitting in front of the desk in Amos' office, Sarah spread out the evidence they had accumulated.

Amos, by the woodstove, picked up the coffeepot. "Would you like some?"

Sarah nodded as she went over the notes. "Yes, please. It doesn't look good for Miss Pembrook, does it? Although I don't think she has the strength to shove what must have been a knife through her mother's ribs, let alone with such precision to pierce the heart."

Amos handed her a cup and sat down behind the desk. "I agree. I also don't think she'd have the presence of mind to try to frame the Shafers. Remember what you said at the coroner's, that it looked like a professional job?"

Sarah let the steam warm her face; then she blew on the coffee and took a sip. "You said that Mr. Marcel wasn't at the hotel this morning. Do you think he left?"

Amos shook his head. "I checked. There haven't been any airplanes or any ships with passenger cabins going out of Juneau in the last week. I told the harbor and the airfield people to let me know if anyone is planning to leave. I did, however, on a hunch, send his name and description to the chief of police in Trenton, New Jersey, by wire."

"Could Miss Pembrook have hired someone to kill her mother?"

"Like I told them at the theater, I'm trying to get all the facts together. I don't think we have enough to come to any conclusions yet."

Sarah thought for a moment. "When I was at the house, Miss Pembrook said her brother introduced her to Mr. Marcel. Maybe I should pay another visit to Mr. Pembrook and ask what kind of business Mr. Marcel is in."

Amos absentmindedly stroked his mustache. "We should go together. I think we can give that cub lawyer something to think about."

Considering the reception Sarah had gotten the last time she talked to Manfred, she thought Amos had a good idea.

Chapter 16

Josh had just finished hammering a board into place when he heard a commotion in the lobby. He and Ivan exchanged glances and hurried out to see what was going on.

Addy stood next to a stack of wall boards, holding one of them upright, while a scowling Zeke scolded, "For the last time, I don't want you lifting those boards. We can take care of this."

Addy set her jaw. "They aren't that heavy. I'm not a delicate flower, and I need something to do. We have to get the ticket booth finished."

"Go help Cora in the kitchen. You may not be a delicate flower, but you're carrying our child. I think I do have some say in that."

They glared at each other for a few moments, while Josh went to Addy and took the board she was waving toward Zeke's head. "I think the four of us," and he indicated Zeke, Ivan and James with himself, "can take care of this without blood being shed." Addy snorted and headed for the restaurant.

Josh shook his head. *Damn, everyone is on edge. This tension has got to come to an end, before we kill each other.* Then he was ashamed of his thoughts. There had been too much killing already; it wasn't anything to take lightly.

****

Muriel was bouncing Jenny on her lap and Cora was peeling carrots when Addy came in, grabbed a knife from the rack, and started murdering another poor root.

Cora put her hand on Addy's arm. "Honey, we

want enough left of that to eat tonight. What's wrong?"

Addy took a deep breath. "Zeke's treating me like an invalid. I'm healthy and strong, but he won't let me help with the construction."

Cora was quiet for a minute as she scraped the carrot. "Addy, I agree with Zeke on this one."

Addy looked up. "But I feel—"

"I felt healthy and strong the first two times I was with child, and I continued to work on the ranch." She leaned toward Addy. "I lost my first two children. I took it easy the next time, and my son was born."

Addy retreated into herself. She sighed. "I'm sorry. I'm so stubborn sometimes."

Cora nodded. "That could be a good thing, but when it comes to the welfare of your children, they have to come first."

Muriel went into the restaurant and brought back the high chair. "Do you have any melba toast? Jenny is teething and that seems to calm her."

Cora took down a tin from the shelf and handed it to her.

As Muriel sat and gave the baby one of the hard pieces of bread to chew on, she asked, "Can I help? There's nothing to do in the office."

Cora gave her another paring knife and a bowl. "You can help with the carrots."

Suddenly, angry yelling and a scuffling commotion came from the lobby. Muriel snatched Jenny from the high chair as the three women ran to see what was going on. They found Ivan and James standing between the two Shafer brothers.

Addy looked at Zeke and Josh. "What happened?" she demanded.

Josh pointed at Zeke. "My jackass brother didn't measure the area correctly. We came up short on the wall boards."

Zeke gritted his teeth. "You're the one who changed the plans without telling me."

Ivan held Josh to keep him from attacking Zeke. "We can order more. We have time before May to get what we need."

Josh glared at Zeke, then stomped upstairs. A door slammed. The women glanced at each other, then at Ivan, who shrugged.

Addy pursed her lips. "Honestly, you two are acting like five-year-olds!"

Zeke waved her away. "Just stay out of it! It's not a woman's concern."

Addy looked like she'd been hit in the gut. "What? I'm as much of a partner in this as you and Josh are."

Cora put her hand on Addy's shoulder. "Let's not add fuel to the fire."

But Addy angrily shook her off. The paring knife Addy had been holding flew through the air and stuck, quivering, in the wooden floor by Zeke's feet before she turned and stalked through the office and into the apartment, slamming the door behind her.

Zeke swallowed hard when he saw the knife only three inches from his shoe. "What the hell is the matter with her?"

Muriel disappeared into the office and tried the door to the apartment. She returned a moment later. "She's locked the door."

Cora shook her head. "This murder is hanging over all our heads like the sword of Damocles, and it's making everyone edgy."

Muriel tapped her foot for a moment. "Cora, could you watch Jenny? I'm going up to see if I can talk to Josh."

Cora nodded as she took the child from Muriel.

Zeke looked uncomfortable. "Maybe I should go up there."

Muriel shook her head. "You two would just end

up fighting again. Let me talk to him. I think you ought to talk to Addy."

Zeke gingerly pulled the knife out of the floor and handed it to Cora. "At least she's unarmed now. Muriel, would you find the apartment key in the desk?" He went to the apartment door and rapped on it. "Addy?" There was no answer. Muriel handed him the key. As Zeke opened the door, Muriel first saw Chloe's eyes glowing from beneath the bed and then Addy's hunched form on the couch.

"Sweetheart, I'm sorry. I was angry at Josh, not you," Muriel heard as she closed the door and headed to the stairs in the lobby. *Zeke can calm Addy down. Let's see what I can do for Josh.*

Muriel hesitated in front of Josh's door, suddenly realizing it wasn't proper to be alone with him in his room. She hadn't considered that when she came up. She'd simply wanted to help him through this. Muriel raised her hand to knock just as the door opened.

Josh gave her a sheepish grin when she jumped. "I heard footsteps stop in front of the door."

Muriel regained her composure. "I came up to see if you were all right."

"Come in."

She bit her lower lip. "Um, can we talk somewhere else?"

He looked behind him. "I see. This is my bedroom." He grabbed her arm. "We can go down the backstairs to the dressing room area. No one is there, as far as I know."

They settled themselves on the couch in the hallway of the dressing rooms. Kata's sewing machine hummed away a few doors down.

As Josh gazed at Muriel, she could see his blue eyes darken. "Everything seems to be turning against us now." He said, taking her hands in his. "Before, we were sailing along, and all fell into place.

The murder was like an omen that we will never get this theater going again."

She squeezed his palms. "I don't believe in bad omens. Josh, I married into a bad family that used stealing, lying, and murder to get what they wanted. The person who did this must have wanted something that Gladys had, and they were experienced enough to be able to frame someone else. I have faith in Sarah Lakat and Sheriff Darcy to find that person."

Josh was quiet for a few moments. "I want to believe that, but I find it hard to believe in anything anymore. My father always called me a failure."

Muriel let go. "Then you'd better listen to me. You're not a failure. You've done wondrous things with this old building and managed to entice a whole staff, including me, to join in your dream." She looked deep in his eyes. "When I first met you, I knew you had the personality to charm a wart off a toad, as my grandpa used to say."

Josh smiled and brushed his fingers across her cheek.

Muriel nearly gasped at the fire ignited by that light touch. She hadn't felt that flame since Tony had bewitched her. Muriel's perception of Josh was changing by the minute.

Josh gritted his teeth. "Muriel, go take care of Jenny." His voice was strained.

"Josh, I—"

"I'm all right. Just go now."

Muriel stood up from the couch and started down the hall toward the kitchen. She glanced back as Josh headed to the stairs.

What is it about me that bothers him? I think I'm beginning to have deep feelings for him. But he keeps backing away from me, ever since that one kiss. Is it because I have a child? He seems to enjoy her. Because I married a Giovanni? He doesn't seem upset about that. He knows I tried to kill his brother when I wasn't thinking clearly. Could that be it? Can he ever trust me? Will he?

****

Sarah stood behind Amos and watched Manfred Pembrook, seated at his desk, glare at the sheriff. "How dare you come in here unannounced." He glanced at Sarah over Amos' shoulder. "And I don't want to see *her* ever again."

Amos crossed his arms over his chest. "Then I want some straight answers out of you. How do you know Mr. Marcel, and what kind of business is he in?"

"He was Amelia's date. Why don't you ask her?"

"Because she said you introduced her to him."

Manfred made an incomprehensible sound and jiggled the papers in front of him. "He came here for advice about opening a business here in Juneau."

"What kind of business?"

"I don't know. He didn't say what kind."

"Was it a legal business or not?"

Manfred slammed his hand on the desk. "I don't know!"

Amos stroked his mustache. "May we ask your receptionist to give us a typing sample?"

"Why?"

"We want to find the typewriter used to type the note found by your mother."

Manfred waved them off, and Sarah got the sample. As they were walking back to Amos' office, he turned to her. "Well, was that the typewriter?"

Sarah shook her head. "I wonder if there's a typewriter at the Pembrook house. I'll go over there after lunch. Care to join me? I usually go to Millie's."

"No, I'd better stay at the office in case a telegram comes in. Stop back after you go to the Pembrooks'."

In Millie's pleasant café Sarah found a table

near the back, where she sat and gave her order. When a couple of men came in and sat at a table behind her, she didn't pay attention to what they were saying until she heard, "Lester, the sheriff has alerted the ships and airplanes to tell him if someone leaves." *I wonder if that's Lester Marcel?* She listened carefully to the rest of their conversation.

"Jack, did you get any takers for the shipments?"

"Some, but not as many as we hoped for."

There was silence for a moment, and then Lester said, "It's too bad the Shafers didn't bite. That would be an easy thing to bring them down on."

"That Zeke Shafer threw me out the moment I said he could buy the finest—" He paused. "Goods for sale. Anyway, the fingers would be pointing at us, Lester. That's not what we want. The sheriff's a rube, but he isn't stupid."

"Look, Juneau is a piss-poor market. We could arrange to be out of here before they can turn around. There may be a tramp steamer that could transport us without anyone stooling to the authorities. I think the Shafers are in trouble now. Even if they're let off for the murder, they're ruined in this town. I don't think people would blink an eye if the Shafers were taken care of. We could do that before we skip out."

Sarah tapped her coffee cup. *I think I'll put off going to the Pembrooks' for now. The sheriff will be very interested in this conversation. Should I confront Lester now to get more information? No, maybe it would be better to let Amos know where they are. I don't have a weapon with me, and they seem like very unsavory characters.* Since her back was to them, she jotted notes of what they said on her pad. Then, smoothly, she put things away and left a tip.

As she was paying the bill at the counter, Sarah

took Millie aside. "Do you know anything about those two?" Sarah nodded toward Lester and Jack.

Millie shook her head. "They're very cagey about what they do. The only thing I know is they're in some type of business, but they've never mentioned what it is."

"Thanks, Millie." Sarah waved as she left.

Amos looked up as she walked into his office. "I didn't expect you back so soon. What happened?"

Sarah settled into one of the chairs. "I was having lunch at Millie's when two men came in and sat behind me." She related the conversation she'd overheard.

Amos nodded. "That sounds like Lester Marcel. He obviously has someone working with him. I have a hunch his business isn't legal. That's probably one of the reasons he's been avoiding me." He was silent for a moment. "I think I'll put one of my deputies down at the docks to keep an eye on comings and goings. And I'll go to Millie's to see if they're still there."

Sarah stood up. "I'll go over to the Pembrooks' now. I should be back in an hour." She saluted Amos as she exited the office.

****

Josh sat in the overstuffed chair by the window in his room. *How am I going to continue to live three doors down from Muriel? I think she has feelings for me, as well. I can still feel that kiss. I keep telling myself she deserves better than me, but every time I'm near her I want her more.* He hit his forehead with the heel of his hand. *I've got to get busy with something else, distract myself. It doesn't do any good to think about her.*

He put on his parka and hurried downstairs. When he ran into Ivan nailing a stud into place for the wall of the ticket booth, he said, "I'm going to the lumber mill to order four more wall boards."

Ivan looked at him closely. "Are you all right?"

Josh stared at the toe of his boot. "Yes and no. I'm trying to make this go. I guess I want to keep faith in myself and this project."

Ivan clapped him on the back. "You have to let this tragedy blow over. It's still too fresh in the minds of the townspeople, but they'll come around, my friend."

Josh gave him a half-smile. "I hope so."

Walking the two and a half blocks to the lumber mill's office, Josh kept his gloved hands jammed into his pockets to keep as warm as possible despite the January winds that cut through him. When he opened the door to the showroom the smell of fresh-cut wood welcomed him, along with warmth from the woodstove in the corner.

A red-haired, freckled-faced young man looked up and grinned. "Hello, Mr. Shafer. Was there anything wrong with the wall boards?"

Josh shook his head. "No, Pete. In fact, I need four more. Could you put that on order?"

Pete's face fell. "I need twelve dollars in advance."

"What?"

"Sorry, it's orders from the boss. He's afraid you'll run out of money and we'll be stuck."

Josh's fist hit the counter. "I've always paid the bills on time."

Pete looked down. "Yes, I know. And if it was me—" His voice trailed off.

Josh pulled out his money clip. Luckily, he had fifteen dollars left. He counted out twelve and slapped them on the counter. "I've never stuck anyone. You can tell your boss that! Let me know when they come in." He whirled around and slammed the door behind him. *Will people stop selling us everything? I'll show them, by God. They're not going to starve us out!*

When Josh got back to the theater, Muriel was waiting for him. She held Jenny, and the minute the little girl saw Josh, she beamed and raised her arms. He smiled and picked her out of Muriel's hands, swinging her up in the air. Jenny burst into giggles.

Muriel cupped his cheek. "She missed you," she said quietly.

Josh hugged the child and quickly wiped away a tear.

Chapter 17

Sarah found Amos pacing his office when she returned from the Pembrooks'.

"Lakat, sit down. When I got to Millie's, Lester and his cohort had already left, but I got back here in time to receive a telegram from the police chief in Trenton, New Jersey, about Mr. Marcel."

Sarah poured herself a cup of coffee before she sat on the chair across the desk from Amos. She put the mug down. "Before you start, the Pembrooks do have a typewriter and, no, it isn't the one." She flipped the paper in front of him.

He took a glance at it, then picked up the telegram. "Mr. Marcel is really Lester Marcelli. That's one of the aliases he uses, and he's a known henchman for the Giovanni family. They're a regular crime syndicate."

Sarah frowned for a moment. "Giovanni. That's Muriel's last name. Do you think she's in on anything illegal?"

"I don't know. She's Adeline Shafer's cousin, but maybe we should pay the young widow a visit."

It was two-thirty and already getting dark when they set out to the theater, and Sarah snuggled her face farther into the parka hood as the sharp wind stung her face. It was a relief to reach their destination, where they found Josh Shafer and Muriel Giovanni in the lobby.

Amos took off his hat. "Mrs. Giovanni, we would like to speak to you in private."

Josh glanced at Muriel. "You can use the office. I'll take care of Jenny for you."

Muriel nodded. "Why don't you put her down for her nap?"

Sarah and Amos followed Muriel to the back. "What can I help you with?" Muriel slid into the chair behind the desk and indicated the chairs on the other side.

The sheriff pulled the telegram from his coat pocket but continued to hold it. "Mrs. Giovanni, we received this from the chief of police in Trenton, New Jersey, about Mr. Marcel."

Sarah watched for any reaction from Muriel, but there wasn't any.

The sheriff continued, "Does the name Marcelli mean anything to you?"

Muriel gasped. "One of the thugs who was killed with my father-in-law, Joe Giovanni, was named Marcelli."

Sarah narrowed her eyes. "You said he was killed? Are you sure of that?"

Muriel took a deep breath. "Addy identified the bodies to the coroner after the raid on my father's house."

Sarah and Amos looked at each other. Amos stood and leaned on the desk. "Maybe you'd better tell me about that."

Muriel hesitated a moment. "You have to understand that Addy, Zeke and I moved up here to escape the Giovannis' reach." She glanced at them sadly. "In Los Angeles, I eloped with Tony Giovanni. At the time, I didn't know anything about his family. I was only eighteen and in love. The Giovannis bought into Majestic Studios, where Addy and Zeke worked, and used it as a front to make bootleg liquor and distribute it through their theaters around the country. Anyway, Addy and Zeke helped the police set up a trap to catch them. Tony died in that raid. Joe later escaped with two of his men and abducted Addy. He tried to...to murder her." Emotion roiled on

Muriel's face. "After Addy was out of the hospital, the police set up a trap at my father's house. That's when Joe and his men were killed."

Amos leaned forward. "Both you and Mrs. Shafer saw Amelia Pembrook's escort on the night of the New Year's party, am I correct?"

"Yes."

"The information I received was that his name is Lester Marcelli and that he works for the Giovanni family."

Muriel turned pale and looked like she was about to faint. "Chester's brother? Oh, my God, they found us." She stood up and dissolved into tears. "The Giovannis want to take Jenny away, and I'm sure they still want to get revenge on Zeke and Addy."

"Why would they want to harm Mr. and Mrs. Shafer?" Amos handed Muriel his large handkerchief, and she mopped her eyes as she answered.

"Because of the trap they helped set up at the studio, and then because my father-in-law and my husband were killed."

Sarah rose and put her arms around Muriel. The poor girl trembled. Sarah looked at Amos and he rubbed his chin. "Where are Mr. and Mrs. Shafer?" he asked.

Muriel blew her nose in the handkerchief. "The last I knew, they were in their apartment, through that door." She pointed.

Amos went over and knocked. "This is Sheriff Darcy. May I see you both in the office?"

Zeke appeared first, and Addy came in behind him. When she saw Muriel crying, she hurried over to her. "What's wrong, dear?"

Sarah stood back as the cousins embraced. Muriel kept saying, "They found us," between sobs.

The sheriff repeated his information to Zeke and

Addy, who stood stunned.

Addy gasped. "I thought he looked familiar, but I couldn't place him. Of course, he resembles Chester."

Amos nodded at Sarah. "Lakat overheard a conversation between Marcelli and a man called Jack that leads me to think the murder was a set-up."

Zeke whirled on the sheriff. "You mean you think he did it?"

Amos shook his head. "We don't have any proof of that, but they are using it to help ruin you."

"What should we do? If they were sent up here to ruin us, we're all in danger."

Sarah put her hand on Amos' arm. "Maybe, since we know there's a threat here, you can spare one of the deputies to watch the theater. Something like a watchman, and if anything happens, he can handle it."

Amos was silent for a few moments, but after some thought he agreed. "I'll send one of the deputies up when I get back to the office. They can work in shifts. I suggest you keep the doors to the building locked."

Zeke flagged down James. "Could you make sure all the outside doors are locked? And give a thorough search inside. We need to be absolutely sure we don't have any unwanted visitors."

James left immediately on his mission.

The sheriff tipped his hat. "I'll get this set up soon. Come on, Lakat."

Zeke nodded. "Thank you, Sheriff."

As they walked back to the office, Sarah looked at Amos. "What do you think?"

Amos pursed his lips. "I read about the collapse of Majestic in the newspaper when it happened. It's as Mrs. Giovanni told us. I do understand that if you cross one of these crime families, they stop at nothing to get revenge. But I can't tie that into Mrs. Pembrook's death, not yet."

"Maybe it's two separate things, but that's more than we had before."

Amos smiled. "I think we found our lead." He flashed a glance at her. "I may be a rube, but I'm not stupid."

Sarah chuckled as they walked into the office.

****

Muriel hurried up the steps to her room. Josh was in the rocking chair by the window and Jenny was sleeping in her crib. "Josh," she whispered, "come out here in the hall."

He closed the door behind him. "What's going on?"

She took a deep breath. "The Giovannis have found us."

Josh held her up as she slumped. "How on earth did they?"

Muriel told him what she had learned from the sheriff.

Josh paled. "Oh, God, what do we do?"

"Zeke had James lock all the outside doors to the building and search the inside. The sheriff is having some deputies work in shifts as watchmen here."

Just then, James came up the stairs from the back and started checking all the rooms. As he approached Josh and Muriel, he told them, "I didn't find anything amiss in the building, and all the outside doors are locked."

Josh clapped him on the shoulder. "Thank you, James. Round up everyone and have them meet up here in the hallway as soon as possible."

Muriel and Josh brought chairs out of the rooms and left the door to Muriel's room ajar so they could hear Jenny if she woke. The little group sat as Zeke explained the most recent news. There was silence as they took it in.

Zeke looked at them. "I realize you don't deserve to get in the middle of this, and I want to apologize for the mess, but we didn't believe we would be followed up here."

Ivan stood. "I think I speak for Kata and me, that we will stay with you."

Kata nodded. "You all have been friends to us. We won't turn our backs on you now."

Cora pounded her knee. "We've been through this before and won. Those gangsters aren't scaring me away."

Muriel felt a swelling of gratitude for these people. She glanced at Josh and saw tears misting in his eyes. Addy was strangely quiet, staring at the floor.

As the others started downstairs, Muriel took Addy aside. "Honey, talk to me. Something's wrong."

Addy trembled, and Muriel hugged her. "Muriel, I don't think I can go through this again. I'd be risking the baby's life as well as my own."

Muriel felt a stab of fear. "You've always been so brave and sure of yourself. We can get through this."

Addy looked her in the eyes. "I'm sure the orders are to kill Zeke and me. Our baby will be a victim then, as well."

"Remember the Giovannis want Jenny, too. We all have to stand together against them."

"If only we hadn't become involved in the first place."

Muriel grabbed her shoulders. "What's done is done, and we have to move on."

Suddenly, Addy giggled. "You sound just like your father."

They both laughed and went toward Muriel's room as Jenny woke up.

****

Josh opened the door to the sheriff and his deputy who, Josh assumed, was their first watchman. The sheriff tipped his hat. "Mr. Shafer, could you gather everyone together in the restaurant?"

Soon, all sat at the tables, with the sheriff and deputy standing before them. "I want to introduce you to Deputy Sam Lindsey. Yes, he's the nephew of our Dr. Lindsey. He will be your daytime watchman, and Deputy Will Strauss will take the night shift, outside, so we won't disturb you. I think because there is so much coming and going during the day, Lindsey should be inside." He turned to Zeke and Addy. "Since there might be a threat against you two in particular, I suggest you take one of the rooms upstairs for now."

Zeke stood. "If you think these men are a threat, why can't you stop them?"

"They haven't really done anything illegal that we can prove yet. You can't arrest a man for talking. So we take precautions, hoping we can draw them out."

Zeke shook his head. "I don't want this to turn out like it did in Los Angeles. The inspector who handled the case there put us in a lot of danger. Addy was almost killed."

"We will do everything in our power to keep all of you safe. In the meantime, carry on your work as usual. We don't want to make them suspicious. You'll notice that Lindsey is in plain clothes for that very reason."

After the sheriff left, Josh helped Zeke and Addy move their things to one of the unoccupied rooms upstairs. When he came back down to work on the ticket booth, he saw Muriel engaged in conversation with the young deputy, and a stab of jealousy hit him. *No. I've turned away from her several times. She doesn't need someone like me. Not until I can prove to myself I can support her.* Josh gritted his teeth and hammered a board into place.

****

Muriel stared at the ceiling as she woke up, still troubled about how Josh kept avoiding her. *Is it something I've said or done? My talks with Sam make me feel like he could be interested in me, but my heart is with Josh. What do I do?* She heard stirrings from the crib, and she rose to get herself and Jenny ready for the day, her mind still pulling every which way over the questions.

She sang to Jenny as they went into the kitchen, where Cora looked up from her perpetual soup on the stove. "Morning, Cora. Mmm, that soup smells wonderful this morning. I may have some of that instead of breakfast. Maybe toast and butter for Jenny."

"Help yourself. You've been in a good mood these past few days, for the cloud we're under. I've noticed you're taking breaks with Deputy Lindsey."

"He is so interesting to talk to. I've learned so much about Juneau. He's lived here all his life. Did you know Dr. Lindsey and Sam's father had a claim during the gold rush?"

"No, I didn't. It must have been as wild a time around here as it was in Tombstone, Arizona, where I grew up. That was a mining town, too."

Muriel came back to the stove with a bowl. "Did you get over to see Amelia like you planned?"

Cora shook her head. "Her aunt didn't let me in. That family is a strange one. I hope Amelia knows we didn't have anything to do with her mother's death." She was silent for a moment. "Have you talked to Josh lately?"

Muriel bit her lower lip. "Outside of taking care of Jenny occasionally, I almost think he's trying to avoid me. Do you think he blames me for the trouble?"

"I think all of these problems are taking a toll on him. Zeke told me their father called Josh a failure from the time he was born. He said Josh was always the happy-go-lucky member of the family, and that was sinful, according to his father. I think the boy is scarred from his harsh treatment." She glanced at Muriel. "He's such a good-hearted young man. You'd think his father would have seen that."

Muriel digested this information throughout the day. She thought about the times Jenny had been colicky at night and Josh would take the baby into his room to let Muriel get some sleep. She remembered Zeke's problem in trusting anyone. How could a father treat his children that way? Her father was strict, but Muriel felt he cared for all his family, including Addy when he'd brought her into their home after her parents were killed.

Muriel spent time with Sam on his breaks and bid him goodnight when he left at the end of his shift. It was a busy day, with the contractors checking the inner roof structure, so there were people going in and out all day.

Ready for bed, she checked on Jenny, who was sleeping peacefully in her crib. Muriel sighed and crawled under the quilts that held off the chill of the January night. She was asleep almost immediately.

She woke to a large hand clamped over her mouth. She was having trouble breathing, or she would have screamed. She felt cold steel against her neck.

"Don't make a sound, Mrs. Giovanni, unless you want to see your baby dead. You're coming with us," a coarse, tobacco-laden voice whispered in her ear. He slapped an envelope on her nightstand.

She raised up to see another man lifting Jenny out of her crib. "What are you doing?" she hissed. "Leave my child alone!" Full-blown panic took her over.

"I mean it, Mrs. Giovanni. It doesn't mean anything to me if you both die." The man holding her shoved her parka and boots at her. "Put these on. Jack, wrap the baby up in extra quilts."

All at once Muriel realized who they were. "Lester, you'll never get away with this. There's a deputy outside watching the building."

He stopped for a moment. "Good, you do know who we are. Then you know where we're taking you. Sofia will be pleased. As for the deputy, we don't have to worry about him." He put a gag in her mouth as she struggled.

Jenny began to cry.

"Keep that brat quiet!" Lester gritted out.

Jack started to rock the baby. "Come on, Les. Let's get out of here."

Lester hauled Muriel onto her feet and hustled her down the back stairs. Just outside the kitchen door she gasped as she saw the body of Deputy Strauss lying face down in a pool of what she suspected was blood. In the dark, it was hard to tell. *What are they going to do to us?*

Les and Jack hustled her down the block to where an auto waited with the motor running. Before shoving Muriel into the back seat, Les tied her hands and feet securely. Then he got into the front passenger seat and held Jenny as Jack drove off.

Suddenly, there was an explosion behind them. Muriel's breath jolted against the gag.

Les turned to Muriel with a smile. "I hope you said a fond goodnight to Mr. and Mrs. Shafer." Then he and Jack laughed as tears streamed down her face.

Chapter 18

The explosion knocked Josh out of bed. He tore out of the room and joined everyone else in the hallway. "What the hell happened?"

Zeke was already running toward the stairs. "I'll go check."

Addy looked around. "Where's Muriel?" She dashed into Muriel's room, and when Josh heard her cry out, he went in after her. Addy had turned on the light and was picking up an envelope next to it. She handed it to him with shaking fingers. "Open it. I can't."

Josh read the note and felt the blood drain from his face. "It says Muriel and Jenny have been abducted, and if we want to see them alive again, we should let Lester and Jack get out of Juneau on the ship in the harbor."

Addy started to cry, and Josh put his arms around her. He was tearing up, as well, and they stood there for a few moments drawing strength from each other.

Before long, however, they heard noises in the lobby, and then the sheriff ran up the stairs. "Get down there with the others, both of you!"

Josh handed him the note, and the sheriff read it as they went. Deputy Lindsey and Sarah Lakat came in the front door as everyone gathered.

Addy threw her arms around Zeke.

"They've taken Muriel and Jenny," Addy blurted, tears still evident on her face. Zeke did his best to calm her, but the worried expression never left.

Cora came from the kitchen, her face stern and sad. "I found Deputy Strauss when I stepped outside for my morning breath of air. It looks like his throat was slit. He's out by the kitchen door."

Josh glanced around. "What was the explosion?"

Deputy Lindsey wiped his brow. "It was a box I found under the bed in the apartment, on my rounds just before I went off my shift. It looked suspicious, so I set it out back, away from the building. I was going to check it out this morning."

The sheriff clapped him on the shoulder. "Good instincts. You saved these people's lives."

Sarah Lakat inspected the note that was found in Muriel's room. "We'd better get down to the harbor before they have time to board the ship."

The sheriff shook his head. "I don't think they went to the harbor. That note is too carefully sending us on a wild goose chase. I'll bet my commission they're going to the airfield. They can't fly at night, so they set us up to buy more time."

Lakat looked impressed. "You're probably right. They wouldn't have left a note if they were trying to sneak off. But the airplanes can't fly in the dark."

The sheriff checked his watch. "It's eight-thirty. It won't start getting light until nine. We'll go to the office and get the auto." He hesitated a moment. "I think I'll send a deputy over to the harbor, just in case I'm wrong. The airfield is twenty minutes away. Let's go!"

After Sheriff Darcy, Deputy Lindsey, and Sarah had gone, Josh dashed to the stairs.

"Where are you going?" Zeke called after him.

"I'm getting dressed." Josh hurried to his room, tearing off his pajamas as he went. He jumped into his clothes and put on his heavy socks and boots, grabbed his parka off the hook by the door, and opened it—to find Zeke standing in his way. "Move over! I have to go!"

Zeke put his hand on Josh's shoulder. "The sheriff can take care of this."

"You don't understand. I have to be there. Muriel and Jenny need me."

Zeke looked deep into his brother's eyes and finally nodded. "I do understand, but be careful and stay back."

Josh started the truck and headed toward the airfield. Juneau was already bustling with its morning business, and the cold crisp January air bit into his lungs. The stars still sparkled in the black sky, but there was a trace of light from behind Mt. Juneau.

From the deep recesses of his mind, he imagined his father chiding him. *And what are you going to do when you get there? You should let the sheriff take care of this. You just want Muriel to see you as a hero. You're going to get in the way and fail again.*

He hit the steering wheel with his fist. "I won't fail!"

He turned the headlights off before he arrived at the airfield. There in the distance, under one of the electric lights, he saw a group of people next to an airplane that stood, warming up, on the field. Two men had their backs to him. One had a bundle on his arm and the other man held a woman. *That must be Muriel.* In the light, he could see the faces of the sheriff, Deputy Lindsey and Sarah Lakat.

Oh, no! The sheriff and the deputy were dropping their weapons to the ground. Josh knew what he had to do.

****

The first gray streaks of dawn were making it slightly lighter over the back of the mountain as Muriel was shoved roughly toward the airplane. Her feet had been untied, but her hands were still bound together, and the gag was in place.

Jack shifted the baby around. "It looks like your

plan worked. I don't see a sign of the sheriff or the police."

"How long before we can take off?" Lester yelled over the engine to the pilot.

"As soon as it's light enough to see. I estimate ten minutes," came the reply.

"Les, someone's coming." Jack pointed at an auto moving toward them on the field.

Muriel thought it looked like the sheriff's patrol in the dim light, and silently she felt a glimmer of hope that she and Jenny were going to be rescued. *Thank you, Lord.*

Les swore under his breath. "The trick didn't work." He tightened his grip on Muriel's arm. "Well, honey, you two are our insurance out of here. Jack, hold your gun on the baby." Then he drew his knife and held it at Muriel's throat as the sheriff's auto screeched to a halt in front of them and its occupants jumped out, guns drawn.

Muriel's heart pounded and she couldn't breathe. *Oh, God, get us out of this.*

Les glared steadily at the group. "That's far enough, Sheriff, unless you want to lose both the baby and her mother."

The sheriff and the others stopped ten feet away.

"That's it, Sheriff. Now would you kindly drop the guns on the ground?"

They hesitated, then let their guns fall. The sheriff stood his ground. "You won't get away with this, Marcelli. We know who you are and can track you down. And not only us. All the information about you is in my office."

Muriel felt the blade against her skin, and a trickle of wetness she knew was blood ran down her neck. Then out of the corner of her eye, she saw a shadowy form come up behind Jack. The bundle was snatched out of Jack's arms, and he wildly fired a shot. Jenny screamed; then her cries were muffled.

Muriel took advantage of Les' surprise and ducked away from the knife blade. She got one boot behind his leg and pushed with her body so that he fell, and in the same moment she saw the sheriff and Sam dive for their guns. The deputy blew the gun out of Jack's hand before he could get off another shot, while the knife flew from Les' hand and skittered on the hard frozen ground. Muriel landed on top of him and felt a sharp pain in her knee, but she rolled away quickly as Les grabbed at her. Although to Muriel everything seemed to move in slow motion, it was all over in only a few seconds.

Meanwhile, the airplane had turned slowly and headed toward the sheriff and the others, its deadly blade slicing the way, but the sheriff aimed toward the pilot's seat and fired. As the aircraft bounced toward them, they ran out of its path to where Lester and Jack were, and the airplane continued down the field to a stone wall across the mountain road. The sound of the crash came a split second after the impact, along with a huge ball of flame as the full gas tanks exploded.

Muriel felt the heat from the blast on her face. Sarah helped her up and cut away the ropes and the gag, while the sheriff and Sam put handcuffs on Lester and Jack. Muffled cries from a few feet away had Muriel in a panic. "My baby! Where is Jenny?"

The dim light of early dawn revealed what looked like a heap of clothing. Muriel's knee protested, but with Sarah's help, she hobbled over to it. She heard a groan of pain as the heap moved with the sheriff's aid. The top quilt wrapped around Jenny was covered with a dark stain, and Muriel screamed.

The sheriff inspected the baby and handed her to Muriel. "The baby is safe, Mrs. Giovanni. Mr. Shafer shielded her with his body."

"But the blood—"

"Mr. Shafer was hit." By this time the sheriff had Josh rolled over and had torn open Josh's parka to find the wound.

Muriel went over to Josh and cradled his head with her free arm while the sheriff put pressure on the wound with material torn from Josh's shirt.

She ignored her knee. It was so much less painful than the thought of losing this wonderful man.

"Josh, oh, Josh," she kept repeating, her tears falling on his face.

The thought of Josh being so brave trying to save both of them, then sacrificing himself, was almost too much for her to bear. With a glance at the baby, quiet on her lap, she continued to sit on the hard, frozen ground, stroking Josh's cheek.

Josh, I love you, my hero. Jenny and I need you. I'd give you my strength to live, if I only knew how.

The sheriff called out to Sam, who watched Lester and Jack. "Lindsey, you and Lakat take those two to jail. Retrieve Mr. Marcelli's knife. Tag it and have it on my desk. I see Mr. Shafer's truck over there. I'll take them to the hospital. Wait until I leave."

While the sheriff brought Josh's truck closer, Sarah kept pressure on the cloth Amos had put on the wound, and Muriel stroked Josh's cheek as she rocked Jenny.

Sam helped put Josh in the back of the truck, where Muriel crawled in beside him, taking over the job of keeping pressure on his wound while still cradling the baby.

On the way to the hospital, Josh opened his eyes for a moment. He took a ragged breath. "How is Jenny?" he rasped.

Muriel swallowed over the lump in her throat. "She's fine."

He nodded and smiled faintly before his eyes closed again.

"Stay with us, Josh," Muriel pleaded. Then she offered a silent prayer.

Chapter 19

Muriel felt the truck stop, and then the sheriff opened the back. "I'll get orderlies for both of you." In a few minutes, two men came out with a stretcher and a nurse wheeled out a chair. Amos helped Muriel out of the truck to be wheeled into the lobby of the community hospital with Jenny in her arms, and from the window she watched Amos help take Josh on the stretcher to the other entrance.

One of the young doctors, who introduced himself as Dr. Curtis, took her into an examining room to check her knee. "It looks like it's a sprain. I'll bandage it and give you some aspirin and an ice pack. You'll probably need crutches for a few days. I'll have one of the nurses bring them to you."

He also cleaned and bandaged the knife cut on Muriel's neck, and when he was finished the nurse gave Muriel a glass of water and some aspirin while Dr. Curtis took a short inspection of Jenny. He soon handed her back to Muriel. "The baby is fine."

He left and returned shortly with an ice pack for Muriel's knee, and the nurse wheeled her back out into the lobby just as Addy and Zeke came in.

Muriel cried out, "I thought you were dead! There was an explosion..." Tears of happiness stung her eyes.

Addy ran to Muriel and hugged her. "Thankfully, Deputy Lindsey found a strange box yesterday evening, under our bed in the apartment, and he took it outside. That's where it exploded, so no one was hurt."

Zeke put his hand on Muriel's shoulder. "How

are you and Jenny?"

"I have a sprained knee and a cut on the neck. Otherwise, we're both fine."

He nodded. "I'm going to go find out about Josh." He inquired at the desk, and the woman there sent him down the hallway.

Addy picked up Jenny and hugged her. "We were so afraid for both of you."

Muriel chewed her lip. "I was worried about you and Zeke. When we were going down the street from the theater, we heard the explosion, and they made me believe you were all dead." A huge lump formed in her throat. "And now Josh—"

Addy gave Jenny back to Muriel. "What happened? Sarah Lakat told us only that you and Josh were hurt."

Muriel told her of the events at the airfield, and Addy's eyes darkened. Muriel took a deep breath. "Josh was hurt protecting Jenny. If anything happens to him, I'll never forgive myself."

Addy put her arms around Muriel. "This isn't your fault. Josh decided to do this himself."

Jenny started to whimper, then cry. Muriel turned to the nurse at the desk. "Is there a room where I can feed my baby?"

Directed to one of the examining rooms, she had Addy wheel her in. After the feeding, when the exhausted child had fallen asleep, Addy wheeled them back into the lobby, where they continued to wait for any word on Josh.

It seemed like hours before Dr. Lindsey came in. "I had the orderly take Mr. Shafer to the men's ward. I want him to stay a few days. The bullet was removed successfully, but it did nick the liver. Thanks to all the clothes he was wearing, it only went in an inch and a half, but he lost a lot of blood."

Muriel and Addy were silent as Dr. Lindsey told them about Josh. Muriel could feel the blood drain from her face. "Can I see him?"

Lindsey shook his head. "I've given him morphine. He should be out for a while. Zeke is going to donate blood, and I'll drive him back to the theater in Josh's truck afterwards. Mrs. Giovanni, I think you should go back and rest your knee."

Addy bit her lip. "We walked over here. Can she make it?"

Lindsey thought for a moment, then turned to a young man working on a ledger at a nearby desk. "Ed, do you have your auto today?"

"Yes, doc."

"Could you take these ladies back to the theater?"

"Sure." He closed the ledger and grabbed his parka. "I'll bring the auto around to the entrance."

Lindsey took a pair of crutches from a cabinet and gave them to Muriel, who handed Jenny over to Addy. "I expect you to use these and stay off your feet as much as possible."

As she took the crutches, Muriel put her hand on the doctor's arm. "May I see Josh first thing tomorrow?" Fear gripped her that she wouldn't see him alive again.

Lindsey patted her hand. "I expect him to be all right. Don't worry. Just take care of yourself." He turned to Addy. "And you, Mrs. Shafer, I want you to get some bed rest after this."

Muriel exchanged a concerned look with Addy. "Thank you, Doctor."

He wheeled Muriel out to the auto, followed by Addy with Jenny. Ed helped them into the auto and headed to the theater.

And Muriel prayed for Josh to get better. *He has to come through this. There are so many things unsaid between us.*

****

Josh drifted in a blackness that seemed to

envelope him. From what seemed like a distance, he heard voices. He couldn't bring himself to open his eyes yet, but what was being said became clearer. "Are you sure he'll pull through?" *That sounded like Zeke.*

The doctor's reply came next. "He's a strong young man, but a bullet can do a lot of damage. He's very lucky. The only thing I'm worried about is the blood loss. The liver is rich with blood, and when it's hit, the bleeding can be severe. That's why we need you. Roll up your shirt sleeve and lie back on the gurney." *What's going on?* "Now make a fist."

Josh felt something go around his arm, and a sharp jab followed. *A needle? Why? Is Zeke giving me blood?* He felt warmth creep into his body. Then he heard his brother say, quietly, "Live, Josh, we need you—I need you."

Love for Zeke overwhelmed Josh. His brother, whom he had always looked up to, needed him. And then the unconsciousness washed over him again.

****

Sarah was helping herself to a cup of coffee when Amos walked into the office. His face looked grim. "I had to tell Will's family what happened. That's the worst part of this job. God, I hate it when a young man goes down."

Sarah sighed. "That's a specter that hangs over all of us in this business."

Amos picked up Lester's knife. "Come on, Sarah. Let's go give Elmer a visit."

They went together into the coroner's office. Elmer Stanton jumped up. "Sheriff, I hope you're done with the Pembrook investigation. Mr. Pembrook is angry that his mother hasn't been buried yet."

"I think he'll be able to have her picked up soon." He waved Elmer into the back.

Elmer pulled the sheet down from the body. The

flesh had corrupted some at the wound site, but the width and length of the cut matched the knife. Amos straightened up. "What do you think, Elmer?"

Elmer rubbed his chin. "It looks right. I'd guess you found the murder weapon."

Amos slapped him on the back. "Ha! We found the killer. Tell Pembrook he can have the body."

Sarah followed Amos back to the office with a nagging thought in her head.

"Sam," Amos called, "add suspicion of murder on Lester's sheet."

Sarah sat down with her coffee and glanced at Amos as he poured himself a cup and sat across from her. "Why did he kill her?"

Amos swallowed wrong and went into a spasm of coughing. "Are you trying to complicate things? We found the murder weapon and the one who owns it."

She shook her head. "It doesn't make any sense. He knew Gladys' son and took out her daughter. What was his motive?"

His mouth pressed in a straight line. "Isn't that motive enough?"

"Amos!"

"Well, what do we know of him? He's from New Jersey, and he works for the Giovanni crime family. He tried to frame the Shafers with the murder, and then he tried to kill them. And he attempted to leave with Mrs. Giovanni and the baby."

Sarah nodded. "He sounds like a hit man. That means someone hired him."

"Wouldn't that be the Giovannis?"

"Possibly. But it could mean there was someone here who tipped them off. Although, I do remember that Mr. Marcelli's brother was killed in a raid at Mrs. Giovanni's family home. It could be revenge, too." She tapped her fingernail on her cup. "I wonder how much Miss Pembrook knows about this. Maybe if I confront her with this new evidence, she might tell us what she knows."

Amos rubbed his chin. "Do you think the blood on the bookcase was hers?"

Sarah nodded. "Dr. Lindsey said her wound looked like a cat scratch. Miss Pembrook might have startled the animal as she took the spear."

Amos pulled on his parka. "Let's go see the young lady."

As they walked to the Pembrook estate, things that had puzzled Sarah started to fall into place. She wished Miss Pembrook hadn't become involved in this. That young lady had been treated badly most of her life, as far as she could see. Everyone in Juneau knew of the abuse her mother gave her, putting Amelia down constantly in front of people. Maybe her age would work in her favor.

They went to the massive door and turned the bell. A maid opened the door and stood looking from one to the other of them. "Yes?"

The sheriff took his hat off. "Could you tell Miss Pembrook that Sheriff Darcy and Miss Lakat would like to see her?"

She nodded. "Wait here in the hall, and I'll tell her."

Amelia's aunt, Martha Davis, appeared at the top of the stairs a few minutes later. "Sheriff, Miss Lakat, my niece has had a very bad night. Is this visit necessary?"

Amos nodded. "I'm afraid so."

Miss Davis' mouth pulled tight, but she turned and said, "Come up."

Amelia was propped in bed with a book next to her. She seemed to Sarah to be less drugged than the last time Sarah had seen her, but Amelia didn't respond when her aunt spoke to her.

Sarah put her hand on Amos' arm. "Let me talk to her."

Amos nodded and brought a chair next to the bed, waving for Sarah to sit.

Sarah leaned forward and put her hand on Amelia's. "Miss Pembrook, we think we found the murder weapon. It looks like Lester Marcel's knife was the one that killed your mother. What do you know about this?"

Amelia stared ahead, with no indication that she heard Sarah.

Sarah chewed her lip and tried something else. "Tell me again how you hurt your arm?"

Glancing at the bandage, Amelia seemed to collect herself. "I cut myself on...glass. Yes, glass." Her voice sounded eerily monotone.

Amos mouthed, "Ask about Lester."

She gently squeezed Amelia's hand. "Where did you meet Lester?"

Smiling slightly, Amelia answered, "I met him at Manny's office. Manny told him I needed an escort for Christmas and New Year's. He is handsome, don't you think? My knight in shining armor. He killed the dragon and set me free."

Sarah knew this was getting out of her depth. She felt this young lady was losing her sanity. Sarah proceeded carefully. "What did Lester tell you about this dragon?"

Amelia trembled slightly, then glanced at Sarah. "He told me he was going to free me. You see, she had to die."

Her aunt shouted, "Amelia, you don't know what you're saying!"

Taking a deep breath, Sarah continued, "Did he want you to help him kill the dragon?"

Amelia regarded her aunt with a puzzled expression before she looked back at Sarah and went on. "He wanted me to find a weapon that belonged to the Shafers, and I remembered the spear from Christmas, and that Mrs. Shafer put it on the bookcase in her parlor. Les told me to get it. I guess I startled the cat, because it bit and scratched me. Les told me not to tell anyone how I got hurt." She gazed at her bandaged arm for a moment. "Oh, no, I forgot that! I shouldn't have told!" She started to cry.

Sarah patted her hand and gave her a handkerchief. "Then what happened?"

"Les took the spear from me and said if anyone asked, he was there at the party all the time. He left and came back a while later." Her eyes grew round. "I told that, too!" She wailed.

"That's all right, Lester wants you to tell me. When he got back to the party, did you notice anything different about him?"

"He changed his clothes." Amelia had a faraway look in her eyes. "He saved me."

Amelia's aunt burst into tears and slumped against the bedpost. "She's delirious! She doesn't know what she's saying."

Amos put his hat back on. "Come on, Lakat, I think we have what we need."

Sarah felt the chills go down her spine as she heard a thin thread of hysterical laughter from Amelia as her aunt sobbed. As they went back to the office, Sarah sighed. "Amelia did contribute to the alleged murder of her mother. You didn't take her in. Why?"

Amos was silent for a moment. "While you were talking to her, I told her aunt to get her to the sanitarium right away. Miss Pembrook needs a doctor's care, not a time in jail."

"Is that for you to decide?"

"I'm a lawman, but I'm not heartless. It will go into my report, and I think the judge would agree with me. Amelia Pembrook has lost her senses."

Sarah was more grateful to Amos than he would ever know.

****

Josh sat propped up in the hospital bed, reading the newspaper the nurse had brought with his breakfast. He felt better enough to grimace at the thin oatmeal that tasted like paste. The sponge bath earlier had humiliated him, but the large nurse had been very insistent, so he gave in and put his mind someplace else. His side felt like it had been clubbed with a large bat. He glanced around the ward; he was one of three patients recuperating.

Dr. Lindsey had come in an hour earlier, to check Josh over. "You'll have some jaundice, a yellow cast to your skin, for a few days, due to the liver injury, but that will fade."

Josh heard voices outside the ward door and Zeke came in, grinning. "Well, if it isn't a visitor from the mystic east! Ah so, Jo Sha."

"Very funny, to kick a brother when he's a different color. If you aren't careful, I'll get that large old nurse after you."

"I would be nice to me, if I were you. A lot of blood in there is mine. I'll cause a mutiny." Zeke patted his shoulder. "Looks like we might be off the hook for the murder. Les is number one on Darcy's list now." Zeke's façade began to crack. With a serious look in his eye he said, "Promise me you won't do something so foolish again."

"I don't make those kinds of promises. I'd do it again if I had to." Josh looked over the foot of the bed. Addy and Muriel were coming slowly into the room. Seeing Muriel's crutches, Josh exclaimed, "What happened? Are you all right?"

Muriel sighed. "I sprained my knee tripping up Lester when you snatched Jenny. I'll be fine. That's the reason we didn't come right in with Zeke. The doctor wanted to look at my knee." She went around the bed and gave him a hug. "My hero."

She smelled like fresh air and sweet soap. Josh felt the blood race to his loins and he raised his knees a bit to hide the physical reaction. "How's Jenny?" he asked, to take his mind off other things.

"She's wonderful, thanks to you. Cora is taking care of her right now." Muriel smiled and ran her hand over his cheek.

Suddenly, he heard a throat being cleared. He looked at Zeke, and Zeke nodded toward the ward door. The sheriff had just entered, and now he strode down the middle aisle with a stern face.

"Mr. Shafer, how are you feeling?"

Josh hesitated a moment. "I'm very sore, but here, thankfully."

The sheriff's eyes flashed. "Good. Now, I'm going to tell you to never again do anything so stupid as you did yesterday. That foolish act of heroism could've got all of you killed. If I ever see you do something like that again, I'm going to throw your sorry carcass in the hoosegow for impeding law enforcement. You got that, boy?" His finger poked the air in front of Josh for emphasis.

Josh felt all the blood drain from his face. "Yes, sir," he said meekly.

Amos' face softened. "That being said," he held out his hand, "that was one of the bravest things I ever saw."

Josh clasped his hand. "Thank you, sir."

Amos turned to Muriel. "I trust you and the baby are all right."

She nodded. "Thanks to all of you. I think we all slept a little better last night, knowing those two are in jail."

The sheriff took his leave of the group. As he left, Addy turned pale. Zeke put his arm around her. "Sweetheart, what's wrong?"

Addy glanced at all of them. "We've thought this before. How do we know it's really over this time?"

None of them had an answer to that.

****

Sarah dug into her breakfast as Amos came toward her table at Millie's. "How is Josh Shafer this morning?" she asked as Amos pulled back a chair and sat.

"He said he was very sore, so I laid the law down to him and then congratulated him on his bravery." After ordering breakfast he turned back to Sarah. "Are you ready to put those two jailbirds through the wringer?"

Sarah smiled. "With pleasure."

They finished up and braved the January winds to the sheriff's office, where they found Sam sitting at the front desk, going through his paperwork.

Amos took the ring of keys off the hook behind the security door. "Anything going on, Sam?"

Sam looked up from the desk. "Just the trays from Millie's this morning."

Amos went through the door to the cells, while Sarah took off her parka. Suddenly Sarah heard, "God damn it all to hell! Sam!"

Sarah followed Sam as he rushed into the back room. The iron cell door was wide open and Amos was bending over two still forms. The breakfast trays were on one of the cots, the coffee cups spilled, their contents making a stain on the floor boards. Steadying herself against the bars, Sarah gasped, "What happened?"

Sam drew in a shaky breath. "I didn't hear anything out of the ordinary." He answered Amos' unasked question.

Amos turned on Sam. "Nobody came in here except the person with the trays?"

"No, sir."

Amos carefully picked up one of the cups, smelled it and handed it to Sarah. "Here, take a whiff of this."

The odor that met her nose was of strong coffee and a slight hint of—almonds? "Cyanide?"

"That's what I'm thinking. Sam, have Luke take over the office, and you go get the doc and the coroner. First, could you give me a description of the person who brought the trays in this morning?"

Sam looked at the floor. "He could've been anywhere between eighteen and twenty-five. He had on a brown uniform. Short reddish-brown hair, greenish eyes. I don't think he was over five-foot-six, slight build. Square face and a short nose."

Amos put away his notebook and clapped Sam's shoulder. "Good man. Lakat, come with me to Millie's."

Sarah hastily put her parka back on and followed Amos back to Millie's. On the way, she tried to remember whether anyone of that description worked at the restaurant.

In the dining area, Amos waved Millie over. "I'd like to talk to the man who took the breakfast trays over to the jailhouse this morning."

Millie stared at him. "Excuse me?"

Amos' eyebrows rose as his mouth became a perfectly straight line. "The man who brought over the trays?"

Millie shook her head. "I didn't send breakfast trays over."

It was Amos' turn to gape. "But, Millie, you always supply the meals to the prisoners."

Millie crossed her arms and tapped her foot. "Sheriff, I didn't send any trays, per your orders."

"What orders?"

She went to the cash register and pulled out an envelope that was tucked next to it. She handed it to him. "A courier brought this in, early this morning. He said it was from you."

Amos opened it and read. He gave it to Sarah and she saw the typed message.

Millie,

Do not send over the breakfast trays this

164

morning. We have made other arrangements.
By order of Sheriff Amos Darcy

Sarah's and Amos' eyes met. He turned to Millie. "I didn't send this. Do you remember what this courier looked like?"

Millie stared into space. "Let me see. He was a short young man. Medium brown hair, and his eyes were green. He was wearing a brown uniform. I assumed it was a company outfit."

Sarah put her hand on Millie's arm. "Do you remember anything else about him?"

Millie shook her head. "He was in and out of here so fast, that's all I noticed."

Amos took the message from Sarah. "Do you mind if I keep this?"

Millie waved her hand. "Go ahead. What happened, by the way?"

"Can't tell yet. You'll find out later."

When they got back to the office, Sarah held out her hand. "Amos, can I see that message again?" He gave it to her and she looked at it carefully, then she shrieked, "This is it!"

"Lakat! This is what?"

"This is from the typewriter we've been looking for. See?"

Amos took the paper and studied it. "What?"

Sarah poked at it with her finger. "The lower case 'm' is broken. This is from the same typewriter that produced the message to Gladys Pembrook."

"The courier is our key. I'm going to put this description in the *Daily Empire* and announce a reward for finding this man."

"Amos, I have another idea. Why don't we just give his description to your deputies and the police department. That way, he won't know we're looking for him."

Amos snorted. "Why get the police involved in this? It's my case."

Sarah patted him on the shoulder. "I'll explain all that at the district, but it will help to have more eyes out for him. I'll just tell the beat police to inform me if they see him."

He rubbed his face. "All right, Lakat, I'll go along with you this time, but if I find out the police—"

"I know. You'll put my sorry carcass in jail." She laughed.

Chapter 20

Muriel knocked on Josh's door, balancing a breakfast tray in her other hand. She'd volunteered to take it up to his room because this would be the first time she could talk to him privately since his injury a week ago. He had come out of the hospital yesterday afternoon with a clean bill of health from Dr. Lindsey, but he was still weak and needed to take it easy for a few days.

"Who is it?"

"It's me, Muriel, with your breakfast tray."

She heard a shuffling, and then the door opened. Josh's hair was disheveled as he knotted his robe's sash. Nevertheless, he looked charming, in her eyes. He relieved her of the tray and set it on the bed, taking a piece of buttered toast to nibble. "Sit down." He waved his hand toward the chair by the window while he sat on the bed, giving her his full attention.

She drew the chair closer. "Do you feel like talking?"

He smiled. "I feel like doing several laps around the building, but all you nursemaids won't let me."

"Good. I want to ask, why did you do it?"

He gave her a wide-eyed innocent stare. "Do what?"

"Put yourself in danger for me and Jenny. You're lucky you're still here."

Josh was silent as he took a sip of warm tea. "Muriel, I've grown to care about you and Jenny. I didn't want you hurt, so I had to do something."

Muriel shook her head and leaned back in the chair. "You have a funny way of showing it. Ever

167

He looked at the floor. "Won't the others wonder if you stay up here too long?"

"You're doing it again. They know I wanted to talk to you, so now you be honest with me. How do you really feel about me?"

He ran his fingers through his hair. "Ever since I met you, I've been strongly attracted to you. I care about you and Jenny, but you've been through so much the past two years, you don't deserve a failure like me."

Muriel gaped at him. "Who ever said you were a failure?"

"My father told me every day how I fail at everything. I didn't finish school, and I didn't want to take over his ministry. He said all I will ever be is a failure, and look what happened. Even with everything I've put into this theater, this is a failure, too."

Muriel couldn't sit still any longer. She was on her feet in a split second, grabbing his shoulders. "You've worked miracles with this old building. You have a personality that draws people to you. You've got oodles of talent. That isn't a man who's a failure." She shook him slightly. "And I love you, silly!" The tears burned her eyes. "I love you."

Tears of his own glistened as Josh stood and took Muriel in his arms. When at last he relaxed his hug, he ran a hand down her cheek. "I was afraid to tell you how I feel about you, after the murder. I figured that would kill any hope I held out to make this theater a success. I couldn't ask you to share in the problems. I feared everything I worked for would fall through."

"But Josh, can't you see? It's more than just you. We're all in this together, not only you but all of us, because we believe in this business. This is a real team, and we can stand together against anything.

Even though Lester and Jack were killed, we seem to have been exonerated of Gladys' murder."

"There are still people in this town who haven't made up their minds."

"Then we'll show them. I've received confirmations for our first month. The show goes on." She looked a long time into his azure eyes.

Finally he drew her into a deep kiss. When he pulled back, she wobbled on her feet. Josh gave her one of his biggest smiles. "I'm very much in love with you, Muriel."

She smoothed his hair back. "I've been waiting a long time to hear you say that." She gave him a little shove, and he sat back on the bed next to the tray. "Now, eat! You have to get your strength back."

****

Several weeks passed, with both deputies and policemen looking out for the mysterious courier who had faked the message to Millie and delivered the fatal coffee to Lester and Jack. At last Sarah received a message from one of the beat policemen that a man of that description had just been seen driving a rig up to the courthouse. She hurried to the square.

The cold slushy snow of early February squished under her boots. Sarah circled the courthouse until she saw a rig fitting the policeman's word sketch. The roan carriage horse was hitched to the public post outside the lawyers' offices on the ground floor. She slid into an alley, in view of the rig but out of the icy breeze, to wait.

After twenty minutes, she saw her quarry come out with someone in an expensive-looking seal coat and fur hat. Sarah squinted to see who it was as he climbed into the back of the rig. The small man they had been searching for took the reins and jumped up to the driver's seat. She flattened her body against the building and watched as the rig went into the street toward her. Putting her gloved hands over her mouth, she recognized the man in the back. It was Mr. Adrian Connor, the wealthy attorney who, Sarah knew from the investigation, was the Pembrooks' executor. *Well, isn't this interesting? I have to go see the sheriff, to plan our next move.* After the rig disappeared around a corner, Sarah headed to Amos' office.

Amos looked up from his desk. "The man is a driver for Mr. Connor?"

Sarah warmed her hands around the cup of coffee. "That's what it looks like."

"We'd better find out who that driver is and arrest him on suspicion of murder. We know he's the one who brought the trays into the jail." He stroked his mustache. "If he's like most accomplices, he won't want to go down alone. Who knows Mr. Connor well?"

"Why can't we ask Mr. Connor who he is?"

"Because I don't want to alert our fine attorney. Who's close to him?"

Sarah made a sour face. "I suppose you could ask Manfred Pembrook. Connor has been very close to the Pembrook family. He was a close friend of Manfred's father."

Putting on his hat and parka, Amos headed toward the door. "Come on, Lakat. Time to see Mr. Pembrook."

She shrugged into her winter gear again. "Are you sure you want me along? He hates me."

He urged her through the door. "I don't give a damn. You're working with me."

Walking into the junior lawyer's office, Amos smiled at the secretary. "I want to see Mr. Pembrook. I have a question to ask him."

Her mouth went into a tight line. "He won't be happy."

Amos leaned over the desk, almost nose to nose

with her. "I didn't come here to make him happy. Now, tell him I'm waiting."

She jumped up and slid through the office door. They heard a roar from inside, and Amos motioned for Sarah to follow him. When Amos swung the door open, Manfred glared at them both.

"What do you want now?" he growled through his teeth.

"Just one simple question, Mr. Pembrook."

Manfred turned umber. "No more questions! I've answered everything I know!"

"Could you tell me the name of Mr. Connor's driver?"

He stood there with his mouth open. "What does that have to do with anything?"

"His name?" Amos was the soul of patience.

"You mean Aubrey Smythe?"

"Thank you, Mr. Pembrook. Ready, Lakat?"

Sarah hid a smile. "Good day to you, Mr. Pembrook." They walked out of the office with Manfred watching them in stunned silence.

Amos turned to Sarah as they walked to the corner. "Lakat, go back to my office. I'm going to make a stop here at the courthouse to pick up a warrant for Mr. Smythe. We'll plan our next move when I get back."

Sarah nodded and sloshed through the slushy snow. She was bringing Sam up to date on the investigation when Amos came through the door. He thrust a paper into Sam's hand. "I want you to get this out to all the deputies you can find. It's a description of Mr. Aubrey Smythe. We think he's a driver for Attorney Adrian Connor. If anyone sees him, they are to come and tell me where he is. Don't speak to him. Got that?"

Sam nodded. "Yes, sir."

Sarah followed Amos into the office. "You have a plan. What is it?"

"I want to talk to Mr. Smythe before Mr. Connor can get to him. I got a warrant for Smythe's arrest on suspicion of murder. Maybe he can fill the rest of the story in."

Sarah sat down with a chuckle. "Now, I know you're devious."

Two hours later, Deputy Luke Ayers came into the office. "Sheriff, Mr. Smythe has been spotted at the Yukon Bar."

"When?"

"Just a couple of minutes ago, the time it took for me to walk here."

"Good man. Stay here, Lakat. I'm going to bring him here." He gave her a slow smile. "We can question him together."

In a very short time, Amos came back holding the small man by the scruff of the neck. Sam tossed Amos the keys to the cells, and Sarah followed them in.

Mr. Smythe was twitching, glancing from Amos to Sarah. "'ere now. What's the meaning of this?"

In answer, Amos called, "Sam, come in here!"

Sam appeared at the cell door. "Yes, sir?"

"Is this the man who brought the food trays in for Mr. Marcelli and Mr. Lozarro?"

Sam looked him over. "He is."

"Thank you, Sam." Sam nodded and went back in the other room. Amos turned to Mr. Smythe, who was sweating profusely. "Now, who put you up to this?"

"I don't know what ya mean."

Sarah took a deep breath. "Mr. Smythe, we have positive identification that it was you who brought in the trays with the poison in the coffee, and I'm sure Millie could identify you as the one who delivered the note to her that morning. Now, you could take the full brunt of the law by yourself, or you can tell us who planned it and ordered you to carry it out."

Amos looked him in the eye. "That means we have enough to hang you for murder. If you had someone directing you to do this, you would get off easier for being an accomplice and probably wouldn't hang."

The sweat was pouring down his face. "Ya gotta believe me, I didn't know nothing about what was in that letter or in the coffee. 'e told me to do it."

"Who?"

Smythe shook as he hesitated. "Mr. Connor. Ya see, I run errands for 'im."

Amos rubbed his hands together as he tossed the keys to Sam. "Lakat, let's go to the courthouse, and then we'll pay Mr. Connor a visit."

A half-hour later, Sarah and Amos burst through the door of Connor's office and past the secretary's protests. Adrian Connor stood and pounded his desk. "What the hell do you think you're doing, Sheriff?"

Amos thrust a paper under Connor's nose. "I'm here to arrest you for your part in the poisoning death of Lester Marcelli and Jack Lozarro."

"What? I had nothing to do with that!"

Amos smiled. "According to Mr. Aubrey Smythe, you did."

For a moment, Connor looked like a beached fish, with bugged-out eyes and mouth opening and closing. Sarah saw his hand snake toward the desk drawer.

So did Amos, and he drew his Smith and Wesson thirty-eight and leveled it at Connor's nose. "Lakat, check the drawer."

She pulled a Remington Derringer out of the desk. While she had her back turned to Connor, she quickly unloaded the bullets and slipped them in her pocket.

Waving the thirty-eight, Amos said, "Mr. Connor, put your hands up and stand here. Lakat, hold the gun on him while I check for more firearms." He patted him down, then moved back. "Now, why did you kill those two gangsters?"

"I don't know what you're talking about."

Amos waved more paper under Connor's gaze. "I think you do. These are search warrants for your office and home. You can either tell us what we want to know or we can go through every ledger and scrap of paper we find in both places." He thumbed the cock on the gun. "And I really don't want to waste my time, but I'll find out what I want to know eventually. You've already been implicated in the poisoning."

Adrian Connor deflated before their eyes. "You've got me in a corner, Sheriff."

Amos waved him to a wooden chair by the wall. "Sit. You can start by telling us how you knew Mr. Marcelli and Mr. Lozarro."

Sarah slipped around to the front of the desk and laid the Derringer on it. She knew that without the bullets the gun posed no danger.

Connor eyed Amos warily. "They were working with the Giovanni ring to sell illegal liquor in the northwest part of the country, from Portland to Seattle and Spokane. They needed a contact to come into the Alaskan Territory."

Sarah interjected, "So they paid you handsomely to look the other way."

He nodded.

She leaned against the desk. "What was the connection to Gladys Pembrook?"

Connor turned pale. "What do you mean?"

Amos watched him carefully. "We believe Lester Marcelli's knife was used to kill Mrs. Pembrook. We have a confession of the theft of Mrs. Shafer's fish spear by Miss Amelia Pembrook."

His eyes grew wide. "Miss Pembrook is in the sanitarium. Her aunt told me she had a nervous

174

breakdown. You can't believe what Miss Pembrook tells you."

Sarah had suspected the young lady was troubled, but she was still sad to hear such news. She wondered if the case would be hampered if Amelia was found an incompetent witness.

"Miss Pembrook had an infected arm from a cat scratch. Mrs. Shafer's cat was in the apartment the night of the party. I found blood on top of the bookcase where the fish spear was kept." Amos shook his head. "My question is, why would someone who was a stranger to Gladys want to kill her?"

Sarah looked straight at Connor. "You knew that Marcelli was a hit man for the Giovannis, didn't you?"

"I did hear that, yes."

"Did you wonder a little bit when you heard the name Muriel Giovanni? And you asked Marcelli about her, didn't you? He told you those were the Shafers who helped set up the trap that killed his brother, right?"

"He wasn't sure at first, but when Mrs. Giovanni came to Juneau with the baby, that sealed it."

"In his will, didn't Jake Pembrook appoint you director of the estate? You controlled the money?" Sarah knew she had hit a nerve.

"Jake didn't trust his wife. And I was giving an allowance to Manfred and Amelia until they each reached the age of twenty-one."

Amos moved toward Connor. "So with Gladys Pembrook throwing all that money around, you had to stop her. In fact, I wouldn't be surprised if you were dipping into the estate funds yourself. We probably could find proof of that, too. There was a hit man in your back pocket, so you hired him to kill her. What did you give in return? A pilot to help them hightail it out of Juneau with Mrs. Giovanni and the baby after they planted a bomb to get revenge on Zeke and Addy Shafer? Lakat, type something on his typewriter."

Sarah grabbed a piece of paper off the desk and typed a sentence on the machine across the room. She smiled and handed it to Amos. "This is the one that was used for the note found by Gladys' body."

Adrian Connor looked around and dove for the Derringer on the desk. Amos reacted, but not fast enough. Connor pointed the gun at Amos, and it clicked on an empty chamber. A look of puzzlement and surprise crossed his face. Amos grabbed the gun.

"I don't understand. It was loaded." Connor shook.

Sarah smiled and drew the bullets out of her pocket. "Do you mean these?"

Amos snapped on the handcuffs. "I think you'd better come with us."

After escorting the culprit to jail, Amos and Sarah went to Western Union to check on outgoing messages. Had anyone sent a message to the Giovannis about the Shafers? All they found was one that read, "We have a surprise for Sofia." Amos said he hoped that wouldn't draw the gangsters up here.

Sarah shook her head. "This is quite a ways for them to come. We can have our two departments keep a watch on the passengers arriving, nevertheless."

"Why don't you go and inform the Shafers what happened, and Sam can search Connor's office. I'll take his house."

Sarah nodded and departed to the theater.

****

Josh sat in the kitchen bouncing Jenny on his knee as he watched Cora and Addy setting up the new refrigerator. It ran on gas and took up nearly the entire wall at one side of the room. He had volunteered to watch the baby while Muriel went into the office to post some new confirmations on performers booked so far. He really enjoyed Jenny. He didn't know if he would like to have children of his own, after growing up in a menagerie, but he loved the way she giggled. Anyway, he figured he was being useful without being yelled at.

Zeke poked his head through the door. "Hey, everyone, Sarah Lakat is here and wants to talk to all of us."

They gathered in the restaurant, sitting in the chairs around the big central table. Sarah stood before them. "I just wanted all of you to hear that the sheriff has arrested a man we think is guilty of arranging Gladys' murder and the deaths of the two henchmen in jail. We have overwhelming evidence against him and an accomplice."

"Who is it?" Zeke asked.

"Mr. Adrian Connor." There was a collective gasp. "Apparently, Mr. Connor was the liaison for illegal liquor. He seemed to be helping himself to the Pembrook estate, as well." She went on to tell them what she and Amos had found out. "The sheriff and I checked the records at Western Union, and it looks like Mr. Marcelli didn't get a chance to get a clear message about you to the rest of the Giovannis. I think you can assume that you are safe for now, but we will have someone watching incoming passengers for a while."

Josh glanced at Muriel and tried to read her face. Worry was still pasted there. He turned to Sarah and extended his hand. "Thank you, Miss Lakat, for everything you've done. Please tell Sheriff Darcy we're grateful to him, too. What do we owe you?"

Sarah smiled. "You're welcome. All you owe me is two tickets to your opening night in May."

Josh nodded. "Done."

When Sarah had gone, Josh turned to Muriel. "Did you order the tickets yet?"

Muriel looked distracted for a moment. "Yes, we should get them next week."

"Good. We'll set up the ticket office and be ready to put them on sale at mid-March." Suddenly he was ready to sail this boat of a theater again. Thank God, the nightmare was over.

Later, in the office, Josh took Muriel aside after she put Jenny in the playpen in the corner. "Something is still bothering you. Would you tell me?"

She sighed. "One, I thought the Giovannis would never find us up here. Two, remember I put an ad in the *Daily Empire* for requests of advance tickets to our opening night—and I've gotten only three requests in the two weeks since then."

Josh pressed his lips together. "Maybe, now that the law has cleared us of Gladys' death, things will change. March is coming up. Why don't you try again next week? You and Addy see some of the townspeople at church every Sunday. How do they act toward you?"

"They're polite, but aloof. The minister is the only one who says anything other than a good morning." Muriel studied his face. "We haven't gone to church since we've been cleared. Maybe things have changed. The same about the tickets. Let's give it another chance."

She pushed him into the desk chair and rubbed his shoulders for a few silent moments. Finally, he reached up and took one of her hands, pulled it around, and kissed her palm.

****

Muriel and Addy agreed it was a relief to have Gladys' murder solved, and together they were determined to try to get everyone back to a sense of normalcy. The rest of their cast would arrive in two weeks—even Roxie, who had written that she got married early so she could be there. The girls were in the kitchen peeling potatoes for the evening meal when Cora came in and bustled around the room, gathering treats and putting them in her picnic basket. Addy looked up from her spud. "What are you doing?"

Cora planted one of her jars of peach preserves in the basket. "I'm going to visit Amelia at the sanitarium. The poor child needs someone to help her through this."

James popped his head through the door. "Are you ready, Cora? Josh said we could use his truck."

Muriel looked at him in surprise. The normally quiet and shy James avoided contact with non-family females. "You're going, too?"

His face flushed. "She should have someone her age as a friend."

The girls looked at each other. Addy just cocked an eyebrow and murmured, "Hmm."

Chapter 21

Muriel sat on the low wall near the entrance to the harbor while Zeke held the reins of the two dapple-grays. The animals blew steam out their nostrils and pawed the slushy snow that was melting fast in the forty-degree weather. He had borrowed the surrey again to convey the new cast members to the theater, while Josh and Ivan had their trucks for the luggage and trunks. The rest of the rooms upstairs would be filled.

The horses were skitterish, so Zeke had sent Addy to greet their friends at the gangplank while he quieted the animals down. Muriel stayed where she was, waiting, unsure how their friends would greet her after the problems in Los Angeles.

The lack of advance ticket sales weighed on her. They had received the tickets from the printers over a week ago, but they'd only sold ten, so far. That wasn't enough to pay for the ticket printing, much less operations and payroll. Apparently there were still repercussions from the investigation. She hoped that would change before the grand opening in May.

Muriel's thoughts were interrupted by a masculine "Hey!" and the sound of a hand slapping a back. She looked up to see Zeke face to face with his friend Nathan Hayes. They grabbed each other's shoulders as the horses shuffled a few steps. "Damn, it's good to see you, Nathan! I've missed you! Where's Babs?"

Nathan gave Zeke a wide grin and his green eyes sparkled. "She's coming up with the others. I see you and Addy have been busy." Nathan poked him in the ribs and Zeke, flushing, calmed the horses again. Muriel rose, shielding her eyes, and saw Addy coming up with three other women, their arms all linked together. Addy's best friends, Anne and Roxie, were on either side of her, and Babs was linked with Anne. As they saw Muriel they greeted her warmly, with hugs and exclamations at how well she looked, and she relaxed. Addy winked at her.

Behind them, Anne's husband, Ray Stewart, and another man, his fedora pulled down so it was hard to see his face, brought up the rear.

Roxie gave Zeke a hug. "Hey, sugar, you look as good as ever!" Her blue eyes flashed with good humor. "I want you to meet my husband."

The man Muriel hadn't recognized pushed back his hat, and Zeke sucked in a breath. A mixture of shock, anger, and surprise played across his face. "Dan? Dan Hanson! You're Roxie's surprise husband?" He looked into the eyes of the man who had been his tyrannical boss, the foremost director of the scandalized Majestic Studios. "What are you doing up here? I thought you'd be directing at one of the big motion picture companies in Hollywood by now."

The hulking, sandy-haired man shuffled his feet. "Like the rest of the employees, I was tainted by being involved with the Giovannis. I couldn't find work in that town. I hoped...thought...maybe your theater would have a place for a good director. I know you and Addy haven't much to thank me for, but I'd like to start fresh." He held his hand out. "Please, Zeke, try to forgive the past and give me a chance to redeem myself?"

Zeke slowly reached to shake his hand. "I know Addy wanted to do Broadway plays and musicals, and if anyone can give us that quality, you can. All right, Dan, since you're married to Roxie, she must think you're okay, so I'm willing to give you a chance." Then, with renewed energy, he greeted the rest of the company and helped them into the surrey.

Back at the theater, Cora hugged Anne and Roxie with delight. "It's like seeing some of my long-lost daughters again!" They were formally introduced to Josh, Ivan and Kata, and then Muriel and Addy helped them settle into the final three rooms upstairs.

****

Josh was dangerously quiet when Zeke came back to the office after returning the surrey. "Zeke, we may owe these people a big apology for getting them to come up here."

Zeke paled. "What do you mean?"

Josh flipped the editorial section of *The Daily Empire*'s rival newspaper to him. "Read the first letter to the editor. The writer didn't even have the courage to sign his name."

Zeke read out loud:

Dear Editor,

I'm concerned with the other newspaper's support of the Golden North Theater. A number of us citizens would like nothing more than to see these outsiders gone. With the murder of one of our own, we know this is not the type of business we want here.

I'm calling for the good citizens of Juneau not to patronize the theater.

Sincerely.

A Concerned Citizen

Zeke moved around the desk to stand next to Josh's chair. "Oh, God, what are we going to do now? What kind of coward would write trash like this? And is this the reason our advance sales are doing so badly?"

Suddenly, the office door flew open and Addy came running in with a film canister. "Zeke! Josh! Would you believe it? Dan Hanson owns the films he directed, and he brought the four films I was in, so we could show them here. Isn't that—" She took in the looks on their faces. "What's wrong?"

Zeke put a firm grip on Josh's shoulder and the two brothers each pasted on a weak attempt of a smile. "Nothing, sweetheart, that's wonderful. We'll give you a premiere here to make up for the one you didn't get in Hollywood."

She pursed her lips. "You two are hiding something from me. What is it?"

Zeke and Josh regarded each other, and Zeke sighed. "I don't want to get you upset, but it looks like someone in Juneau is trying to blackball us." He showed her the newspaper.

"Oh, no!" Addy sat on one of the side chairs to read. "Well, that's bad. What should we do?"

Ivan tapped on the door frame. "If it's all right with you, Kata and I are going to her sister's in Douglas for a couple of days." He glanced around at the glum faces. He saw the newspaper and nodded. "You saw the letter, eh?"

They all nodded.

"I've been thinking on that. There's a town hall meeting next week. Would you mind if I brought this up for discussion? I know how to handle the townsfolk, and I know the mayor."

Josh listened carefully. "Do you want us to come with you?"

Ivan shook his head. "I don't think the people would talk freely if you were there. Let me try to bring them to your way. Maybe I can get some help from the ones on your side, eh? A few can get under thick hides and into thick heads."

Josh didn't know how good at speeches Ivan could be, but he'd give anything a chance. He turned to Zeke. "What do you think?"

Zeke massaged his temples. "I'm willing to let him try."

Ivan came over and slapped the brothers on

their backs and gave Addy a wink. "Good. I'll make sure they hear the best about you, my friends."

Josh buried his face in his hands. *Can things get any worse?*

****

Sarah Lakat opened the door of her home to Kata. "Kata, come in! I heard you were to your sister's. How are the twins?" They went into Sarah's cozy parlor with the whitewashed walls and simple furniture. Kata sat on the bentwood rocker and Sarah settled on the couch as they talked family.

"The twins are growing so fast. They're starting to walk and Mary is trying to keep them out of trouble."

Just then a whistle from a steam kettle in the kitchen sounded and Sarah stood. "I was warming some water for tea. May I offer you some?"

Kata nodded. "Please."

Returning with the tea tray, Sarah gave her a cup. "Do you have a reason to come and see me, or is this a social stop?"

Kata took a sip and set the cup on the table beside her. "Did you see the letter to the editor in the weekly newspaper a few days ago, the one about the theater?"

"Yes, I did. The writer didn't even post his name."

"Well, Ivan is going to bring the theater up for discussion at the town hall meeting Wednesday next, and we are trying to get the people who know and like the Shafers to come out for them. Will you?"

Sarah frowned. "You know we aren't considered citizens. You and I can't vote on anything."

Kata set her jaw. "I know we can't vote, but this isn't something that needs that. The Shafers are good people, and they are innocent of any wrongdoing. Working with them this past year has eased my views on white Americans. Addy knows how it feels to be judged by what you look like. I think if we tell the citizens who the Shafers are and what they want to do with the theater, they might give them a chance."

"Didn't they do that at the sample show last September?"

Kata shook her head. "That was just for the people who could back them. This information should get to all the people of Juneau."

Sarah stirred her tea, then set down the spoon with a clink on the saucer. "We have to come with citizens, or they won't let us in. You've got Ivan, of course."

Kata bit her lip. "Maybe you could come with the sheriff. He's always at the meetings."

Sarah smiled. She'd been looking for a reason to talk to Amos again. "I'll ask. I can tell him the reason."

Kata gave her a sly glance. "I'm sure he'll escort you. You two make a good team."

Sarah just looked heavenward.

****

Wednesday evening, a knock came on Sarah's door. When she opened it, there was Amos, hat in hand. "Are you ready, Miss Lakat?"

With Amos' help, she slipped on her warm coat. He offered his arm and they walked with purpose to the town hall a few blocks away. There was a sizeable crowd there, in this town of over a thousand, and the hall filled up quickly.

There were some angry glances thrown at Sarah, but she continued on with Amos and they found seats on the right side of the aisle. She was sure if she hadn't been with Amos she would have been asked to leave. The heated atmosphere contrasted with the chill of the March breeze coming through the doors.

The plain rectangular public building was large

enough to seat two hundred and fifty people, but many stood around the perimeter of the room, making an interesting human wainscoting pattern. The room hummed with loud murmurs until the sharp crack of the gavel brought everyone's attention to Mayor Robertson at the raised platform.

The usual business was carried out in a strict meeting agenda. Then, under new business, the Mayor called on Ivan Nikolaevich to address the crowd. "He has concerns regarding a letter that appeared last week in one of our newspapers. Mr. Nikolaevich?"

Ivan went to the podium, looking more uncomfortable than Sarah had ever seen him. He cleared his throat. "My friends and fellow citizens of Juneau, many of you have known me for a long time. I've helped with construction work all over the city. You know I've been honest and trustworthy and would never lie for anyone. So believe me when I tell you, what some of you are doing against the Shafers and their family and friends is wrong. Yes, Gladys Pembrook losing her life was a terrible thing, but it has been proven that the Shafers had nothing to do with it."

"But they're outsiders!" a man in the back shouted out. "Gladys was one of our own."

Ivan pointed at him. "Most of us were newcomers at one time. Juneau was founded just forty years ago. I'm sure there are many who weren't born here and came from someplace else. Well, the Shafers did the same thing. They came here for a fresh start, and they want to do something for the community."

There was a rumbling of agreement sprinkled around the room.

"Wasn't that Mrs. Giovanni married to the mob?" a woman called out.

"From what I understand, Muriel Giovanni was

very young and eloped with the boy she loved, who happened to be a son of the mob boss in the Los Angeles area. She came here to escape that family after her husband was killed and the family threatened to take her child."

"That seems to be something any mother would do," another woman called out.

"She should've known what the gangsters were about," a man chided.

"And there was that ugly fight between Mrs. Shafer and Gladys. Mrs. Shafer doesn't seem very ladylike, and I heard she was a—an actress." Some of the crowd gasped.

"Those of you who are the dirt spreaders should be ashamed of yourselves! Addy Shafer was defending her marriage. I hate to speak ill of the dead, but as many of you know, Gladys Pembrook was no saint. She was after Zeke Shafer and tore Addy down whenever she could. I know. I saw her do it many times. I'm sure many of you, uh, ladies would've done the same in her place, eh?" There was some assent from a few of the women. "And as for Mrs. Shafer being an actress, she's a very good one. She was featured in several films before the studio collapsed." Ivan stopped for a few moments and mopped his brow with a handkerchief. "All I ask of you good folks is to give them a chance. Go to the opening. If you enjoy the show, swell. If you don't, stay away after that. Either way, don't reject them out of hand. That's all I have to say."

Kata looked proudly at her husband and stood, starting to clap. Sarah followed suit. In a few moments, most of the room was standing and applauding. Some didn't respond, and a few others walked out in disgust while Ivan strode back to his seat.

Mayor Robertson took the podium again and quieted the crowd. "I know there isn't a vote connected with this, but I second what Mr. Nikolaevich had to say. The Shafers put a lot of work in on our old theater, and I think it looks better than when it was built. I, for one, will be there at the opening." He cracked the gavel down. "Next, on new business?"

After the meeting, while Kata beamed, Sarah and the sheriff congratulated Ivan.

Amos shook his hand. "Ivan, I'm impressed. I didn't know you had it in you."

Ivan looked down. "My friends needed my help. I did what I could."

On the walk to Sarah's house, Amos spoke up. "I'd like to see opening night myself."

Sarah smiled. "I have two tickets to it. Would you like to escort me?"

Amos studied her for a moment. "Uh-huh, and I think I figured out who you were working for in the investigation."

She let out a breath that floated in the frosty air and rolled her eyes. "You're quite a detective."

Up on her porch, Sarah thanked Amos for going with her to the meeting. He turned to her and put both hands on her shoulders. "Lakat, would you consider becoming one of my deputies?"

She hesitated for a moment. "I thought only men could work in the sheriff's department."

"Rules can be changed. You're a damn good detective, Lakat."

She chuckled. "All right. As long as you think we won't end up killing each other."

They regarded each other for a few moments. Then Amos took a step back. "Goodnight, Lakat. I'll let you know when you can join us."

Sarah might have been mistaken in the dim porch light, but Amos looked like he blushed.

Chapter 22

Josh knew Ivan was confident they would see a line of ticket buyers after the town meeting, but there was still a knot in his stomach when he got out of bed Saturday morning. Their ticket booth was finished, ready and waiting, as was the whole theater. The outside scaffolding had been taken down, and the white Victorian building gleamed like brand new. With James' genius, they had large electric light signs installed high on the flat roof and, above the lobby doors, a theater sign with a place for changeable letters.

Muriel had the preprinted tickets, and she and Addy were going to manage the booth that morning from nine to one. He deeply hoped they wouldn't be wasting their time as well as their money. They had delved into the budget and saturated the newspaper with ads and put posters up around town.

At the washstand Josh poured water from the pitcher into the basin. As he washed his face and hands, he glanced in the mirror at the dark circles traced beneath his eyes. This stress was aging him. Stirring the soap in the shaving mug, he lathered up. *Might as well look presentable.*

When he had finished shaving, he toweled off his face, looking deep into his eyes in the mirror. His father's icy blue eyes stared back at him accusingly.

Suddenly, squaring his shoulders and firming his jaw, Josh knew what he must do. "No! I'm not going to let you ruin my life anymore! I've done a good job on this building, with the help of everyone. I'm finished with the melancholies and feeling like I can't do anything right. We're going to go out and give these people a damn good show." He shook his finger at the mirror. "I'm not going to let you downgrade me. From now on, I'm rid of you!" He hit the reflection with his squared fist, firmly but not hard enough to break the glass. "And I'm going to ask Muriel to marry me. I *am* worthy of her. I'll be able to take care of her and Jenny." With that resolved, the weight that had been on his shoulders for so long lifted.

Buoyed, he marched down to the restaurant where Muriel and Addy were engaged in conversation over breakfast. Jenny was chewing on some toast. "Muriel," he demanded in a voice he didn't recognize, "come with me. I have something to say to you."

Muriel looked at him in amazement. "Jo—Josh?"

He whirled on Addy. "Take care of Jenny. You need the practice."

Addy, eyes wide, was stunned to silence.

He sighed. "I'm sorry, Addy. Could you watch Jenny for a while?"

"Yes, but we have—"

Josh took Muriel's arm and hurried her out, not hearing Addy's words. He led her to the deserted dressing room area and locked the door behind them, then turned and put his hands on her shoulders. "Sit on the couch. I want to talk to you."

Muriel's face was a mixture of surprise and concern. "Something's wrong, isn't it?" She sank onto the cushion.

Josh sat next to her. "No, everything's wonderful! I'm not going to be ruled by my father anymore."

"What?"

He related his conversation with the reflection in the mirror as he caressed first her hands and then her face. "Don't you see?" he asked, searching her eyes, "It was my memory of his hateful words to me all my life that kept me from fully believing in myself and this theater." He kissed her forehead. "My father was the one who made me believe I wasn't worthy of you and Jenny. Now, I won't let his words hurt me."

Muriel gazed at him silently.

"I don't know if this theater is ever going to make money, but I will do my best to make it go. You need someone to love you and help you raise Jenny. Let it be me. I adore you both and want you to be a part of my life." He swung down on one knee. "Marry me, Muriel, please?"

Muriel ran her fingers through his hair and her eyes glistened. Her lashes closed over her eyes, and the tears flowed. She was silent.

Josh gritted his teeth. *What's wrong? Did I misjudge her feelings for me? Is she afraid to make a commitment again? Why* is *she crying?* "Say something, Muriel. What is going on in your mind?"

Muriel sighed and opened her eyes again. He looked into their brown depths, not daring to glance away. "Josh, I will accept your offer of marriage. I will be your partner in any business you choose to go into, and together we will raise Jenny and any future children that come along. Will you accept my offer to you?"

He took both her hands in his. "I accept, Muriel. It's easier for two to stand together than one alone. And I don't plan to stand alone any longer."

Drawing him up to sit next to her, she gently cupped his face in her hands and kissed him deeply. Josh felt every nerve in his body telegraphing to his brain as the blood rushed to his loins. His fingers ran down her sides and his breath came in rasps. He tried to clear his head of the lustful fog that gathered there. He pulled back. "We shouldn't—"

Muriel shushed him by kissing him again. In

between kisses, she said, "I've wanted this for some time...I'm not a little virginal girl...I was married before...and, Josh, I'm at a safe time of month."

Clothes were shed. A breast revealed here, hands working to unbutton a fly there. A white bead formed on her nipple and he gently lapped it. Tasting her sweet milk spiraled him faster into pure passion. He eased her back on the couch and looked deeply into her eyes, finding acceptance. Gently pushing in, he felt her soft folds surround him as a moan escaped her lips. Josh had to stop and gain control again. He started moving. He couldn't help it; it was instinctive. Building, then slowing and building again. The one short leg on the couch made a tapping sound every time he moved, but he didn't hear the symphony of squeaks and bangs that accompanied their lovemaking.

Muriel shuddered underneath him and held him tighter. Drawing in a rough breath, she let go with a low wail and dug her nails into his back, and that released him. They clasped each other and rested their sweaty foreheads together.

Josh brushed her hair away from her face. "I love you."

She sighed, a contented look in her eyes. "You are magnificent, my love." She glanced at the clothes in a heap. "I'd better collect myself, if I'm going to sell tickets in a hour."

They made themselves presentable, still finding it hard to keep their hands off each other, Josh stealing a kiss with almost every piece of clothing put back in place. Finally they unlocked the door and stepped out from the dressing area into the theater.

Everyone was gathered on the stage, all trying hard not to stare at them. Addy's glance had an amused glint. She handed Jenny to Cora. "I tried to remind you, Josh, of the rehearsal this morning."

Josh felt his cheeks warm. "I guess I forgot." He cleared his throat. "Since you're all here, let me announce that Muriel and I are engaged to be married."

Addy ran to embrace Muriel, and Zeke slapped Josh on the back. "It's about time, little brother, but did you have to put on such a performance to go with it? We could hear you all the way across the stage." Zeke grinned knowingly at him and winked.

It took a moment for Josh to absorb that information. When it dawned on him what Zeke meant, Josh pointed at him. "To use your words, keep your dirty thoughts to yourself!"

With a muted groan and heated cheeks, Muriel grabbed Addy by the arm. "Let's go set up the ticket booth. Cora, could you take care of Jenny for a while?" At Cora's nod and chuckle, Muriel pulled Addy out of the theater.

Josh shouldered his banjo and turned to Dan Hanson. "Well, Mr. Director, let's get started." He turned to Zeke. "Isn't Addy going to be in the show?"

"I don't know if she'll have the baby before then. I don't want to put a lot of things on her at once."

Dan broke in. "I think she can pick up any of the acts in a few days. Anyway, we've got Roxie and Babs to fill in the musical numbers."

Josh walked on air as they set up the number he and Zeke were doing.

****

Muriel and Addy dug through the boxes of tickets in the office and set them up in the ticket booth, where there were two stools in front of the table facing the small windows. The blinds were pulled down to shield any view inside the booth until they were ready to open. They set up the bricks of tickets and two cash boxes with change on a shelf under the table.

Suddenly, Addy hugged Muriel. With tears in

her eyes, she exclaimed, "We're going to be real sisters now, dear, like we've always dreamed."

Muriel smiled. "In my mind, we've always been sisters. Even if we weren't by parentage, I've never thought of you as anything but a big sister." When they pulled apart, Muriel peeked through the blinds and gasped. There was a double line of people for as far as she could see. "Addy, take a look at this."

Addy did so, and glanced back over her shoulder with a wide grin. "Tell Josh to come out here."

Muriel hurried to the theater. "Josh, all of you. You've got to see what's outside."

As Addy and Muriel opened the box office, the rest of the group stepped outside the lobby doors. Muriel watched Josh's face as the people in line at the front saw them and applauded. He, in turn, registered surprise, then gratitude, with a large grin and a wave.

Muriel and Addy sold all but ninety-six of the four hundred tickets. After the box office closed, Muriel piled the forty-five dollars and sixty cents in front of Josh and Zeke in the office just as Cora brought in a bottle of ginger ale and some glasses. "I sure wish this was champagne. We deserve it."

Everyone was in the midst of toasting their good fortune when a knock came on the office door. Josh looked up and called, "Come in."

Ivan ushered in Millie. She sighed and took them all in. "I wanted to speak for the rest of the townspeople who have come back to your side. We want to say how sorry we were to treat you the way we did." She patted Ivan's hand. "He did a swell job putting us in our place at the town meeting. And I, for one, wish you only the best in your business."

Josh moved around the desk and planted a kiss firmly on her cheek, then grasped her arm. "Would you like to see your ad?"

Muriel and the others followed them into the

theater, where Millie took a look at the gaily colored square on the right side of the curtain, her lips trembling. "It looks wonderful. Thank you."

When she had gone, cast and crew together had a celebration, and Muriel and Josh raised a toast to each other and to their future.

****

Muriel sat back in the wings of the stage, watching the rehearsal. She bounced Jenny on her knee, and the little girl seemed to enjoy the music.

Addy sat on the makeshift pier after the "By The Sea" number with a perturbed look on her face. Two days before opening night, and the baby still hadn't come. Addy, Roxie, and Babs had worked up an act of "Blonde, Brunette, and Redhead." Addy, of course, was the brunette, sunny Roxie the blonde, and Babs the redhead, with her glowing auburn hair.

Dan looked concerned from his seat in the theater. "Are you sure you're all right, Addy? I don't think you should be in the show if your time hasn't come yet."

"She's not going to be in the show!" came a voice from the back. Zeke came down the aisle. "Sorry, Addy, but you shouldn't be out in public in your condition."

Addy put her hands on her hips. "But I can't miss opening night!"

"No!" Zeke thundered and stalked out.

Dan nodded. "I agree. Roxie and Babs will be able to do it."

Addy scowled as she started backstage with Roxie and Babs. She picked up one of the prop beach balls and bounced it as she went. Suddenly, she stopped, studying the ball. "Roxie, Babs, come and stand over here, and I'll go on the platform over there." Addy knelt on the scaffold with the ball in front of her. "Does that cover my stomach?"

Roxie and Babs looked at each other. "Yes,

but—" Roxie started.

Addy beamed. "That's the way I can do the number without my condition showing. I'll just keep the ball in front of me while you do the dancing. I'll only sing."

Muriel shook her head. "Zeke said no."

Addy set her jaw. "I have to be in opening night. Now, don't any of you tell anyone. Swear!"

They all sighed and solemnly raised their right hands. "Swear."

Muriel put her hand on Addy's arm. "You know he's going to find out. Somehow, he'll stop you."

Addy picked up Jenny and tickled the baby until she giggled. "I have to try."

Muriel couldn't help being amused. Addy would stop at nothing to be a performer.

Chapter 23

Muriel hurried to Addy as she came out of the dressing room area. "Addy, the vaudeville troop is here. Sophie Tucker is the headliner! Wow! We're getting a star of her magnitude to open our theater? And there are animal acts, and a magician, and musical and comedy acts along with our entertainment—what a show!"

They headed toward where Zeke and Josh were talking to Miss Tucker. Zeke saw the girls and waved them over. "Miss Tucker, I want you to meet my wife—she's a co-owner of the theater—Mrs. Addy Shafer, and her cousin, my brother Josh's fiancée, Muriel Giovanni."

The voluptuous star turned and greeted the girls. "Pleased to meet you. We were expecting a little dump of a theater up here. But you've got the Palace on the run. Congratulations on all your work."

Muriel and Addy each said, "Thank you," before Miss Tucker went on into the theater to inspect the stage. As they turned toward the office, a young couple slipped over to them. The woman was pretty, with a sweet but mischievous look about her, while her companion, dapper in his new suit, wore a perpetual smile and puffed on a large Havana.

The man spoke up. "We were told that all of you are the owners of this fancy joint. I have to say, I'm stunned. Most owners are aged just this side of Methuselah." He held out his hand. "By the way, I'm George Burns, and this is my partner, Gracie Allen. We just got started as an act this year."

As the Shafers introduced themselves, surprise was written on the couple's faces. Gracie raised an eyebrow. "Aren't you the ones involved in the Majestic Studio scandal a couple of years ago?"

Zeke nodded. "That's right. We met my brother up here to help him rebuild the theater and to escape the crime family's wrath."

Josh clapped George on the shoulder. "What's your act?"

George shrugged. "A little singing, a little dancing, a little patter in between."

Gracie added, "I do a dumb-Dora act."

Addy smiled. "I'm anxious to see it. I'll be in the wings tomorrow."

Gracie regarded Addy's girth. "Are you sure you'll make it?"

"I have to be here on opening night." Addy glanced at Zeke, who frowned at her. "Even though I can't be in the show like this."

Muriel knew she was lying through her teeth and wondered whether Zeke knew her well enough to tell that, too.

****

Sarah carefully fastened the buttons on her emerald green silk dress. Her one good outfit for going to parties was a little passé, but she felt wonderful in something other than her police clothes. Brushing her newly cut bob, she was delighted that it went into place so easily. The straight black hair fell along her jaw line and shone in the light from the lamp on her vanity. She settled a green headband with sequins and a striped pheasant tail feather on the modern hairstyle and assessed herself in the mirror—striking. Her jade necklace completed the aura of a sophisticated lady.

Pulling on her gloves, Sarah heard a knock at her front door. She opened it and was caught off balance for a moment. There, fedora in hand, stood what must be Amos. Only this being was clean-shaven except for a neatly trimmed mustache and oiled-back hair. The black suit with a white shirt front and a black bow tie completely transformed him. Sarah found her voice. "My, Amos, you clean up nicely." She picked up her pocketbook and shawl.

Amos gallantly took the shawl and put it around her shoulders. "There's a chilly May breeze out there. I've never seen you so dressed up before. You are—beautiful tonight." He hurriedly cleared his throat. "I can transfer you from the police department to the sheriff's next week. I'll be happy to have you on the staff. There's a new case I want to talk to you about."

The corners of her mouth edged up. "A girl could never resist a proposition like that. Come on, we'll be late."

She and Amos strode the walkway to the street, he offered his arm, and they chatted all the way to the theater.

****

To say Josh had the opening night jitters would be kind. He was a walking white knuckle. He busied himself setting up here, tearing down there, until Ivan told him to get out of the way. Finally, everything was ready to go.

Josh peeked out into the theater, where people were filing in. He saw Cora and James shepherding Amelia to a seat. Amelia was recovering slowly from her nervous breakdown, with the diligent help of Cora and the support of James, who, Josh was sure, had fallen in love with the girl. After seeing her carefully settled, James came up on stage and went back into the wings to where Josh stood.

"Are the lights all ready?"

James checked the panel. "All ready to go."

"How's Amelia?"

James hesitated a moment. "She's doing better.

She can leave the sanitarium for a few hours at a time. The doctor said he was hopeful for a full recovery."

"Do you think it was wise to bring her to the theater? This was where her mother was killed. We don't want to cause a relapse."

James shook his head. "She seems all right as long as Cora and I are with her. If anything comes up, Cora will take her back. The doctor thinks it will help her to face her fears a little at a time."

Suddenly, angry voices were heard in the direction of the dressing rooms. Josh hurried to check what was happening and found Zeke standing next to the couch in the hallway, his hand gripping Addy's arm. She was dressed in an old-fashioned bathing suit costume, complete with a gathered cap, and held a large beach ball.

Zeke pulled her back to the dressing room. "No, you're not going on like that!"

Addy shrugged out of his grip. "I can't miss—" Then her eyes grew large and she said, "Arrgh—oooh!" and squeezed the beach ball into a figure eight.

Zeke stared at her. "What?"

Josh's alarm went off. "Muriel! Come out here!"

Muriel appeared from helping in one of the dressing room and went into action after one quick look at Addy's face. "Josh, Zeke, find out if Dr. Lindsey is here. I'll take her around to the apartment."

Even as she spoke Muriel was guiding Addy out the stage door, as Addy complained, "Not now! The baby can't come *now*!"

Zeke stood watching all this with his mouth open, seemingly stunned to silence, until Josh turned him and pushed him toward the theater. "We've got to find Dr. Lindsey!"

At the far end of the stage Josh hollered out, "If

Dr. Lindsey is here, please meet us in the lobby," and then he dragged Zeke up the aisle. A few seconds later, the doctor joined them, his medical bag in hand. "It's Mrs. Shafer, isn't it?"

Zeke nodded.

"I thought I'd better be available, just in case. Where is she?"

Josh pointed toward the office door. "Muriel took her to the apartment." He turned his brother and pushed him in the right direction. "Zeke will take you back there." He chuckled a little to himself as he watched his normally lucid sibling stumbling toward the office.

Finding Roxie and Babs backstage, Josh gave them the news. "It looks like your 'By The Sea' number is a duet."

Babs shook her head. "I had a feeling this was going to happen. Addy made us swear we wouldn't tell she was planning to do the number in spite of Zeke."

Roxie agreed. "This is the only thing that would keep her from being on stage for opening night."

Soon Zeke appeared backstage. "The doc and Muriel are going to stay with Addy. I was chased out of there."

Josh glanced at Zeke. "Who's watching Jenny?"

"She's in her playpen in the dressing room, and Kata is keeping an eye on her."

The two-hour extravaganza went off wonderfully, in Josh's opinion. He and Zeke made it through their Gay Nineties medley without too many minor mistakes on Zeke's part. They also backed up Nathan and Babs' dance act, which included some pretty fancy tapping. The energetic pair made their feet fly. The young couple they'd met earlier, George and Gracie, asked about Addy and gave Zeke congratulations in advance, as well as complimenting Josh and Zeke on how well the theater was run and how well things were going.

The acts came and went fairly smoothly. The magician had some trouble rounding up some of his doves after the curtain closed, and the comedy quartet hadn't told Josh about the buckets of confetti they would throw at each other, but Ivan and James did quick work with a broom and a large pail to clear it off before the next act.

Roxie and Babs dedicated the beach number to their absent partner, followed by Anne and her husband, who performed the balcony scene from *Romeo and Juliet*.

The comedy of George and Gracie was fresh and very funny. Zeke and Josh applauded resoundingly from the wings. But Sophie Tucker was the climax of the show. She brought down the house with her song, "Red-Hot Mama."

After that finale, Josh nodded at James and waited a few moments to allow James and Cora time to shepherd Amelia out. They would miss the last announcement as they took her back to the sanitarium, but the doctor didn't want to risk her reaction to the last piece of business for the evening.

Finally Josh and Zeke appeared in front of the audience, who were still applauding wildly. Josh waved his hands. "May we have your attention, please!" When people had quieted some, Josh continued, "There is a person we would like to honor, because I don't think we would have gotten this theater off the ground without her. Unfortunately, she met an untimely end before this night. We will honor her memory by naming this stage the Gladys Pembrook Memorial Stage."

Josh and Zeke went over to the edge of the proscenium, where a small curtain hung over a square. Zeke ceremoniously pulled it off to reveal a bronze plaque that announced the name. Silence filled the theater, and then someone started to clap.

The applause grew to a thunderous roar, and Josh knew they had done the right thing.

Two hours later, after James and Cora returned, the permanent staff were celebrating in the restaurant, toasting their success, when Muriel appeared at the office door with a bundle. "Zeke," she said softly, "I want you to meet your son."

Zeke looked like he was trying to swallow a boulder as he made his way to Muriel. He held the baby for a moment before he turned to hold the boy for all to see. "The name Addy and I agreed on is Tomas Lorenzo Shafer." Zeke put his finger in the tiny palm, and little Tom grasped it.

There were congratulations all around, and then Zeke carried the little one back to the apartment. Muriel, meanwhile, Josh at her side, picked up Jenny from Kata's lap.

Muriel said, with a special smile, "Thank you for watching Jenny for me."

Kata patted Muriel's hand. "She is a delight. Anyway, I'd better get used to babies."

Muriel took a breath. "You're—?"

Kata smiled and blushed. "Uh-huh. I found out yesterday."

Josh shook his head. "And I thought my childhood home was a menagerie. Well, congratulations to you and Ivan."

Jenny, tired, began to whimper, and Muriel nodded toward the stairs. "We'd better put Jenny to bed. It's late," she said to Josh.

Tucked into her nightie and clean diaper and snuggled into her crib, Jenny fell asleep almost immediately. Muriel and Josh left the door to her room open and stepped out onto the second floor porch right next to where the sleeping baby lay.

As they settled onto the wicker couch there, Josh put his arm around Muriel and felt deep in his heart that this was where he belonged. Muriel and

Jenny had become as much a part of his life as the theater.

A cool salty sea breeze gentled over them and the stars twinkled in the shortened night span. Already there was a hint of the late spring sunrise.

Josh was tired, but wonderfully so. The opening had been a success. He kissed Muriel's earlobe. "When do you want to get married?"

Muriel rested her head on his shoulder. "As soon as possible. We can get married at the courthouse."

"You don't want a big wedding this time? You eloped before."

She sighed and linked her fingers with his. "Both our families are far away, and usually people have big weddings for the loved ones. Anyway, I can't very well wear white." She gave him an impish smile.

Josh grinned. "The courthouse it is, then." He put his fingers under her chin and lifted her face to his. The kiss was deep and long. Gray streaks of dawn laced the sky before they went inside.

Chapter 24

Morning came, with the rare Alaskan sun shining through the windows. Josh and Muriel came downstairs with Jenny after a very short sleep. It was their own fault, really—the urges couldn't wait—but he knew they had to clean up the theater before the next performance. Josh felt a warming, reminded of last night with Muriel. He had to stop thinking about her like that or he was going to embarrass himself.

Everyone at breakfast in the restaurant looked equally drawn out. Josh and Muriel ran into Cora coming through the office door. "I took a breakfast tray into the apartment for Addy. She's awake, if you want to visit her."

They nodded. "Thanks, we will." Muriel led the way to the apartment door and knocked.

Zeke opened it with a smile. "Good morning! You both look like something the cat dragged in." As if on cue, Chloe meowed.

Josh snorted. "You seem more chipper than you appear, yourself. How's Addy?"

"Exhausted, but still here," came a voice from the bedroom.

The trio went in to greet her, and when Jenny saw the baby, she pointed and babbled, "Baba, baba!"

Addy grinned. "She's talking up a storm, isn't she? Now, with Kata expecting, we're going to have plenty of little ones running around."

Zeke gazed tenderly at Addy and little Tom. He sat on the edge of the bed and put his arm around her. "I'm so proud of Addy. We have a fine son."

She looked at Muriel and Josh. "You know, Muriel, Zeke and I were talking last night. We should think about finding a couple of houses. We can't raise these children in this theater. It's nice for adults, but not for families."

Zeke shook his head. "We don't have the money for it yet. I don't want the backing money to go for our own use, but we should think about paying ourselves wages. With Josh and Muriel getting married, this business has to support a number of families as well as single people."

Josh hesitated a moment. "Does anyone know how much we made last night?"

Zeke sat up. "Well, Addy and Muriel made about fifty on advanced ticket sales, but then we were sold out when everyone came for the show, so I think, between that and the restaurant, we might have close to a hundred."

Addy smiled tiredly. "We keep doing that, we'll have a home by fall."

"Whoa, Addy, you forget we're closed Sunday and Monday and just have motion pictures Tuesday through Thursday. Fridays and Saturdays will be our big money makers. The restaurant is just open a few hours each night." Zeke sighed. "And it may not be a big sellout every time."

Muriel handed Jenny to Josh and picked up Tom. "Well, we can worry about this another time." Josh peered over her shoulder at his new nephew. Jenny was equally as curious. Tom waved his arms around, then set to sucking his fingers.

Muriel grinned. "Uh-oh, it looks like someone's hungry." She gave Tom back to Addy. "We'll visit you again after we've all had breakfast."

In the restaurant, at the big table with the others, Josh, Muriel and Zeke helped themselves to some of the eggs, toast and sausage that Cora had whipped up for everyone. Muriel set Jenny in her high chair and gave her a little of the egg and a few inch-square pieces of toast.

After wolfing down a good share of his breakfast, Josh spoke up. "Muriel and I decided to get married at the courthouse next week. Since Monday is our day off, I think we'll do it then."

Everyone looked at them as if he'd said they were going to fly to the moon in a couple of days. Cora pressed her lips together. "We can't plan something like that in two days!"

Josh shook his head. "There's nothing to plan. We don't want fuss. It's just going to be a quiet ceremony, and that's it. We don't have the funds for a celebration."

Cora looked like a thundercloud as she crossed her arms and tapped her foot. "Have you thought this out thoroughly? For example, who will be your witnesses?"

Muriel put in, "Why, Zeke and Addy—oh, I see what you mean. I don't think Addy will be able to go to the courthouse in two days."

Underneath, Josh was saying, *Damn, damn, damn!* He glanced at Zeke. "Do you think Addy will be up and around a week from Monday?"

Zeke watched Josh's frustration with an amused expression. "I think she can make it to the courthouse then. If you think you can wait that long." He chuckled and applied his fork again to the food on his plate.

Breakfast over, Josh, Muriel and Zeke headed toward the office, planning to get the change for replenishment of the cash boxes. On their way, they were met by James, who handed Josh an envelope. "This was wedged between the lobby doors."

Puzzled, Josh opened it and read the handwritten note:

If you agree to close the theater within a

month's time, nothing will happen to any of you. If not, there are people who want back what is theirs.

  The Concerned Citizen

Josh felt the blood drain from his face. "Oh, no. Now what does this mean? Could it mean the money for backing?"

Zeke took the paper from Josh's hand. "I wonder if this is the same person who wrote the letter in the weekly newspaper? It looks like someone is trying to get rid of us one way or another."

Muriel pressed her lips together as she placed Jenny in the playpen. "What do we have that isn't ours, besides money? We had many backers, so which one could it be?"

Josh shook his head. "I think if one of our backers was unhappy, they would come and ask us for their money back to our faces. Maybe we should take this to the sheriff."

Zeke nodded. "I agree. I don't think we should tell any of the others about this yet. Not until we find out more. No need to cause worry." He paused for a moment. "That includes Addy."

Josh turned to Muriel. "Take care of the cash. We'll be back as soon as we can."

"What should I say to Addy, if she asks where you are?"

"Just tell her we had some business in town we had to take care of."

Grabbing their spring coats, the brothers started for the sheriff's office. They knew Amos made a point of being in on Saturday mornings if at all possible.

The May sun was shining on the harbor, helping it to come out of the winter freeze. Here and there in the shadows were small piles of stubborn snow that hadn't melted off, and snow was still visible on the mountaintops, but the air was crisp and clean, with a tang of springtime. Josh and Zeke strode into the main office and nodded to Sam, who sat behind the desk.

Josh spoke up. "Morning, Sam, is the sheriff in?"

"Morning. I'll tell him you're here. How was the opening last night? I plan to go tonight, since I was on duty yesterday."

Zeke half-smiled. "It went very well."

Sam knocked at the sheriff's private office, stepped in, and returned quickly. "Go on in."

They thanked him, and Sam closed the door behind them. The sheriff was going over papers on his desk, but he looked up and greeted them. "I was impressed with the show you put on last night. How is Mrs. Shafer?"

Zeke grinned. "Delivered a bouncing baby boy."

Amos stood up and offered his hand. "Congratulations! Now what do you two boys need?"

Josh took the envelope out of his coat pocket. "James found this in the lobby doors this morning."

Amos frowned when he read it. "Have any of your backers come to you about this?"

Josh shook his head. "We were discussing that earlier. We figured any of them would come to us if they were unhappy. We wondered if it had any connection to the 'Concerned Citizen' who wrote the letter against us in the weekly newspaper."

Amos stroked his mustache. "I'll take this, and if you get anything else, let me know. I'll see if the weekly has a record of who put in the original letter."

"All right, Sheriff. Thank you." The brothers left the office.

As they re-entered the theater, Josh and Zeke heard singing coming from the stage. "Look for the silver lining, whenever clouds appear in the blue..."

They looked at each other. Zeke's mouth tightened. "That sounds like Addy." He marched down the aisle. "What do you think you're doing?" he yelled.

Addy went pale but stood her ground, her hands on her hips. "I'm rehearsing for the show tonight."

"No, you're not going to be in the show tonight. Now get back to bed!" By this time, they were standing practically nose to nose. "Where is the baby?"

Addy pointed to Muriel in the front row with Jenny on her lap and Tom on her right arm. Muriel wiggled her fingers at him. Addy stuck out her chin. "I'm feeling fine, and I couldn't stay in bed one more minute. Anyway, I had to miss the show last night."

"I thought you were exhausted."

"I want to be on stage tonight. One song isn't going to tire me out!"

Josh made it to the stage and put his hand on Zeke's shoulder. "The song is a slow one, and she doesn't have to move around. She can sit on a stool."

Zeke whirled on him. "Are you trying to placate her? She only just gave birth last night!"

Josh shrugged. "I hear oriental women give birth in the fields and go right back to work."

"Addy's not a peasant out in the fields!" He turned his wrathful gaze on her again.

She smiled her biggest and brightest. "Please? I can relax on the couch backstage, do the song, then go directly to the apartment after the show. I'll be good, I promise."

Zeke sputtered a few seconds. "What about the baby?"

Muriel spoke up. "I can take care of him."

Zeke gave her a withering glance. "Am I outnumbered here?"

Josh slapped him on the back. "I think so."

Zeke sat on the piano bench. "All right, one number, but I'll be your pianist."

Josh saw Addy give Muriel a conspiratorial smile and wink as she went back to rehearsing.

Chapter 25

Sitting across the kitchen table from Cora, Addy was thoughtful while she helped Cora peel potatoes for their dinner. "You know, we *could* probably get a reception ready for Josh and Muriel next Monday. It doesn't have to be a fancy gala. Just some of our friends and a cozy celebration." Tom started whimpering, and Addy picked him up from his cradle.

Smiling slightly, Cora nodded. "I think we might arrange something. We could have a surprise reception for them when they get back. Since you and Zeke are going as witnesses, you can make sure they get here."

"Zeke was thinking of giving them a stay at the honeymoon suite in town, but I could suggest that they come here first before they go to the hotel. Oh, and I could hand out invitations to our close friends for a reception."

Cora shook her head. "You really shouldn't be up and around, much less handing out invitations. You get them ready, and I'll go out this afternoon. I was planning to go see Amelia, since this is our day off."

Addy put Tom back in the lightweight cradle of Alaskan cedar Ivan had made for them and carried him toward the apartment. "Swell! I'll get them ready. Thank you."

Zeke was reading in the parlor when Addy came in with Tom. He put down his book. "I wish you wouldn't carry that cradle around. Get someone to help you."

Addy made a disapproving face. "Zeke, I gave

birth, not broke my neck. I feel fine."

"Most women spend a week in bed. You know you have enough help. You could just spend time with the baby."

"You heard my uncle, when he was here—I was never the delicate lady. Anyway, I have to talk to you." She told him about the idea to have a surprise reception for Muriel and Josh. "Did you get the reservations for the honeymoon suite?"

Zeke pointed to an envelope on the writing desk. "I was planning to give them that after the ceremony."

"Hold off. We can use that as an excuse to come back here. What do you think?"

"Sounds good, sweetheart. You'd better get going on those invitations."

Addy grinned and kissed him. "I love you, you know." She sat at the desk and took out her stationery.

****

Muriel smiled and stretched when the alarm went off on the morning of her wedding. Her first thoughts were of how much she loved Josh. She hadn't thought she could ever love again when Tony was killed, but in Josh she had found her perfect man. Since getting rid of his melancholy he was becoming more and more confident and strong. That one note they'd found after opening night and given to the sheriff would have devastated him a few months ago, but now he was handling the uncertainty.

She heard, "Ma-ma-ma-ma," coming from the curtained partition in one corner. That would be Jenny's area now that Josh would be sharing her room. The child beamed when Muriel picked her up.

"Mama is here, love. You'll get used to this sleeping arrangement. I'm just around the curtain from you, and so will Josh be."

"Ja-ja-ja-ja," Jenny said with a big smile.

"Yes, you like Josh, don't you? Well, he'll be your daddy after today."

"Da-da-da-da," the baby sang.

Muriel laughed and swung her around. She heard a knock. "Are you up?" came Addy's voice. Muriel opened the door.

Jenny pointed at Addy. "Ad-da!"

Addy grinned and kissed the pudgy finger. "Yes, it will be Auntie Addy after today." Addy gave Muriel the clothes she carried. "Here's your flowered dress. I picked it up from the laundry for you."

Muriel handed Jenny to Addy and hung the dress on a hook. "Thank you. I'll get Jenny changed and you can take her down to breakfast. I'll be down in an hour. Is Kata going to watch both children while we're away?"

"Uh-huh. She said she would be delighted. Zeke is taking care of his brother right now. Josh has been up since four o'clock. I think the nerves got the best of him."

Muriel finished getting Jenny freshened up and dressed. When Addy swept out with the child, Muriel could hear Jenny giggling as they went downstairs.

Muriel drew her bath and settled in the tub. She sighed in contentment as the warm fragrant steam played around her nose. *Mrs. Joshua Shafer. I'll soon shed the Giovanni name. Tony was a love, but he was a murderer like his relatives. Well, Jenny will be raised in a home where there is no killing to get what you want.*

Muriel finished her bath and went back to her room. She oiled and dusted her skin before putting on her clothes. The dress had pale pink blooms over it, and draped sleeves that came to the elbow. The perfect spring frock. She grabbed her light spring coat and pale pink broad-brimmed hat, then did a quick primp in front of the mirror and put a little rouge on her lips and cheeks before she hurried to the restaurant and looked around.

Addy gave her a little twitch of a smile. "Josh and Zeke went ahead to the courthouse to start the paperwork. That way, all you have to do is sign it when you get there."

Cora waved her to the table. "Sit! Eat something. You don't want to faint in the middle of the vows."

"Where is everyone else? You usually have a full breakfast going here." Muriel picked nervously into her scrambled eggs and ham.

Addy and Cora glanced at each other. "Oh, they ate earlier," was all Addy said.

When Muriel had finished, Addy picked up Muriel's spring coat and helped her into it. "I could get it myself," Muriel protested.

Addy brushed off a bit of lint. "I'm your Matron of Honor. You attended me, so I'll repay the favor. And if you say I just gave birth last week, I'll knot the sheets on your bed." The two laughed at the childish prank they used to play on each other.

Cora gave Muriel a hug. "You deserve to be happy, and Josh is a very good man. He'll make sure you and Jenny are taken care of, and he'll be a good father."

Muriel smiled. "Both Jenny and I love him very much." She adjusted her hat. "Come on, Addy, it's time to go."

Muriel and Addy walked out the lobby doors into the crisp spring air of the sunny May morning. The mountainside looked plush in its coat of fresh green, with birds of every kind soaring joyfully in the blue sky.

Josh was pacing back and forth, wearing a hole in the floor of the courthouse. He glanced at Muriel and Addy as they came in. "Where have you been?

Our appointment with the judge is in ten minutes! Go sign the papers at the desk."

Muriel gave Addy a questioning look, and Addy shrugged. Muriel went to the desk and the clerk showed her where to put her name. Addy signed as a witness next to Zeke's signature.

Muriel gave Josh a small smile. "I love you, too."

Josh deflated before her eyes. "I'm sorry. I didn't mean to do that." He took her hand and squeezed it. "You're absolutely beautiful."

Zeke stood with an amused glint. "He's been like this since we've been here. I thought he was going to snap my head off a couple of times."

A young man appeared at the courtroom door. "Joshua Shafer, Muriel Giovanni, the judge is ready for you." He held the door as the four went inside.

Josh offered Muriel his arm and, as they walked up to the bench, she knew that this was where she always wanted to be, standing by this man, for the rest of her life. She gazed warmly at him and his eyes reflected her love.

The vows were simple and short. A 'Will you, Joshua' and a 'Will you, Muriel.' She glanced at Addy, who was wiping tears off her cheek. Then the judge said, "By the power invested in me by the Territory of Alaska, I now pronounce you Mr. and Mrs. Joshua Shafer." The hated Giovanni name was gone. Josh took Muriel in his arms and gave her a kiss that buckled her knees.

Addy couldn't contain herself any longer. She grabbed both of Muriel's hands. "My sister! How wonderful that sounds!" Then she hugged Josh. "And I have a brother, too!"

Zeke slapped Josh on the back. "Congratulations to the both of you." Then he kissed Muriel on the cheek. "Let's go back to the theater. I have your gift waiting there."

Josh gave him a glare. "I told you, you didn't

have to get us anything."

Zeke punched his arm. "I know, little brother, but I didn't listen."

As the newlyweds stepped out into the brilliant sunshine, Addy and Zeke hit them with handfuls of rice. Muriel's heart sang all the way to the theater, her arm held firmly by her handsome husband.

Zeke led them through the door of the apartment, saying, "I left it in the parlor." Once there, he handed them an envelope.

Josh opened it and gasped. He showed the paper to Muriel. "You gave us a night in Juneau's finest hotel? We can't take this."

Zeke refused to take it back. "You two deserve something special tonight. Anyway, it's back to work tomorrow."

Addy grasped Muriel's shoulders. "Now, you must have some lunch before you go," and Muriel and Josh had no choice but to follow her through the office and into the darkened restaurant, Zeke behind them.

Suddenly, the lights blazed on and colorful banners and balloons were hung everywhere and, in the middle of the room, a huge banner proclaimed, "Congratulations, Mr. and Mrs. Josh Shafer." A large cheer went around from all of their friends. Muriel's heart was in her throat and tears in her eyes. She instinctively hugged Addy. "Oh, my dear sweet co—sister! It feels so good to say *sister*."

Cora, at the forefront of the wellwishers, congratulated Josh and then Muriel before handing over a telegram. "This came for you while you were out."

Muriel opened it and read out loud:
DAUGHTER STOP MOTHER AND I RECEIVED NEWS STOP KNOW YOU WILL BE HAPPY STOP GIVE LOVE TO JOSH STOP FATHER

A wave of homesickness welled in her heart. How she wished the rest of her family could have joined her on this happy day. Deep down she desperately would have liked her mother to be here, but she knew Mother was thinking of her. She could almost feel the dear woman beside her.

With a tender look at Muriel, Josh put his arms around her, seeming as always to know what she needed.

Ivan had brought his gramophone and played music throughout the luncheon. Muriel couldn't take her eyes off Josh; he filled her with such joy.

The table groaned under sliced ham, turkey, and fresh fish. Potatoes, rolls and vegetables shared the space with relishes of many kinds. For dessert, Cora brought out her spice layer cake with white icing, and Muriel and Josh cut and shared the first piece, accompanied by the cheers of the guests.

Finally, at three o'clock, Muriel and Josh thanked all their guests and went to pack. Josh and Zeke brought Jenny's crib down to Zeke's apartment for the night.

Muriel cuddled the child. "Now, Jenny, be good for Aunt Addy. We'll be back tomorrow."

Jenny patted Muriel's cheek. "Ma-ma-ma-ma."

Muriel gave Jenny to Addy, and the little girl put her thumb in her mouth and sadly watched Muriel go. Muriel almost went back in when she heard Jenny cry.

Josh put his hand on her arm. "She'll be all right. Addy can take care of her."

Muriel and Josh opened the lobby doors and there, right in front of them, was Zeke in the driver's seat of the neighbor's surrey. He tipped his hat with a grin. "Going my way, folks? I thought I'd take you to the hotel in style."

Josh shook his head. "If you don't watch out, you're going to become our permanent driver." He put the suitcase under the seat and helped Muriel up into the surrey, then swung in next to her.

The clip-clop of the horse's hooves beat out a cheerful rhythm until Zeke pulled up to the grand entrance, where the doorman in his crisp uniform greeted them. Zeke hopped down and put the suitcase next to his brother, shook Josh's hand and gave Muriel a kiss, and was on his way again.

Opening the impressive oak door, with its colorful stained glass inlays, the doorman ushered the pair into a plush lobby. There was an air of the frontier in the décor. Massive wooden beams directed attention to a fieldstone fireplace large enough to have held a small cabin yet dwarfed by a large Kodiak bear, fortunately stuffed, on its hind legs nearby. Potted plants stood everywhere, interspersed with other stuffed animals of many sorts posing somewhat unnaturally on stands. "It's like we're in a forest," marveled Muriel. Otters, foxes and rabbits watched them from the lower walls, and on the upper shelves owls and eagles peered down. Several polar bear rugs were scattered about. The sturdy wooden furniture had leather cushions, with Indian blankets placed carefully over the backs of chairs and sofas. Muriel wandered around in amazement as Josh registered at the desk.

Josh came to her and clasped her hand. "We can go up to our room now."

Muriel squeezed it, still looking about her in wonder. "I've never seen a place quite like this one."

He cupped her face in his hands and gazed into her eyes. "It's beautiful and unique. Like you."

Laughing, she gave him a quick kiss. "Let's go, my Alaskan prince."

They followed the bellboy carrying their suitcase into the elevator, where a gray-uniformed attendant operated the controls that took them up to the third floor. There the bellboy led them into a suite whose sitting room also had a fireplace, one quite a bit smaller than that in the lobby. The doorway to the bedroom framed a magnificent white iron bed with a polar bear fur as a comforter. Muriel again was lost in wonder while Josh gave the bellboy a tip and sent him on his way.

As Muriel took off her hat and put it on the rack, she felt Josh come up behind and enfold her. "I'm at my beautiful wife's disposal tonight." He traced his lips down to the nape of her neck, then rubbed her back.

Muriel turned. "Mmm, are you sure about that?" She put her arms around his shoulders and rubbed her pelvis into his hardness as she gave him a deep kiss.

He worked the buttons open down her back and slipped his hands inside, giving her a smooth caress on skin that was tingling in anticipation. Clothes lightly billowed to the floor, settling here and there. Josh drew his fingers down to her waist, alerting every nerve in her body, before he swept her up and took her to the white fur on the bed and lay next to her. He gently played with her breasts, teasing the tips.

Their lovemaking was slow and sensual. Josh made her mad with want before he raised up and settled between her thighs, driving home. They both moaned. Muriel moved her hands over his stomach, watching his tight muscles ripple. He closed his eyes and gritted his teeth. "You're going to make me lose control."

Muriel gave him a smile. "There's plenty of time for a rematch."

Josh clamped his mouth firmly on hers and completely pushed her over the edge. Her body exploded in different colors, an explosion she felt from her head to her toes. Josh seemed to try to hang on, but she felt him contract and a deep moan escaped.

They lay together for some time on the fur as if they didn't want to let go of the feeling of it or of each other. Then Josh rolled over and looked at her with love. "You inspire me to new feelings I didn't know I had." He moved his hand back and forth on her arm. "One thing I have to thank the Giovannis for is driving you up here. Otherwise, I probably never would've met you."

A troubling thought entered her head. "You wouldn't have gotten shot, either."

He laughed. "They failed. I'm still here and in love with you." They cuddled on the fur for a long time and happily consummated their marriage again.

In the morning, Muriel and Josh gazed at each other over a leisurely breakfast of ham and eggs in the hotel restaurant. Muriel spread butter on her toast. "You know, there are still some things I don't know about you."

Josh took a sip of coffee. "Oh? Like what?"

"What's your middle name? I didn't see it on the marriage license."

"I don't have one. Neither do Zeke or any of my other siblings. My father thought it was vain glory. The way we were named, he flipped open the Bible to a page, then went down the column until he had a boy's or girl's name. He said the Almighty named us."

Muriel shook her head. "All the preachers I've known have been good men and not the horror you've described your father to be."

"To the congregation, he was an upstanding man of God, although a strict one. For some reason, he thought his family should be perfect. He lived by 'spare the rod and spoil the child.' He beat us if he considered we were disrespectful of his wishes. Zeke and I tended to balk the most."

Muriel put her hand over his. "I'm so sorry for both of you. And glad that you and Zeke have turned out all right after that rough start."

When they had finished their meal, they found Zeke waiting for them in the lobby. Zeke smiled, but he had a worried look. "Good morning, you two! Are you ready to get back to work?"

Muriel and Josh glanced at each other. Josh gripped Zeke's shoulder. "What's wrong? Something's bothering you."

Zeke hesitated a moment. "I didn't want to put a damper on your special day, but this morning someone threw a rock through one of the lobby windows. There was a note attached to it that said, 'You've been warned.'" He picked up their suitcase. "Come on, we'd better get back. The sheriff is there."

They climbed into the surrey, but the festive atmosphere of yesterday had evaporated.

Muriel's stomach knotted. This was getting serious. Who was the "concerned citizen" who wrote these threatening notes?

At the theater, Josh and Zeke talked with the sheriff while Muriel sought out Addy in the apartment. When Jenny saw Muriel, she raised her little hands. "Ma-ma-ma-ma!" she sang out. Muriel whisked her into her arms and held her tight, suddenly afraid.

Addy searched Muriel's face. "Zeke told you?"

Muriel nodded. "He and Josh are with the sheriff now. I wish whoever did this would come out and tell us what he wants, instead of scaring us to death."

"I have a feeling he's trying to drive us away. He's too cowardly to do it to our face."

Muriel sighed. "Well, I guess we'll have to carry on and hope this person will either give up or come forward." The two mothers sat with their babies, hoping for the best.

Chapter 26

Josh stood, hardly breathing, as Zeke told the sheriff what he'd found that morning when he investigated the sound of breaking glass. Amos had brought the other note and was comparing the handwriting.

Amos looked up. "It seems to be the same person."

Zeke pursed his lips. "Did you check to see who wrote the letter in the weekly?"

"Both Sarah and I went through their records and found the name Sven Jorgenson connected to the Concerned Citizen letter, but we couldn't find anyone by that name in the city rolls. They didn't remember what the fellow looked like. They said it was a while ago, and many people come through their office."

Josh gave him an angry glance. "That means you have no idea who's doing this."

Amos regarded him for a moment. "Not now. We have to wait for him to show his hand."

Josh hit the wall with his fist. "We have a bunch of frightened people living here. We don't know if this is just a crackpot or if we're in real danger!" His voice rose to a yell.

Zeke clamped a hand on Josh's shoulder. "Calm down. Sheriff, what should we do?"

Amos stroked his mustache. "There's a place in town that hires out night watchmen. I could send one of them your way. I believe they charge six bits a night."

Zeke nodded. "We can do that. Thank you,

Sheriff."

Amos took the evidence. As they closed the lobby door behind the sheriff, Zeke motioned for Josh to follow him to the office. Zeke closed and locked the door. He pointed to one of the chairs. "Sit. I want to talk to you."

Josh settled across the desk from Zeke. "What?"

Zeke sighed. "You've been very short of temper lately. Yesterday, you snapped at me and Muriel before the wedding, and today you just about lost control of it, talking to the sheriff. You almost sound like Father. I know you'll say the situation warrants it, but I want you to be careful anger doesn't take you over."

"I've been under a lot of tension lately. What with the opening of the theater, getting married, and now putting up with an insane person trying to ruin us, of course I'm short of temper. How dare you compare me to Father!"

Shaking his head, Zeke continued, "Instead of remembering him chiding you, you're now making decisions as he would have—with anger. Anger ruled him, and it's starting to rule you, too. I had a problem with that when I got so angry with the inspector in Los Angeles. Now I have to think before I say or do anything. Even with the melancholy you had before, you pressed on, thinking things through."

Josh sat in thought for a long moment before looking up. "Will you help me with this? I need you to lean on."

"I'll be there for you, as I am now. I had to go through a dark time to learn to trust again. Father did a lot of damage to me, too." With a long look into each other's eyes, as though silently pledging mutual assistance, the two rose from their chairs and met in a tight brotherly embrace.

****

Muriel hurried through the stage door, her heart breaking. On stage, Addy, Babs and Roxie busily worked out their new number, "I Wish I Could Shimmy Like My Sister Kate," for Friday and Saturday. Dan blocked the dance steps from his usual seat in the audience while Zeke and Josh accompanied them on the piano and banjo.

She paused by the cradle where little Tom was snugly ensconced in a corner of the stage with Jenny next to him, happily playing in her playpen. The sight of the children was a bright spot in her sad quest, but then she went on and appeared at the right wing of the stage where the dancers could see her as she slumped against the wall. "Addy, I need to see you...and James," she gasped, putting a hand over her face.

As James came around from the lighting panel, Addy ran to her and held her tight. "Dear, what's wrong?"

In answer, Muriel thrust forward the telegram clutched in her hand. While Josh held Muriel, Addy and James looked at the telegram, and Addy read aloud:

JAMES MURIEL ADELINE STOP GRANDMA PASSED ON TODAY STOP FATHER AND UNCLE

James teared up and reached for his handkerchief.

Addy buried her face in Zeke's waiting arms and sobbed. "No! It hasn't been that long since Grandpa died. We can't lose her, too."

Muriel wiped her eyes. "Grandma must have been very lonely since then. Losing Grandpa would have broken her heart."

Addy nodded, looking at Zeke. "I know I wouldn't like going on without you."

Muriel sighed. "Grandma and Grandpa were together for so many years. To suddenly be alone like that—but now they're together again." Muriel suddenly felt strangely happy for Grandma.

****

A month went by. One morning as Muriel picked up the mail from the post office one of the clerks called to her, "Mrs. Shafer, I have a registered letter here for you and Adeline Shafer and James Carter. I need your signature."

Muriel took the card, signed it, and handed it back to the clerk. The envelope was thick, brown and legal-sized. She looked at the return address: an attorney's office in Los Angeles. *I wonder what this could be?* It looked so important, almost forbidding, she decided to wait until she returned to the office, to open it with the others present.

Seeking out James and Addy and herding them into the office, Muriel put the envelope on the desk. "This came by registered post, and it has all our names on it. I thought we should be together when it's opened."

Addy picked it up. "I'll open it." She extracted a packet of papers clipped together. As she read the top sheet, her eyes widened and her hand rose to cover her mouth. "This is a copy of Grandma's will."

James nudged her. "What does it say?"

"The attorney is the executor of the estate, and he says we each get a thousand dollars. Grandma and Grandpa had a lot of money stashed away in banks, and in stocks and bonds. Each of the grandchildren get a thousand and the rest goes to your mother." The three of them jumped up and down, cheering. "Do you know what that means? We have enough to get a house!"

Muriel, Addy and James hugged each other, laughing out loud. When Josh and Zeke came in from the theater to find out what was going on, Muriel showed them the letter.

Josh broke out in a wide grin. "I never met her,

but thank you, Mrs. Applegate!"

Zeke pounded him on the back. "I did, and believe me, this gift is something that gracious lady would do."

Addy ran into Zeke's arms. "Those two houses Muriel and I were looking at in the residential section were each fifteen hundred. We could easily get a mortgage for a few hundred dollars."

Zeke looked at her critically. "You've got this all figured out, haven't you?"

Addy stood back and put her hands on her hips. "You bet I do! Muriel and I always dreamed we would live next to each other."

Josh shook his head. "Well, who are we to break up an act like that?"

They quickly got out the ledger and started making their plans.

****

Sarah blew on the hot coffee as she sat on her lookout at the harbor. This was the part of the job she hated, but even the boring stakeout was important. Amos wanted to watch the passengers who came in for a few more months. He knew the mob didn't give up easily, and he strongly suspected the trouble at the theater might be tied to them.

August was a busy month for tourists coming up to look at the wilds of Alaska, the place where their fathers and grandfathers didn't find a fortune in gold. Just a few had gotten the best claims on the gold fields. Now, even the mining companies around Juneau were closed down, except for the Alaska-Juneau mine that chopped the gold out of rock.

Suddenly two passengers disembarking from the liner caught her attention. They were dressed in cheaper clothes than a trip on the liner would warrant, for one thing, but more obvious was the fact that there at the end of the ramp was Manfred Pembrook greeting them.

The man was large, dressed in dungarees and a blue flannel shirt; unusual for this time of year. The woman was much younger than the man, possibly his daughter. But her expertly done hair and makeup belied the plain brown dress and sweater.

Taking out her notebook, Sarah put down a description of the couple, thinking she and Amos could ask Mr. Pembrook who they were. It might be nothing, but something in her gut told her to make note of it. These weren't the type of people Manfred usually bothered with.

The note on the rock through the theater window was still itching in her mind, also. She had looked into the background of the Giovannis and families like them. They didn't let go of slights easily. Somehow, Sarah too was sure this "Concerned Citizen" might have a connection to the Giovannis. Could it be Manfred? He had worked with Adrian Connor, after all.

Luke came to relieve her, and Sarah told him what she had observed, reminding him to keep an eye on the other passengers who came off the liner. He took down the descriptions she had before she headed to Amos' office.

Sarah sat back in the chair facing Amos after telling him what she'd seen at the harbor. "What do you think? Could Manfred still be trying to drive the Shafers away?"

He shook his head. "I don't think we should jump to any conclusions. After all, the only crime is a broken window, and we don't have any proof that Manfred was the one who did it."

"Could we ask him who those people were?"

"He'll probably tell us to mind our own business. Nothing has happened."

Sarah took a sip of coffee. "I wish we didn't have to wait for something to happen, but I understand you can't question someone without a reason."

"Let's just keep an eye on our young lawyer."

Sarah paused for a moment. "Isn't Adrian Connor's trial supposed to start tomorrow morning?"

Amos checked his calendar. "Yes, the judge asked me to escort him to the courthouse. Do you think there's any connection between that and the people Manfred met?"

Sarah tapped her cup. "I don't know, but I have a feeling of doom I can't seem to shake." She met his eyes, and he looked as worried as she felt.

The next morning, Sarah and Amos met at his office. Newspaper reporters and curious spectators lined the two blocks from the sheriff's office to the courthouse.

Standing at the door to the street, Amos motioned to Sarah. "Lakat, I want you to go ahead of me. If you see anything suspicious in the crowd, let me know."

He turned to Sam. "Sam, you're going to be the eyes in back. Watch all the windows and rooftops." At their nods, he said, "All right. Ayers, bring Connor to me."

Luke brought out Adrian Conner in shackles. Amos took out a key and unlocked the leg bands. "Conner, I warn you, if you try to escape, we won't hesitate to shoot. The shackles go back on at the courthouse."

Connor looked at Amos with hatred seething under the skin. "I'm not going to forgive you for making me stay in this filthy rat hole until the trial. If I get off, you'd better watch your back."

Amos grabbed his arm. "Good one, Connor, threatening a lawman. That ought to look swell on the list. Come on, Lakat, after you."

Sarah took a breath and opened the door. A murmur went through the crowd as she led the way out, and the people opened a path for the little parade. Sarah squinted through the morning sun already far up over the mountain. A gray blanket of sea fog waited in the harbor, however, ready to cover the town. She knew it wouldn't be sunny for long.

Sarah imagined movement behind every window ahead. She hadn't shaken that dread she felt yesterday. Suddenly, she heard a shout from Sam and then a gunshot from the rear. A bullet ripped through her sleeve, skimming her bicep. She whirled. Pandemonium was already running through the crowd. Several women screamed and she heard vomiting from others as she saw what was left of Adrian Connor's face. Amos was cussing a blue streak even as he eased the body to the pavement. Blood and brains were splattered over everyone within range, including herself. A wave of nausea went over her, but she shook it off, watching Sam take off in weird slow motion toward a building behind them, his gun drawn.

Amos checked over Connor's body and shook his head at Sarah. "There isn't any way he would live through getting his head blown off." His expression changed when he saw her arm. "You were hit!"

Sarah tore her sleeve down and used the material to put pressure on the wound. "It's just a scratch. The doc can fix me up."

Sam ran back to them, weaving through stunned citizens. Some were running toward the courthouse, but most simply stood with their mouths agape. Sam's face was pale as he sagged against the building. Between catching his breath, he told them, "I saw which window it came from...that empty building back there...gone when I got there...saw the high-powered rifle barrel out the window."

Amos glanced at Sarah. "It had to be a professional assassin."

She pursed her lips. "Like a hit man?"

Amos took a knowing look. "Yeah."

"Someone didn't want any testimony coming out

of this trial."

At that instant, Dr. Lindsey came running up with the coroner. The doctor proclaimed Adrian Connor dead, and the coroner's staff put the body on a cart to take back to the morgue while Lindsey took a look at Sarah's arm. "You'd better come back to my office with me. I'll patch you up. Do you feel like walking?"

Sarah nodded. "It's almost stopped bleeding. I'll make it." She glanced at Amos.

Waving his hand, Amos answered her unasked question. "Sam and I can start on the investigation. We'll catch you up on it when you get back." He looked at his blood-soaked clothes. "And after I clean up."

Sarah's mind raced as she headed to the doctor's office. *Could the Giovannis have slipped in somehow? This was the kind of hit the crime families would do to keep their actions quiet.* The people Manfred Pembrook met at the harbor popped into her mind. *How closely did Manfred work with Connor?*

Two hours later, Sarah sat in the sheriff's office. "Did you or Sam find out anything?"

Amos tapped the desktop impatiently with his pencil. "No one we talked to saw anything, or at least nobody is owning up. The best we got was several people who noticed a figure coming out of the alley behind the vacant building. A large man wearing a long black coat and a black fedora. Nobody saw his face, that we could find."

"Do you think we could use that as an excuse to check with Mr. Pembrook about those two people he met?"

"You think Pembrook has a connection with the Giovannis?"

"Working with Connor, it's entirely possible. I wonder if the Shafers are in danger again?"

Amos nodded. "There might be a connection there with the one who sent the threatening note after opening night at the theater and the one later who threw a rock through the window." He took the two pieces of paper out of his file folder. "Lakat, does the writing look the same to you?"

Sarah studied the notes, then nodded. "The writing is from the same person, I'm sure."

A few minutes later Amos and Sarah entered Manfred Pembrook's office and were met by the secretary's glare. "What do you want now, Sheriff?"

He sidled up to her desk with the face of patience. "Good morning, my dear. I suppose you have heard by now of the shooting of Mr. Connor. Because Mr. Pembrook worked closely with him, we would like to ask him a few questions."

Her lips disappeared in a tight line. "Just a moment." She huffed as she knocked at the door of the inner office and went in. A very unhappy sound came billowing out, and then the secretary slunk back. "He said to make it short and sweet. He's a very busy man."

"I'll bet he is," Amos said under his breath to Sarah just before they stepped through the doorway. "Mr. Pembrook." Amos nodded to the man behind the desk. "We're conducting an investigation on the shooting of Mr. Connor this morning."

Manfred scowled. "I see the sheriff's office is very efficient, as usual."

Amos seemed to ignore that. "We're checking on some of the new arrivals here in Juneau. You were observed greeting a couple yesterday. Who were they?"

"What are you spying on me for? Can't I conduct my business without the law nosing in?"

"Answer my question, Pembrook."

Manfred hesitated for a moment. "It was a man with his wife. They wanted me to help them get a fishing business license."

Sarah shook her head. "The woman looked too young to be his wife."

Manfred turned a glare on her. "That's not any of my business."

Amos took out his notepad. "What are their names?"

"Jake and Mary Cassidy, if you must know. Now, get out of my office. I don't know anything about the shooting."

"I figured as much. Good day, Mr. Pembrook." Amos gave Sarah a glance as they exited the office building. "Let's find out if a business license has been issued in this name, shall we?"

At the courthouse, Amos greeted the clerk in charge of licenses. "Pete, can you check in your files if anyone has applied for a license for a fishing business in the past week?"

Pete went over to the file cabinet and took out a folder. "Here's the past week's applications. They haven't been put in the main cabinet yet."

Amos and Sarah sat at one of the tables and divided up the papers. When he came to the end of his stack, Amos sighed. "Any luck?"

Sarah thumbed her stack. "I've some business applications here, but none for a Cassidy."

"Same here. I think Pembrook sent us on a wild goose chase."

Sarah was frustrated. "Back to his office?"

"What do you think?" Amos snapped. He shoved the papers back into the folder and handed it to Pete before striding out of the building with Sarah in close pursuit. Amos was not a happy man when he found that Manfred had taken off. His fist came down on the secretary's desk. "Where did he go, and when is he coming back?"

"I don't know, to both questions. He didn't say." She stared daggers back.

"Tell him I have to ask him a few things. Got that?"

"Yes, Sheriff." She went back to her typewriter.

On the way to Amos' office, Sarah looked at him. "Do you think Manfred was behind the shooting?"

Amos nodded. "Either that or he had a big hand in it. Meanwhile, we need to keep an eye on the Shafers. If the Giovannis have come up here, they may want to complete some unfinished business. We probably should check the theater every few hours."

Sarah shuddered as she followed him into the building. "Do you think we should check at Manfred's home to see if he's there?"

Amos gazed at her thoughtfully. "Good idea. And if he isn't, we can check with his wife, Lettie, to see if she knows anything."

At the elegant townhouse on the edge of the city, Amos' heavy knock at the large oak door brought a maid to open it. "May I ask if Mr. or Mrs. Pembrook is at home?"

The girl hesitated for a moment. "The missus is in. Just a minute." She closed the door without inviting them in.

Amos and Sarah glanced at each other on this seeming breach of etiquette. In a moment Lettie Pembrook opened the door. "Yes, may I help you, Sheriff?"

"May we speak to you about the whereabouts of your husband?"

"I haven't seen him since the day before yesterday," she said tersely.

Sarah studied her carefully. "Did he say where he was going? We just saw him at his office this morning."

Lettie seemed to be going through some inner turmoil. "Well, you know more than I do. Good day." She closed the door with a bang.

Amos scratched his cheek as they turned. "Any

idea what that was all about?"

Sarah shook her head. "Someone's hiding something." She didn't like having to wait until something else happened, but they had no choice. Or would there be anything more? *Did Manfred have it in him to kill Connor on his own? What would it gain him to do something so foolish?*

Chapter 27

Muriel and Addy carried out the appetizers while Cora made other preparations for the outdoor dinner party at Addy's new house. Both Shafer families had moved, only a few weeks before, into a pair of almost identical two-story clapboard houses in the residential area right outside the downtown area. The buildings were both white with green trim and shutters. Two driveways to garages, with a hedge down the middle between them, were all that separated them. The girls had immediately found an opening in the hedge for a shortcut between their back doors. A beautiful oak stood in one front yard and a maple tree in the other.

Muriel relaxed after moving out of the theater, but the killing of Adrian Connor had set her on edge again. *We haven't had any more threats since May. I thought maybe the concerned citizen was just a troublemaker who gave up when he couldn't chase us out. But now...*

No one was living in the theater now. Cora and James had tried to stay on, but Cora said there were too many noises in the empty building to suit her. While the other couples got apartments not far from the theater, Cora was staying in one of Zeke and Addy's upstairs bedrooms until she could find a place of her own, and James had moved in with Josh and Muriel for the time being.

The days were still quite long in August, but there was a crisp hint of fall in the air as people congregated for the double housewarming. As expected, James brought Amelia. She was more animated than Muriel had ever seen her before, and she even smiled repeatedly, mostly at James and Cora, occasionally at the others when they engaged her attention.

Zeke had set up a table outside where everyone helped themselves to the food all had contributed. There were lawn and folding chairs in a conversation circle in the tiny backyard, and some of the men simply sat cross-legged on the grass.

Anne and Ray Stewart were next to Addy and Zeke, with Muriel and Josh facing them, when Ray leaned toward them and announced, "Anne and I have something to tell you. We're going to be leaving at the end of the month."

Addy sat up straight. "Why?"

Anne looked at her plate. "We don't fit with singing and dancing acts. We're mostly drama trained."

Ray took it up. "I have a friend in New York who wants the two of us in a play he's written for the stage. I took the offer, with Anne's blessing."

Josh shook his head. "You've helped us out so much. We're grateful for that."

Zeke put his hand on Ray's shoulder. "We'll miss you, buddy, but thanks to the both of you."

Addy couldn't resist jumping up to embrace Anne before she said with a sigh, "I hate to see you go, after everyone is back together again, but this is a wonderful offer. Don't forget to stay in touch."

As the party went on, one of the main topics of conversation was the killing of Adrian Connor only a few days earlier. Something in Muriel cringed about that, although she couldn't say why. Maybe because he had been in cahoots with the Giovannis.

She couldn't shake a feeling of dread as she and Addy bade goodnight to their guests and then joined Cora to clean everything up. At last, with all in order, Cora also said goodnight and made her way upstairs. Muriel watched at the door as Addy settled little Tom into his crib in the main floor bedroom Addy shared with Zeke. The crib was on the far side of the room from the slightly raised window, where the moving air wouldn't be too much for the baby. Muriel knew because she had placed Jenny's crib the same way. With the baby asleep, the girls stood silently by the door for a moment while the gentle summer breeze billowed the lace curtains. Addy leaned against Muriel and shuddered.

"What's wrong, dear?" Muriel asked, putting an arm around her cousin.

"I don't know, but that whole thing with Adrian Connor is bothering me, for some reason."

"I don't think we have anything to worry about. That whole vendetta might have been someone who thought it was a perfect time to get even with Connor for something."

Addy paused. "We both know the Giovannis prevent people from talking by killing them."

"I'm sure the sheriff would tell us if anyone suspicious was looking for us."

Addy quieted, and Muriel knew there had been too many times in the past years when she'd thought it was all over—and it wasn't.

****

Josh finished putting away the folding chairs brought back from next door just as Muriel came into the parlor after settling Jenny in her crib. "Has James come from taking Amelia back to the sanitarium?" She turned out all the lights except the small desk lamp.

Shaking his head, Josh said, "No, not yet. I'm sure he can find his way upstairs without us. I'm tired." He put his arms around her in a weary embrace.

"Stand right where you are and don't make a sound," came a voice from behind them.

They both whirled to face a large man training a gun on them. "Aldo?" Muriel gasped.

His features turned into a cruel smile. "Someone told me I looked like my late brother, Joe. Yes, and you must be my former niece-in-law, Muriel."

"What do you want?" Josh cut in angrily.

"We came to take back what is ours."

The words seared into Josh's brain. Those were the words from the first note they gave to the sheriff. It wasn't money they wanted, he realized suddenly, and just at that moment he heard Jenny cry out. A young woman appeared with the child.

"No!" Muriel screamed. She flew at the woman, but Aldo stepped between them and shoved the muzzle of the gun next to Jenny's head.

"You probably remember your former sister-in-law, Gina. Now, if either of you tries to stop us, I won't hesitate to shoot the brat."

Josh watched this unfold like a bad dream. *What can I do? If I try to rush them now, they could kill both Jenny and Muriel. I've vowed to protect them. What kind of a man am I?*

Jenny and Muriel were both crying hysterically as Aldo took Jenny, holding the flailing child awkwardly on one arm. "Gina, put those two chairs together back to back. Then take the loop of cord from my coat pocket." Still with the gun pointed toward the scared child, Aldo commanded Josh and Muriel, "Sit."

If I'm going to do something, it better be now. Josh launched himself at Aldo, who smashed the gun down on the side of Josh's face. The pain was sharp, but not enough to cause unconsciousness. He felt the blood trickling on his chin as Gina tied them to the chairs.

"Where is the young man who lives upstairs?" When no one answered, he cocked the gun next to the baby.

"He's out," Muriel said through her teeth.

"That's all right, then. You'll both be dead by the time he gets back. We have someone taking care of the Shafers next door, and then he'll take care of you two."

Suddenly they heard a gunshot, followed by a scream—it sounded like Addy—and then there was another shot. Muriel was beside herself. "You bastards! I curse your whole family!"

Josh turned the air blue, calling Aldo every name in the book. *Maybe father was right about me. I can't help Muriel and Jenny. My brother's family is dead, and I can't even help myself!*

Aldo and Gina moved toward the back door, and Aldo tipped his hat as he gave Gina the crying child. "We're going to take Jenelle Giovanni back to Sofia, where she belongs."

As they went through the back door, Josh could hear a plaintive cry of, "Mama, mama!" A few moments later, an auto engine fired from somewhere on the street, and he heard it take off. His heart twisted. Then he heard the door open again. He shut his eyes tight, ready to be executed in his own home. Instead, someone knelt by the chairs and cut his bonds.

"Are either of you hurt?" It was the welcome voice of James.

"How long have you been here?" Josh snapped.

"Long enough to hear what was happening."

"Then why didn't you do something to stop them?"

James finished with Josh and started cutting Muriel free. "They had a gun. I figured if I stayed in the shadows outside until they left, I had a better chance of rescuing you."

Josh sputtered. "Of course, you're right. I'm sorry, James."

James finished with Muriel's bindings and

hurried upstairs, calling over his shoulder. "I've got my radio equipment in my room. The Giovannis will probably head to the harbor. I can send a message there and to the airfield. They can let the sheriff and the police know what's happened."

As Josh held Muriel, who was still crying hysterically, he glanced out the window at Zeke's house, only to see a figure come out the back door there and head toward his own home. Anger flaring within him, Josh grabbed the poker from the rack by the fireplace. "Stay down and be quiet, Muriel. I think the hit man is coming."

Muriel's eyes grew wide. "But, Josh—"

"Hush!" he hissed. Josh made his way through the darkened kitchen to the back door. He watched as the figure inched through the gap in the hedge.

Opening the door just enough to slide out, Josh dropped noiselessly into the shadows next to the porch. He gripped the poker tight as he watched the man come slowly to the back of his house. *I'm going to kill you, you bastard!*

As soon as the man was in range, Josh bolted with his head low and hit the man in the stomach with all the force he could muster. The man let out an "Oof!" and hit the ground gasping for air as Josh stood over him, the poker already swinging in an arc to crush the murderer's head. A light went on behind him.

"No, Josh! That's Zeke!" Muriel screamed.

In the light from the porch, he saw his brother paralyzed with fear at his feet. Josh couldn't stop the poker, but with a twist of his arm, the tip buried itself in the lawn three inches from Zeke's head. The two stared at each other, their chests heaving. Josh's knees buckled and he let out a wail that could have come from the bowels of hell. "I almost killed you!"

Zeke reached to hug his distraught brother. "I didn't know if all of you were dead." He leaned back to get a look at Josh's face. "You're hurt."

"Just a bruise and a cut. But how are you still alive? We heard shots from next door, and Addy screamed."

"We had gone to bed. Cora was still up and heard noises downstairs and came down with her shotgun. She caught a man coming in through the back door. She said he fired at her but missed, and she fired back. She didn't miss. What happened over here?"

Muriel was next to them by this time, and Josh stood and put an arm around her as she began sobbing again, barely able to get out, "It was the Giovannis...they took Jenny...the hit man Cora killed...he was supposed to kill us next."

Josh, with a deep breath, tried to shake off the fact he had almost killed his brother. He gave a hand up to Zeke. "Seems they were going to finish what was started in Los Angeles." He put his arms around Muriel. "James is radioing the harbor and the airfield."

Zeke looked at them in horror. "My God, they abducted Jenny? Cora went to get Doc Lindsey and alert the sheriff's department, but she won't know about this. Addy's at home with Tom."

Just then James ran out the back door and stopped short when he saw Zeke. "You're not dead?"

Zeke shook his head. "I wish everyone wouldn't keep asking me that. We're all alive except the hit man. Did you get anything back?"

"One of the ships in the harbor said they saw a pontoon airplane warming up on the other side of the bay. A rowboat with a man in it was waiting nearby. The operator said that looked suspicious for this time of night, since airplanes don't fly in the dark. They'll watch for a couple with a baby."

Josh bolted for the garage. "I'm going down there."

Zeke called after him, "I'll go with you."

As the truck roared out into the driveway and halted beside them, Josh at the wheel, Muriel laid a hand on Zeke's arm. The fierce determination in her eyes spoke more than her words. "No, you stay here and take care of Addy and Tom. *I'm* going with Josh. Jenny will need me."

Zeke hesitated before agreeing. "You're right, but you two let the sheriff take care of things. Stay safe, both of you." Zeke opened the passenger door for Muriel and gave her a quick kiss on her cheek.

Josh glanced at her. "Whatever you do, stay down."

She grasped his hand. "We'll be all right."

Josh exhaled a shaky breath and put the truck in gear. He hoped she was right.

****

Sarah and Amos leaned over the radioman's desk while he communicated with James Carter. He finished writing down the translation of the Morse code. "Carter says a hit man was killed by Cora when he tried to break into Zeke's home. Dr. Lindsey is on his way there. Josh and Muriel are on their way here in the truck."

"Why would they come down here into danger?" Amos slammed his fist on the desk.

Sarah put her hand on his shoulder. "Their daughter was abducted. You can't expect a mother to sit home and wait."

He whirled on her, his eyes flashing. "Then it's up to you to hold them back and keep them safe. They'll probably be coming down the main drive. You can head them off."

Sam ran in. "Sir, a couple with a child just got into that rowboat across from the airplane."

Amos grabbed Sam's arm and headed for the door. "Into the motorboat, now!"

Speeding to the top of the main drive, Sarah saw

the headlights of a truck coming toward her rapidly. She stood her ground in the middle of the road, and the truck braked to a stop only inches away from her. Josh and Muriel got out.

"Why are you in the middle of the road?" Josh's agitation was evident. His arms flailed, and his fingers kept running through his hair.

Sarah clamped a hand on Muriel's arm when Muriel looked like she was going to bolt. "The couple was spotted. Amos and a few of the deputies are after them. You are to stay here out of danger."

Muriel started crying, "My baby. My Jenny!" as Josh folded her in his arms.

In the light of the three-quarters moon, the three could make out the shadowy outline of the rowboat nearing the airplane. Amos' motorboat had just left the pier with four of his deputies aboard, and Sarah doubted it would reach the rowboat before the couple with Jenny would be into the airplane and able to escape.

Then a remarkable thing happened. A large fishing boat idling nearby suddenly gunned its engines and blocked the airplane in front. Another steamer chugged over and hemmed in the airplane near the shore.

"What's going on out there?" Josh wondered.

Sarah shook her head. "It looks like those two ships are determined to stop the airplane from getting away."

The motorboat swung between the two ships, and then two figures jumped from it into the rowboat. Sarah heard a gunshot and shouting. Someone from the motorboat pulled two people out of the airplane. Another shot was fired and more struggle ensued.

Muriel was beside herself, her words completely incomprehensible in her fear for her child. Josh attempted to quiet her even as he looked on in amazement at the battle before him. When the motorboat started back toward the town, Sarah realized she hadn't been breathing and gasped a huge gulp of air just as it docked across the road from them.

One of the figures got out and headed toward them, and in the headlights of the truck Sarah recognized a bloodied Amos with a bundle in his arms. Muriel twisted out of Josh's hold and ran to Amos to clutch the bundle close with hugs and tears.

With the child out of his arms, Amos sagged against one of the fence posts along the road, and Sarah left the family tableau to make her way to him. "Amos, you're hurt."

He waved her off. "Just grazed in the shoulder. I have to help the others get the prisoners to jail."

She put her hands on her hips. "They can handle it." Sarah called to Josh. "Can you drive the sheriff to the hospital? He's been hit."

Josh nodded. "I'll be happy to pay him back."

Sarah started toward the dock. "I'll tell the others and be right back."

She saw Josh take Amos by the arm and help him into the back of the truck. When she got to the end of the pier, Sam and Luke were putting not only the Giovannis into the paddy wagon but also Manfred and Lettie Pembrook.

Sarah waved at Sam. "I'm going with the Shafers. They're going to drop off the sheriff at the hospital."

Sam returned the wave. "Tell him we'll put these guests in our finest rooms."

Sarah grinned. "See you later." She hurried to the waiting truck and crawled in the back with Amos. As the truck pulled out, Sarah shook her head. "I wouldn't have believed it if I hadn't seen for myself who was on that airplane."

Amos gave her a glance. "I have to say I'm not

entirely surprised. When Manfred did that disappearing act, I suspected he had a hand in the harassment of the Shafers. But I didn't think he would call the Giovannis up here." He grimaced as the truck went over a bump, and he kept pressure on his shoulder with cloth torn from his shirt.

****

Back home after leaving the sheriff and Sarah at the hospital, Josh and Muriel found Zeke and James waiting outside and told them what had happened.

Josh ran his hand over his eyes. "It was the damnedest thing I ever saw. Two of the ships blocked the airplane to keep it from taking off."

Looking at each other with a grin, Zeke pointed at James. "He was talking to the two radio men on those boats and told them what happened. The men asked their captains to trap the airplane. Once they explained there was an abducted child involved, there was no problem."

Josh put his arms around both of them. "I've got the two greatest brothers in the world. Thank you."

Muriel silently hugged Zeke and James, then took Jenny into the house. Josh slapped them both on the shoulders. "We'd better get some sleep before we open tomorrow." He couldn't help feeling there was light at the end of the tunnel.

Chapter 28

The next morning, the residents of the two neighboring houses went to the theater together. At the door, Josh had started to get out his key before he noticed it was already unlocked and ajar. He took a deep breath and looked at Zeke standing next to him. "Something's wrong."

Zeke waved Addy, Muriel, Cora and James back. "Stay out here. I'll see if it's safe to go in." He gently pushed the door open and paled. "James, go get the sheriff."

As James set off down the street, Zeke showed the others what waited inside. In the lobby, the potted plants were overturned and the pictures slashed. Paint splattered the walls and carpeting. A stunned group met the sheriff, his arm in a sling, and Sarah as they came up the street with James.

"Mr. Carter tells us there's a problem at the theater." The sheriff glanced at the somber group.

Josh waved at the building. "The door was unlocked this morning, and this is what we found when Zeke opened it."

The sheriff and Sarah stepped inside the lobby as the others gathered just outside. Amos shook his head. "I thought you hired a night watchman for the place."

Josh felt a little sheepish. "We let him go when everyone moved out."

As they searched through the building, they realized the theater had some damage but the main destruction followed a path to the office. There they found the vault open and the bank bags of money gone.

Zeke turned to Muriel. "Do you know how much money was in the vault?"

Muriel sought out the ledger on the floor next to the overturned desk. She took a quick scan. "Three hundred sixty-six dollars and fifty-nine cents, in three bank bags."

Sarah plucked an empty bag from the floor. "Were the other bags like this one?" On the canvas was the name of the bank and a printed "GN" on the top.

Muriel nodded. "Those are the bags the bank gave us to make our deposits."

Sarah and Amos glanced at each other. Amos put his hand on Josh's shoulder. "I think we solved this all ready. We discovered a number of bank bags stowed on the airplane last night. I saw yours among them."

Sarah continued. "It looks like Manfred Pembrook was trying to make off with not only the entire Pembrook estate, but with as much money from you as he could get. He closed out their account and took Amelia Pembrook's share, too."

Josh frowned. "Do you think he did the destruction, as well?"

"Most likely. He still blamed all of you for taking money from his mother when she backed the theater. By the way, that was his handwriting on the threatening notes, and he was probably the one who broke the window of the lobby."

Amos stroked his mustache. "Well, we can add this to the list against them. I don't think any of them will see the outside of prison for a long time." He took the bank bag from Sarah. "May we take this in as evidence? This will prove to the judge that those others are a match."

Nodding, Josh motioned toward Amos' arm. "How's your arm this morning?"

"Stiff shoulder, but it should heal in a week or so."

"Thank you for getting Jenny back for us." He struggled to control the break in his voice.

Amos slapped him on the back. "Just doing our job. You're welcome. How's the little girl this morning?"

"Quiet, but I think she'll be fine. The doc took a look at her when we arrived home. He and the coroner were taking away the hit man."

Amos chuckled. "They shouldn't have come up against Mrs. Hutton. Where did she learn to shoot like that?"

"She was raised in the Arizona Territory near Tombstone."

"Good bodyguard for all of you. I'm never going to criticize her cooking."

As the sheriff and Sarah took their leave, the other members of the theater staff arrived and viewed the mess. Finally they all met in the restaurant, where Zeke faced them, waving them to silence. "I know this looks like an impossible cleanup job, but if we each take a section, I think we can do most of it by tonight. Addy and Muriel, take the office. The rest of the girls can help Cora clean the restaurant, all except Kata." He turned to her. "Some of the seat cushions in the theater were slashed. Could you repair them?"

"Sure I can." Kata ran to get her sewing kit.

"The theater isn't in bad shape. James, Dan, Ray and Nathan, you boys give it a close inspection and clean it up. Josh, Ivan and I will take care of the lobby. Ready?"

Everyone nodded and set to their tasks. Josh was relieved that Zeke organized things so easily. The theater and restaurant would be ready in time, despite the efforts of their ill-wisher.

As Josh began cleaning up the potted plants in

the lobby, he heard a knock on the outer door. Opening it, he found a group of twenty-five or so people outside, headed by Millie. He shook his head. "We had a problem here last night, and we won't be open for business for a while."

Millie smiled. "Yes, we all heard what happened, and we're here to help you clean up."

A rock lodged firmly in Josh's throat, but he croaked out, "You want to help us?"

Mayor Robertson stepped forward. "You're one of our neighbors. That's what we do for one of our own."

Zeke and Ivan stood beside Josh by now, and the three of them glanced at each other with tears misting their eyes but grins breaking out as well. Josh held the door wide and let the neighbors in.

Epilogue

Muriel hummed to herself as she mended clothes from the laundry basket. Josh studied the new sheets of music he'd ordered from the mercantile. The evening had been quiet since Jenny went to bed. It was Sunday, a day that seemed to have a way of bringing contentment. Home was beginning to feel safe to them again, after the episode of last week; however, now they always locked their outside doors.

Moving the basket so he could sit beside her, Josh took Muriel's hand and kissed it. "Honey, I was thinking, I'd like to adopt Jenny. I know you want her to know about her real father, but I think it might be better if she didn't have the Giovanni name. We could tell her after she's old enough to understand."

Muriel closed her eyes for a moment. "I know Tony would have loved and protected her, but I do understand about the Giovanni name. It stands out like a beacon. I don't think they'll try anything more, now that the law is alerted about them." She squeezed his hand. "You're the only father she's ever known. She should be a Shafer along with her brother or sister."

Jolted, Josh stared at her. "Brother or sister? Are you—?"

Nodding, she drew him into a long, sweet kiss before he broke away with a yell of happiness.

****

After dinner, Muriel and Josh joined Addy and Zeke on their porch in celebration of Muriel's news, watching the sun settle below the horizon. The wicker swing squeaked back and forth, and Zeke put his arms around Addy as the cool breeze played about them.

"We should all go inside," he said.

"We did it again." Muriel smiled.

"What?" Josh asked sitting up.

"Fought the Giovannis and won. We can survive anything, I think."

"I know one thing." Zeke stood and gave a hand to Addy. "I'm not going to keep running from them. We've found a home here."

The other three agreed as they all went into the welcoming warmth of the house.

A word about the author...

Ilona Fridl was born in West Hollywood, California, where she developed an interest in the movie industry. *Silver Screen Heroes* came to be from her love of silent movies. When she was in her twenties, she moved to Wisconsin where she lives now.

She always had a love of writing, but a hatred of typewriters, so she started writing when she got her first computer. She sold short stories to magazines, but always dreamed of selling a novel.

She credits her family and friends as her biggest cheerleaders.

Contact Ilona at

www.ilonafridl.com

Thank you for purchasing
this Wild Rose Press publication.
For other wonderful stories of romance,
please visit our on-line bookstore at
www.thewildrosepress.com

For questions or more information,
contact us at
info@thewildrosepress.com

The Wild Rose Press
www.TheWildRosePress.com

Other Vintage titles to enjoy...

DON'T CALL ME DARLIN' by Fleeta Cunningham: Santa Rita, Texas, 1957: Carole faces library censorship and a pyromaniac. Will the County Judge who's dating her protect or accuse her?

BLACK RAIN RISING by Fleeta Cunningham: The courageous daughter of a radio station owner signs a country singer accused of murder, who also has a little girl in need of an operation in order to live.

ELOPEMENT FOR ONE by Fleeta Cunningham: Hiding from an abusive, controlling fiancé, Troy discovers more than love from an unexpected source.

SOLILOQUY by Janet Fogg: A broken figurine reveals the story behind the disappearance of Erin's aunt at the end of World War II. Can Erin save her and still find the only love she's ever known?

SOURDOUGH RED by Pinkie Paranya: At the end of the gold rush, a sea captain and a disillusioned doctor help Jen search for her twin in Alaska's wilderness.

SCHERESADE by Ronit Lèvy: Erika's new life in America is full of promise. So why have nightmares returned? A passionate young neurologist and an embittered Holocaust survivor help her unravel the mystery of her past and discover true love.

WILD OATS by Margaret Tanner: In this prequel to THE TROUBLE WITH PLAYBOYS, the effect of World War I on the life of an Australian country girl is catastrophic. Will the father of her child ever come back? Will she ever see her child again? And what about the child of the man she loved and lost?

THE VICARAGE BENCH by Mimi Barbour: An entertaining trilogy centered on the bench and the magical rosebush beside it. First, time travel deals a blow to a spoilt model suddenly in the body of a chubby librarian. Second, same rosebush, different victims! Third, a new angle on the rosebush as a Las Vegas hero and heroine try to escape a death threat.